MW01075264

Ruthless

Villains

ALSO BY MARION BLACKWOOD

Marion Blackwood has written lots of books across multiple series, and new books are constantly added to her catalogue. To see the most recently updated list of books, please visit: www.marionblackwood.com

CONTENT WARNINGS

The *Ruthless Villains* series is intended for mature readers. It contains graphic violence and sexual content. Not to mention that the two main characters are villains who do immoral things both to others and to each other. If you have specific triggers, you can find the full list of content warnings at: www.marionblackwood.com/content-warnings

Ruthless Villains

Ruthless Villains

Book One

Marion Blackwood

First edition

ISBN 978-91-988023-2-0 (hardcover)
ISBN 978-91-988023-1-3 (paperback)
ISBN 978-91-988023-0-6 (ebook)

Editing by Julia Gibbs
Dust jacket design by Claire Holt with
Luminescence Covers (www.luminescencecovers.com)
Hardback design by Franziska Stern from
www.coverdungeon.com - IG: @coverdungeonrabbit

This is a work of fiction. Names, characters, places, and incidents either are the product of the author's imagination or are used fictitiously. Any resemblance to actual persons, living or dead, events, or locales is entirely coincidental.

www.marionblackwood.com

*For everyone who always ends up
falling for the villain*

CHAPTER 1

Audrey

T hey say that poison is a coward's weapon. I say that they have never known the intoxicating rush of power that comes from watching a man beg you for mercy while your poison slowly chokes him to death.

A glittering green cloud hung in the air around the guard. I cocked my head and watched as my poison magic forced its way into his lungs where he sat, kneeling before me. His hands clawed at the damp grass, and choking sounds gurgled from his throat.

"Please," he gasped, but it only made him inhale more poison. Tremors racked his body as he coughed repeatedly before looking up at me with pleading brown eyes. "Please. Mercy."

I flicked my long black hair behind my shoulder and watched him fight for breath for another few seconds before clicking my tongue. "I could be persuaded to spare your life... if you let me in through the back door to the kitchen."

Putting a hand to his own throat, he nodded desperately while sucking in strangled gasps. I arched an unimpressed eyebrow at him. How a dark mage could have hired such a pathetic excuse for a guard was beyond me. Glancing up, I studied the sprawling mansion set into the lush grasslands ahead. This truly proved that a stronghold was only as secure as its weakest link. I would have to go over the security of my own mansion again when I got home. But first, I had an enemy to kill.

The guard at my feet let out a panicked gurgling noise. Blowing out an annoyed breath, I pulled back my poison magic and allowed him to breathe once more. He sucked in a deep breath and coughed a few more times before looking up at me again.

I jerked my chin. "Get to it, then."

While blinking his eyes back into focus, he struggled to his feet and then staggered towards Callan Blackwell's mansion. I followed behind, a threat looming at his back to make sure that he didn't try to warn the other sentries. But no calls of alarm came from his throat. Only the occasional wheezing cough. I studied the mansion while we snuck closer.

The white marble structure sat like a pale jewel on the thick green grass. Gleaming windows were set into its sides to let in the light, and a few stone steps led up to the grand oak door. Trees dotted the landscape between the mansion and a stable visible farther behind. I narrowed my eyes at the classy style of the building. It had always annoyed me how similar Callan's home was to my own. As if we would ever agree on anything.

"This is it," the guard whispered as he edged open a small wooden door at the back of the great house. "This will take you into the kitchen."

"Excellent."

I touched my hands together to call up my magic again, and then sent another cloud of poison straight at him from behind. He only managed one surprised gasp before he crumpled to the ground. The poison was enough to knock him out, but not enough to kill him. He was a weak link in Callan Blackwell's security, and if this didn't work, I could probably use the guard again next time. If Callan let him live, that is.

While withdrawing my magic again, I stepped over the man's unconscious form and slipped in through the door.

Pots clanked from the kitchen up ahead. I cast a quick glance at the overcast summer sky outside. Sunset was close, which meant that I had timed this perfectly.

Bright firelight illuminated the spacious kitchen as I strode across the threshold. For a moment, the kitchen staff only continued bustling about. Then the first person spotted me. It was a woman with curly brown hair pulled up in a bun, and an apron stained with flour. She sucked in a gasp and dropped the ladle she had been holding. Wooden clattering echoed through the room as it hit the counter before her. The others whipped their heads towards me.

I swept hard eyes over all of them, daring them to do anything to stop me. They shrank back. Only silence followed me as I strode into the corridor beyond and continued towards the dining room at its end. Apparently, Callan's kitchen staff didn't get paid enough to try to take out a dark mage.

A tall man with bulging muscles appeared as I turned a corner. Two swords swung from his hips. However, he was currently looking in the wrong direction. I touched my hands together and sent a cloud of poison magic straight at him before he could turn back.

Dull thuds sounded as he hit the floor. Dead. The cooks might not get paid enough to try to stop me, but this guy certainly would have.

The glittering green cloud dissipated as I stalked through it.

Candlelight flickered from up ahead, and there was a faint clinking sound. As if someone was eating.

A smirk slid across my lips. *Perfect.*

Drawing myself up against the wall, I glanced around the edge and into the dining room on the other side. Victory sparkled inside me. There he was. Callan Blackwell.

He was seated alone at the head of a grand table. The scent of grilled meat and fried potatoes hung in the air as he cut a strip from his steak and brought it to his mouth. Candlelight painted gilded streaks in his black hair and set his dark brown eyes glittering. Touching my palms together, I summoned my magic while I continued glaring at him. With his sharp cheekbones and lean muscled body, I had to admit that he was fucking hot. The problem was that he knew it. He knew that he was attractive and powerful, and he moved and spoke with the confidence of that. And that made me hate him even more.

I flicked my wrist, and poison magic shot through the air.

Wood clanked as Callan threw himself sideways, knocking his chair over in the process, and rolled across the floor to evade my magic. Moving into the dining room, I sent another poisonous attack straight at him. He touched his hands together while rolling to his feet.

I leaped aside. A second later, a wall of force magic hurtled past me. Slamming my palms together, I called up another cloud of poison and threw it at him while his gaze at last locked on me.

Surprise and rage flashed in his brown eyes.

While dodging my attack, he sent another force wall at me. I jumped back to avoid it while he took off across the floor, but the force wall he shot had only been a diversion. Realizing it a moment too late, I only managed to partly twist aside as another blast took me in the shoulder. The strength of the hit sent me flying into the wall behind me.

I sucked in a gasp as my breath was knocked from my lungs when my back hit the marble wall. The bodice of my dress was made of metal armor, so it helped lessen the impact a bit, but not nearly enough. Throwing out a hand to brace myself against the cool stone, I managed to keep myself from crumpling to the floor. While still trying to refill my lungs, I scrambled to bring my palms together.

Strong fingers curled around my right wrist and slammed my arm up against the wall next to my head while another hand wrapped around my throat. Dark brown eyes stared down at me.

"Audrey Sable," Callan drawled while his iron grip kept me pinned to his dining room wall. "I should have known."

"Yes, you should," I replied with a smirk as I raised my eyebrows at him. "Given how easy it was for me to get in here."

He matched my cocky smile. "Did you ever think that maybe I wanted to draw you in here? Alone. In the middle of my stronghold."

As if on cue, men with swords appeared from the doorways at the front and back of the dining room. Callan's grip on me tightened.

"You can't touch your palms together now." He pulled my hand forward a little and then slammed it back against the wall next to my head as if to prove the point. "Which means that you can't do magic. So, what are you going to do now?"

I let my one free hand drop down at my side as Callan increased the pressure on my throat. My fingers brushed against my black and green skirt.

"Oh I have been wanting to kill you for so long," Callan continued, that smug smirk still on his lips as he looked down at me. "Why did I spend all that time trying to break through your defenses when I could just have you walk right into your own execution?"

A strangled breath fought its way down into my lungs. Callan shifted his grip and placed his thumb under my chin, forcing my head back to expose my throat. Leaning down, he slanted his lips over mine.

"This is the part where you start begging me for mercy," he breathed against my mouth.

My fingers finally curled around something hard.

Drawing the dagger I had strapped to my thigh under my skirt, I rammed it into his side.

Shock pulsed in his eyes as I yanked it out again.

His grip on me loosened as he staggered back a step and pressed a hand to his side. I ripped my wrist free of his grip while shifting the blade in my other hand so that I could slam my palms together. Glittering green poison bloomed in the air. I shoved it towards Callan while he smacked his hands together and brought his arm down.

I stopped.

As did he.

Tension crackled through the beautiful dining room as we locked hateful eyes on each other.

A twisting cloud of poison hung in the air right in front of Callan's face while a force blade hovered above my own shoulder. Both attacks had stopped just shy of actually hitting.

Callan's force magic had the gray color of half-translucent steel and looked like shifting air, but I knew that he could make his force blades vibrate to the point where they could cut through both flesh and bone.

"You move that poison cloud one inch closer to me, and I will cut you in half," he warned as he stared me down from the other side of the glittering green mist.

I let out a mocking laugh and made a show of looking down at the wound in his side. Blood welled up from it and ran down to drip onto the floor. The palm he had pressed against it was also smeared red.

"Oh, I don't need to use my magic to kill you anymore," I

replied as I met his gaze again. "That wound will do it for me. All I need to do is stand here until you bleed out."

Callan narrowed his eyes at me. Raising his red right hand, he motioned towards the men with swords who now surrounded us. "Except if you do that, my people will kill you afterwards."

"But you will still be dead."

"So will you."

While keeping the poison cloud in place, I flicked my gaze around the room, calculating whether I could kill all of these people before one of them managed to ram a sword through my body. The problem was that there were a lot of them and they were standing close to us, which increased the odds that at least one person might be quick enough to strike me before I could touch my hands together and call up another poison attack. I sucked my teeth.

"How about this?" Callan began. "I let you leave. Just this once."

I slid my gaze back to him while nodding towards the wound in his side. "So that you won't bleed out while we just stand here."

He lifted one shoulder in a nonchalant shrug. "Unless you'd rather die with me?"

Glaring up at him, I flexed my fingers on the hilt of my dagger. While I most certainly wanted Callan Blackwell dead, I had no plans on dying myself to make that happen.

"Fine," I said. "We'll consider tonight a draw."

He gave me a slow nod.

Keeping the force blade above my shoulder, he moved both of us a step towards the doorway on my left. I held the cloud of poison in front of him while he backed me across the room and into the corridor that would take us to the front door. The men with swords followed after their master.

Blood ran down Callan's side. Muted drops hit the floor, leaving a red trail behind us as we walked. While still holding the force blade with his left hand, Callan pressed his other palm against the wound to stop the bleeding. I flashed him a wicked grin. The promise of vengeance flickered in his brown eyes.

My back hit the closed front door with a soft thud. Keeping my eyes locked on Callan, I slid my dagger under my flowing black and green skirt, returning it to my thigh holster, before I reached out and grabbed the handle.

Air smelling of damp soil and grass filled the room as I opened the front door. I backed out onto the porch and then down the white steps while Callan followed. He stopped on the final step. Red drops splattered the pale marble behind him.

Power rolled off his lethal body as he stared me down. "I will see you soon, Audrey."

A smile dripping with threats slid across my lips as I disappeared into the grasslands. "Yes, you will."

CHAPTER 2

Callan

P ain shot up my side. I sucked in a breath between my teeth as I shifted so that Henry could reach the wound. Fucking Audrey Sable. Thinking she could kill me in my own home. If there was one person I was going to torture to death before the end of the year, it was her.

"Boss," Henry began as his gray eyes shifted from the wound and to my face. "It's deep."

I forced out an irritated breath. "Then get Sam."

He inclined his head before barking the order to some of the guys still lingering in the hallway outside. Boots thudded against the wooden floorboards as one of them raced towards the front door. Another wave of pain washed over me as I draped my arm over the back of the chair next to me. Without saying anything, Henry leaned down and pressed the ball of fabric to my bloodstained skin again.

Henry had worked for me for many years, and he was one of the few people whose loyalty I never doubted. He was one of the first people I had hired after I decided to screw over the city-state of Eldar and become a dark mage instead of

9

following their pathetic path of holding hands and singing while bunnies farted rainbows, or whatever they did during their bloody graduation ceremony. Sharing power equally? That had to be the dumbest shit I'd ever heard. Power comes from hard work and cunning. It has to be earned. Not just given to anyone in the name of *fairness*. Because guess what? Life isn't fair.

"Do you want me to send out a team to hunt her down?" Henry asked as he continued pressing the now red cloth to my wound.

"No," I growled. "I'll deal with Audrey fucking Sable. I am going to personally make her beg for her miserable life before I give her the privilege of dying at my feet."

Henry nodded in acknowledgement.

I stifled another wince as I reached out to grab the glass of whiskey still sitting on the table. Bringing it to my lips, I downed the whole thing. The liquid burned pleasantly as it disappeared down my throat. A soft thud sounded as I set the glass down next to my half-finished dinner that had now gone cold. Oh, I had such plans for Audrey indeed. As soon as my wound was healed, I would end our drawn-out war.

"Boss," came a voice from the corridor. "He's here."

Before I could reply, two people strode across the threshold. One of them was the guard who had called out, the other was the person I had sent for only a minute ago.

I frowned. "That was fast."

Sam Foster strolled across the floor with a carefree look on his face while his gray eyes took in the state of my dining room. "Yep. I was already on my way here."

After a nod from me, Henry straightened and moved aside. He raked a large hand through his brown hair as he withdrew to allow Sam to approach me. Henry was a mountain of a man. Tall and muscular, he towered over the skinny blond guy who sauntered over to take his place. But Sam didn't look the least bit worried. And there was a good reason for that.

"Why?" I asked as Sam frowned down at the bleeding hole in my side.

"That looks painful," he said instead.

"Yeah, I had a little disagreement with some cutlery."

"I see the cutlery won."

I let out an involuntary huff of amusement. Mirth sparkled in Sam's eyes as he grinned at me while plopping down on the chair that Henry had just vacated. His pale brows furrowed slightly as he studied the wound up close.

"I assume this is why you had planned to send for me," he said.

It was more of a statement than a question, but I still nodded in reply.

"Since I was gonna come here anyway, I'll give you the usual rate instead of the rush rate."

I wasn't sure whether to laugh or shake my head, so instead I just snapped my fingers at Henry while saying to Sam, "I appreciate that."

While Henry disappeared out the door, Sam touched his hands together and then drew them apart. Shimmering magic of a turquoise blue color appeared between his palms. Keeping his eyes on my wound, he held his hands above the bleeding hole. A warm sparkling sensation spread through my side.

This was the reason why Sam never had anything to fear from his fellow dark mages. While the rest of us killed each other indiscriminately, no one ever laid a finger on Sam Foster. Because he was a healer. And between our battles amongst ourselves and Eldar's attempts to return us dark mages to the proper path, injuries were a rather common part of our lives. Healers in general were rare, and since no one was ever allowed to keep their powers after graduation, powerful healer mages were practically nonexistent. Which meant that a dark mage healer was worth more than the entire city-state's treasury. So... no one touched Sam.

"You said you were already on your way here," I prompted while Sam continued healing me.

"Yeah, we need to have a meeting," he said without looking up.

"We're having one right now."

Tearing his eyes from his work, he met my gaze. "No, I mean all of us."

"What for?"

"It's better if I explain it to everyone at the same time." When he saw me about to protest, he shook his head. "Callan... I'm serious. This is important. We're all in danger. More than we have ever been in before."

I heaved a sigh. "Fine. When and where?"

"Six o'clock tomorrow evening. Peter Essington's mansion."

A huff of laughter escaped my throat. Of course we were meeting in Essington's old place. He was a dark mage with the ability to cast wards. Or at least, he had been before another dark mage killed him three years ago. But his house still stood because it was warded against magic, which meant that it was the only place we could meet where none of us would be able to use magic to attack the others. Clever. And highly necessary.

"Boss," Henry said as he returned with a thick pile of cash.

Jerking my chin, I motioned for him to give it to Sam. It produced a small thud as Henry set the stack of money down on the table next to Sam, who continued working on my wound.

"Alright, six o'clock tomorrow evening at Essington's old place," I confirmed.

Sam nodded. "Good."

Silence fell while he finished up his work. Once he was done, he rolled his shoulders and cracked his neck. I shifted my arm and twisted my torso from side to side, testing it out. No pain. No loss of movement. Only a thick scar was left as a reminder of where Audrey's dagger had punctured my skin.

Blowing out a satisfied breath, Sam rose and scooped up the pile of cash. He flashed me a grin while running his thumb down the edge of the bills.

"Always a pleasure doing business." Lifting his hand in a salute, he swung around and strolled towards the door. "See you tomorrow."

"Yeah."

"Oh, and Callan?" he tossed over his shoulder while he walked across the threshold. "There will be no violence at the meeting."

His blond head thankfully disappeared out the door before I could reply. Because if Audrey was going to be there, I was making no promises.

CHAPTER 3

Audrey

Sunset painted the dark wooden mansion with red and golden streaks. I swung down from my horse and tied the reins to one of the crooked posts. There was only one other horse there, meaning that only one other dark mage had arrived so far. Probably Sam Foster, since he was the one who had called the meeting.

I had been surprised when I returned from my assassination attempt at Callan's house to find Sam waiting for me. Once he had explained what he wanted, I knew that he had been to see Callan as well, and that he had probably healed him too. Pity.

Brushing down my flowing dark skirt, I strode up the steps to the front door. As soon as I crossed the threshold, a strange feeling enveloped me. It felt like my whole body was wrapped in a thick wet blanket, smothering all my magic. I rolled my shoulders to shake off the feeling. Peter Essington had been a particularly troublesome dark mage to deal with since he could create places where we couldn't use our magic. Good thing someone had managed to kill him in the end.

14

The mansion lay dark and deserted as I walked through the hallway, peering into a few different rooms. Cracked mirrors and fractured furniture still stood where their now deceased owner had left them. My fingers carved a line in the dust atop a side table as I trailed my hand over it. Wiping them off again, I turned the corner and stepped into what had once been Essington's dining room.

Dark brown eyes met me.

I froze.

A vicious smile spread across Callan Blackwell's lips. "Hello, Audrey."

"Callan." I let a mocking expression slide home on my face as I started forward again and sauntered farther into the room. "You're looking spry for someone who was bleeding all over your own floors last night."

"Yes." He drew a long knife from the thigh holster of his dark leather armor. "I thought I might return the favor."

A flash of alarm shot through me unbidden. In here, without my magic, I was at a severe disadvantage. I was both shorter and lighter than him. Not to mention that my skills with a blade were only mediocre at best. But running was out of the question. Dark mages never showed any fear or weakness. Those who did rarely lived very long, because our reputation was all we had.

So I buried the flash of worry deep and instead unsheathed my own dagger. Spinning it once in my hand, I let out a derisive snort. "Come try it."

He shot across the floor. I leaped aside to evade the knife coming for my ribs. The blade whooshed through the air a mere inch from my body. Whirling around, I rammed my dagger towards Callan's neck.

Metal clanged as he yanked his knife up and parried the strike. Before I could disengage our blades, he grabbed my wrist and twisted it up behind my back while his closed fist slammed into the spot between my shoulder blades. Air exploded from my lungs as the force of his moves made me crash down onto the table. With an iron grip forcing my knife hand up my back, Callan pushed my chest harder down against the wood where he had me bent over the tabletop. Cold steel kissed my throat.

I yanked against his grip, but the difference in strength was ridiculous. Instead of me gaining even an inch of space, Callan twisted my arm farther up my back. I had to bite my tongue to stop from crying out in pain.

"Now," he began, "I believe I promised you the taste of a knife."

Steel scraped against my skin as he trailed the tip of his blade from my neck and down my arm until he reached my hand. Panic crackled through me as he positioned the tip against the back of my hand and pushed down slightly.

"Unless you want to beg me for mercy?" Callan taunted.

Gritting my teeth, I yanked against his grip again, but he only forced my arm farther up. He leaned down over me so that his hard body pressed into mine.

Smug victory laced his voice as he placed his lips next to my ear and whispered, "Just one word. *Mercy.* And I will let you go with your hand intact."

My heart thumped in my chest, but I wouldn't give him the satisfaction so I kept my mouth firmly shut.

"Well..." He let out a dark laugh. "Have it your way."

"Callan," a sharp voice came from somewhere behind us. "Sam said no fighting during this meeting."

"This doesn't concern you, Malcolm," Callan replied as he straightened slightly.

With my cheek pressed into the table, I could just barely make out a tall man with brown hair and eyes.

"Oh, come on," another voice said. "Didn't I say no

fighting?"

Relief fluttered through me as Sam strolled into the room. Callan met his gaze for a second before shifting his attention back to me. A low growl rumbled from his throat but then he shoved me harder against the tabletop before finally letting me go. I rolled my shoulder to relieve the tension while straightening from the table. For a moment, I considered using the opportunity to stab Callan, but in the end, I just sheathed my dagger and drew a hand through my long black hair before sitting down in the nearest chair.

Golden light from the low-hanging sun illuminated the deserted dining room and made the dusty furniture look a bit grander. Pulling out a chair, Sam plopped down on the other side of the round table. Callan flashed me a sharp smile before sitting down as well. After brushing his hands down his impeccable dark suit, Malcolm Griffith took the seat between them, leaving the two chairs on either side of me empty.

"I don't like the way my body feels in this house," yet another voice said.

Turning my head, I watched a young woman with long red hair and beautiful citrine eyes stride into the dining room. She swept her gaze over the four of us before unceremoniously dropping into the chair on my right.

"It makes me feel like I'm being suffocated," she finished.

"Everyone feels that way, Sienna," Sam answered with a small smile. "It's just a safety precaution."

"Where's Grant?" Malcolm grumbled as he looked towards the empty doorway.

"Right here," said a very average-looking man with brown hair and blue eyes, as he strolled into the room.

Malcolm narrowed his eyes at him. "You're late."

A clock chimed from somewhere farther into the building, informing us that it was now six o'clock.

"I'd say I'm right on time," Harvey Grant, who preferred to go by his last name, answered with a nonchalant shrug as he took the final seat on my left.

Malcolm let out an annoyed huff before turning to Sam. "Alright, Sam, we're all here. What is it?"

Furniture creaked as the rest of us turned towards the healer as well. Golden light fell across his face and made the worry present there even more noticeable. I frowned at him. What in the world had made him this anxious?

"We're all that's left," Sam said at last.

"Of what?" Sienna asked, her brows creased as well.

"The six of us are the only dark mages left in Eldar right now."

Callan shot me a mocking look. "Which begs the question, how the hell are *you* one of them?"

"I wasn't the one getting ambushed in my own dining room last night," I sniped back.

"Enough," Malcolm snapped, and cut a scathing look at the both of us. "Sam called this meeting, so let him speak."

I held his gaze for a few seconds. Malcolm Griffith was a shadow mage, and he was the oldest one of us. The death rate among dark mages was rather high, which meant that at only thirty-five, Malcolm was the most senior one in Eldar. He was followed by Callan at age twenty-seven, Grant a year younger, and me at twenty-five. Sienna, who had only been a dark mage for a bit over two years, was the youngest at twenty-two, while Sam was two years older than her. I didn't feel like starting a war with someone like Malcolm over something that Callan had goaded me into, so I just clicked my tongue and motioned for Sam to keep going.

"Thank you." Sam swept his gaze around the room to see if anyone else planned to interrupt. When no one did, he went on. "Like I said, there are only six of us left. And that's because we've both been fighting amongst ourselves as well as trying to fight off the rest of Eldar. It's time to set our differences aside and stop killing each other."

"Why now?" Sienna asked. She sounded genuinely curious.

"I have a contact who works at a low level in the parliament, and if we don't work together to stop the threat that's coming, we're all going to get wiped out."

"We?" Callan said. His dark brows were furrowed in skepticism. "*We* are going to get wiped out? By the *heroes*?"

A ripple of laughter came from both Malcolm and Sienna.

We mockingly called the leaders of Eldar *heroes*, because that was how they saw themselves. As heroes who fought against injustice and inequality and turned the world into glitter and rainbows. And they did that by forcing all the mages to share their magic.

Only a portion of the population was actually born with magic. The rest didn't get anything. Those who were born mages were sent to a special school where they spent a decade developing their powers to make them as strong as possible. When the mages turned twenty, they graduated from the academy and went through the graduation ceremony. That ceremony was the most illogical thing I had ever heard of. After spending over a decade developing their powers, the students were expected to go through with the ceremony and *share* their magic with everyone.

The graduation ceremony draws the magic out of the mage and feeds it to something called the Great Current so that everyone can use it instead. People who are born without any powers are able to wield magic thanks to this Great Current, and the mage can also use its power because the ceremony links the student to it.

In the heroes' mind, it sounds like the perfect dream. Magic is shared equally among all people so that no one has more than anyone else. The problem is that it also dilutes the magic.

Every mage is born with *one* power. The most common ones are fire, water, wind, and lightning mages. But there are also other powers that are much rarer. Like my poison magic.

The graduation ceremony adds that mage's power to the shared pool, which means that everyone can use every type of magic in it. However, the strength of that magic is based on how many mages of that particular kind has added their power to the Great Current. While everyone might be able to wield fire or water magic to a relatively decent degree, no one can effectively use poison magic or healing magic because there are too few mages like that who have added their power to the shared pool.

Those of us who refused to share our powers, who escaped before we were forced to complete the graduation ceremony, have been dubbed dark mages. The leaders of Eldar are constantly trying to capture us and bring us back so that they can make us do the ceremony. But because we still have the undiluted power we were born with and were trained to develop for years, we are much stronger than them in terms of magical ability. Which is why it was unlikely that they would be able to wipe us all out.

"Yes, we are," Sam said. His gray eyes had a panicked look to them as he swept his gaze over all of us. "Listen to me. My contact told me that there is a guy called Lance Carmichael at the academy. He's got an incredibly rare power, and he turns twenty in a few months so his magic is really strong too because he has trained all this time but he hasn't graduated yet."

"What kind of power?" Grant asked.

"He's a Binder."

Shock rippled through the room as several of us sucked in a gasp.

CHAPTER 4

Callan

I stared at Sam in stunned disbelief. A Binder? There hadn't been one of those in what? Decades? If this was true, we were in serious shit.

Sunlight reflected off the glass cabinet behind me and hit Sienna's face, making her citrine eyes look like yellow flames.

"What's a Binder?" she asked, confusion blowing across her beautiful features.

"Someone who can bind other people's magic," I answered slowly.

Grant's gaze shot to Malcolm. "What about the artifact?"

"It's still secure," he replied. "But it doesn't matter. We don't know what this Lance Carmichael looks like, so he could hide in a crowd when they attack, and all he needs is one touch and we're done."

"Exactly," Sam picked up. "And my contact in the parliament told me that they're planning to launch a full-scale attack on us all, with this Lance guy leading the charge. They are going to bind all of our magic and then drag us back before undoing the binding so that they can force us to complete the ceremony, effectively wiping out dark mages in Eldar."

Malcolm dragged a hand over his face. "Bloody hell."

"Yeah. And I don't know about you, but I like being a dark mage." He flashed us an unapologetic grin and spread his arms. "Because I like freedom... and money."

"Okay." Malcolm swept brown eyes dripping with authority over all of us. "Our internal fighting is hereby finished. Now, how do we stop them from sending a Binder after us?"

I hated when that bastard tried to give us orders, and besides, Audrey was still due a lesson in humility so I was about to argue that I would not be ending any wars with her. But the awful truth was that the threat of a Binder was too great to dismiss, so in the end, I only gave him a curt nod in acknowledgement. The others did the same.

Grant scratched his chin. "When are they launching this attack?"

"In about two weeks," Sam answered. "So what we need to do, or rather what you need to do, because this isn't exactly my area of expertise... is to get into the city and abduct this Lance Carmichael so that *we* can use him against the heroes instead."

"That's a sound plan," Malcolm said while drumming his fingers against the tabletop. "There's only one problem. The moment I set foot inside the city, I'll be arrested. I waged a rather bloody war on the Chief Constable about ten years ago."

"I know. I actually had someone else in mind." Sam's gray eyes shifted between Audrey and me. "I think the people most suited for this mission would be Callan and Audrey."

"What?" I challenged.

"You're the only ones who can openly walk the city because no one knows what you look like."

"He's right," Sienna added. "My face is plastered across

wanted posters too."

"How is it my problem that you burned down two whole city blocks?" Audrey sniped back at her.

Sienna Hall was a fire mage, and two years ago, she had apparently set a portion of the city on fire when she escaped the academy at her graduation.

"Because we can't send people who are instantly recognizable," Malcolm reasoned. "You and Callan are not on any wanted posters. They don't know what you look like."

"Neither is Grant," I pointed out while cocking an eyebrow in challenge.

"No," Sam said. "But Grant's power is not lethal enough for this kind of mission." His gray eyes darted to the mage across the table. "No offense, Grant."

Harvey Grant, whose magic gave him the power to manipulate people's emotions, raised his hands in a casual gesture. "None taken."

"Between you and Audrey, you have both powerful in-your-face magic and sneaky poison magic," Sam said as he turned hopeful eyes on me. "Which is why you are the best people for this job."

"I agree," Malcolm said with a nod.

Anger flashed in Audrey's green eyes as she snapped, "I think I missed the part where this was a fucking democracy."

For once, I actually agreed with the infuriating poison mage. However, before I could say as much, Sam spoke up again.

"Please." He shifted his pleading gaze between me and Audrey. "I don't want to give up this life, and I don't think you want to either. So if you don't want to do it for me or for us, then do it for yourselves. To save yourselves. Please."

For a while, the only sound to break the silence was the faint ticking of a large clock somewhere on the other side of the wall. Both Audrey and I were looking at Sam, while the rest of them watched us.

Blowing out a breath, I raked a hand through my hair and leaned back in my seat. "Fine."

A smile lit Sam's face. He turned to the scowling poison mage. "Audrey?"

Her sharp eyes slid to me. I raised my eyebrows and shot her a challenging smirk that dared her to say no. To show the others that she was too afraid of me to agree. A vicious smile curled her lips.

"Alright," she said at last.

"Fantastic." Sam clapped his hands together. "Then you will go into the city and figure out a way to kidnap Lance. I'll send over all the information my contact gave me. And in the meantime, the rest of us will get this mansion ready so that we can imprison Lance here and break him until he does our bidding instead."

The other five of us nodded in agreement of the plan.

Wood scraped against wood as we pushed our chairs back and stood up, ending this unprecedented dark mage meeting. While the others filed out to start making arrangements, I stalked after Audrey. She moved with confident steps, but I knew that she was trying to get out of the house and its oppressive wards before I could catch up with her. In here, she was completely at my mercy. And she knew it.

A wicked grin spread across my mouth as I picked up the pace. My longer legs ate up the distance between us and I reached her before she could enter the final hallway. Grabbing her by the shoulder from behind, I spun her around and slammed her up against the dark wooden wall. Her back hit the worn panels with a thud, but she only glared up at me in silent defiance as I took a step closer.

"So, looks like you and I will have to work together," I said as I pushed farther into her space, forcing her to press herself against the wall. Reaching out, I traced my fingers over her jaw. "But as long as you do as I say, we won't have a problem."

She slapped my hand away while a cold laugh ripped from her throat. "Follow your orders?" Cocking her head, she lifted her hand and patted my cheek. "I don't think so, pretty boy."

Pretty boy? My hand shot up and wrapped around her wrist. Forcing her hand away, I leaned down until our faces were so close that I could feel her breath on my skin. "What was that?"

"You heard me. You might be used to people begging at your feet, but let me burst your bubble right now. That is not something you will ever get from me."

I slanted my lips over hers, just shy of touching. "We'll see about that."

Audrey only glared up at me. I kept her trapped like that against the wall for another few seconds, just to really drive the point home that I held all the power right now. Then I let go of her wrist and took a step back.

"We need to meet up and make a plan before we ride to the city," I said and threw her a grin dripping with challenge. "Come to my mansion at sundown tomorrow, if you dare."

She scoffed. Her shining black hair fluttered behind her as she swept past me. It smelled faintly of jasmine.

Standing there in the hallway, I watched as she made her way to the front door. The armor bodice of her dress clung to her figure while the black and green skirt flowed around her legs as she swished her hips. A malicious grin decorated my face as I studied her.

This was the perfect opportunity.

We would go into Eldar and get this Lance boy. And if Audrey just so happened to be captured by the heroes in the process, then, well... that wouldn't be my fault, now would it?

CHAPTER 5

Audrey

The midday sun shone brightly from the pale blue heavens. I huffed in contempt as I stalked up the stone steps to Callan's front door. *Come to my mansion, if you dare.* As if I would be afraid to face him in his own stronghold. I had broken in here and stabbed him only two days ago, hadn't I? And telling me to come at sunset. Oh, I didn't think so. I would come when I damn well pleased.

"Stand aside," I ordered the two guards by the door.

They exchanged a glance. However, before they could reply, the door was opened and a mountain of a man became visible on the other side. His gray eyes seared into me.

"Audrey Sable," he said at last.

Since I didn't know his name, and didn't care enough to ask either, I just stared back at him with my eyebrows raised expectantly.

He flashed some kind of hand signal to the guards outside the door and then jerked his chin at me. "Come with me."

I narrowed my eyes at his presumptuous tone, but stalked across the threshold and followed him into Callan's mansion.

As we walked, I ran my scrutinizing gaze over the rooms and corridors we passed. The dark wooden floors were now clean and shiny again. No sign of the blood Callan had dripped all over them during my last visit. In fact, the whole building was neat and clean. With well-organized bookshelves and smooth tables, the entire mansion had a classy feel to it. And yet, it was also strangely homely. As if Callan truly valued this home he had built. It made me want to destroy it even more.

"Wait here," my tall guide said as we reached a hallway upstairs.

Touching my palms together, I summoned a cloud of poison. The glittering green swirls twisted around my forearm as I cocked my head and locked eyes with the disrespectful guard. "Watch that tone."

He rolled his eyes, actually rolled his eyes, at me before he strode over to a door a little farther down and pounded his fist against it. I considered killing him where he stood for his insolence, but decided against it. I didn't have surprise on my side this time, and taking on Callan's entire household all at the same time might prove troublesome.

"What?" Callan Blackwell barked from the other side of the closed door.

"It's Henry," the muscular guard answered. "Audrey Sable is here."

A smirk stretched my lips. I wondered what important business I had managed to interrupt by showing up several hours too early. Brushing a hand down my flowing skirt, I huffed out a silent laugh. If Callan thought he would be the boss during our temporary partnership, he was sorely mistaken.

Callan's dark laugh echoed from inside the room. "I see. Well, send her in then."

Turning back around, Henry twitched his fingers at me. Poison magic still twisted around my arm so I sent it straight at him. His eyes widened as his air supply was suddenly blocked off. While forcing the glittering green tendril deeper into his throat, I stalked over and glared up into his angular face.

"Next time, remember your manners," I said, my voice cold and vicious.

Then I pulled my magic back and yanked open the door. Henry sucked in a deep breath, but it was quickly cut off as I crossed the threshold and slammed the door shut behind me.

I jerked back. Blinking at the scene before me, I stopped dead on the floor while trying to get my brain to process what I was seeing.

The room I was in was mostly bare, except for a set of drawers and a large four-poster bed. It looked like a spare bedroom rather than Callan's own room, or the office that I had assumed it would be. But that was not what made me stare in bafflement.

There was a naked woman on the bed. She was lying on her stomach, and her wrists were tied to the bedposts before her while her legs were attached to some kind of metal bar that kept them spread wide. Callan had raised her hips so that her knees were braced against the mattress. He was on his knees too. Behind her. Pounding into her.

I gave my head a few quick shakes as I tried to readjust my assumptions about how this meeting would transpire.

The muscles in Callan's forearms shifted as he gripped the dark-haired woman's hips and adjusted them while continuing to thrust into her with savage strength. A rolling moan of pleasure came from the woman's throat. With her hands still bound, she curled her fingers, gripping the sheets hard. Resting one cheek against the mattress, she kept her eyes closed and let out another dark moan. There was pure bliss on her face.

My brows furrowed in a scowl. She had to be faking it.

Probably because she was afraid to displease him. I studied the expression on her face for another couple of seconds.

Sex was so overrated. Sure, I'd fucked guys from time to time, but I'd never understood what the big deal was. First of all, the whole situation in itself puts people in a very vulnerable position. So I'd had to make sure I only fucked guys who presented no threat to me. And then the act of the guy just thrusting his cock into me? It didn't exactly blow my mind. I could accomplish far more with my own fingers.

"I thought I told you to come at sundown," Callan tossed over his shoulder while he continued pounding into the moaning beauty.

"And I thought I made it clear that I don't take orders from you," I replied.

He let out a dark chuckle. "Oh, you will."

A smirk still played over his lips as he changed up the rhythm of his thrusts. The dark-haired woman pulled at her restraints and clenched her hands while her chest heaved. I wanted to stalk out of the room and slam the door behind me, but if I did that, Callan would know that he had won. He was trying to throw me off my game with this, I knew that. I'd tried to get the upper hand by arriving earlier than I should have, and this was his response. This was how he tried to show me that it hadn't fazed him in the slightest. So in the end, I just painted a bored expression on my face and arched an unimpressed eyebrow while Callan made the beautiful woman come apart underneath him.

Her body shook and she let out a shuddering cry as she climaxed. Or at least pretended to do so, I assumed. Callan followed shortly after, a rough groan ripping from his throat as he thrust into her one last time. A bead of sweat ran down his muscled chest as he tipped his head back and closed his eyes.

I kept the bored and unimpressed look on my face as he

pulled out of her and rose from the bed. The woman slumped down on the mattress, her chest heaving.

My eyes drifted over Callan's lethal body and dipped below his waistline while he straightened. Damn. He was well equipped.

He drew a hand through his messy black hair as he advanced on me, still completely naked. There was a smug smile playing over his lips. "Did you enjoy the show?"

Standing my ground, I just flicked a lazy glance at the woman still tied to the bed. "Is she an actress from the theater? Because I've never seen anyone fake it that well before."

He smirked. "I bet you'd know all about faking it."

My fingers curled around the hilt of my hidden dagger. Callan kept coming. Since I refused to let him back me across the room, I remained firmly in place as his powerful body almost mowed me down. I yanked out the blade.

Callan stopped abruptly as I flicked my wrist, placing the cold edge of the knife against his cock. Challenge danced in his dark brown eyes.

"I came here for a business meeting." Keeping the blade steady, I held his gaze. "So stop playing with your little toy before I decide to cut it off."

A smile dripping with threats curled his lips. "Oh you and I have unfinished business, indeed. And I can't wait to get started with it. Now, go wait in the dining room like a good girl."

I pressed the blade harder against his sensitive skin.

He cocked his head. "Unless you want to join me in the shower?"

With a mocking smile on my lips, I cast a pointed look at his cock. "Why would I do that? I have already been grossly underwhelmed once today."

Before he could answer, I turned around while sheathing my dagger and then strolled out the door.

Henry was still standing in the corridor outside. His sharp eyes tracked me as I stalked right past him and made my way downstairs. The heavy footsteps behind me informed me that he was following.

Once I reached the dining room, I unceremoniously took the seat at the head of the table. Henry narrowed his eyes at me but said nothing.

Leaning back in the dark wooden chair, I drummed my fingers on the smooth tabletop and waited for the arrogant force mage to show up.

When he at last did, he was once more fully dressed. But not in the dark leather armor he usually wore when he was out. Instead, he wore a pair of dark pants and a loose white shirt that he had rolled up the sleeves on, exposing his forearms. His black hair was still wet from the shower, and he dragged a hand through it as he sauntered into the dining room.

A sharp glint crept into his eyes when he found me sitting at the head of the table. But instead of commenting on it, he strolled over to the couch on the other side of the room and dropped down right in the middle of it. Leaning back, he spread his arms and draped them along the backrest. He smirked at me as if saying, *your move.*

Ignoring the implied challenge, I instead brought the topic back to our mission. "So, we need to abduct Lance Carmichael."

"Yes." Callan kept his eyes on me, but the smugness on his face was replaced by serious consideration. "But going after him at the academy is out of the question."

"I agree. It's the most well-guarded place in all of Eldar. Frankly, I'm surprised that Sienna even managed to escape during the actual graduation ceremony. Most of us run while we're back in the city, visiting our family."

"Indeed. Which means that we will need to grab him when he's outside the academy too."

"Did you read the notes Sam sent over?"

"Of course."

"Anything stand out?"

"Yeah. The grand ball to celebrate the start of their campaign."

I nodded. "I was thinking the same thing."

"But according to Sam's contacts, they're using those fancy invites that send up a little sparkle of fireworks when they're opened on the day of the ball."

"Which means that we can't just forge a couple of invitations," I finished.

"So we need to find a way to get invited to the ball instead. And once we're inside, we use your poison magic to knock him out and then we get him out of the city."

"Yeah. But to get invited, we need to establish ourselves in their social circles."

"Agreed." He narrowed his eyes at me. "Sam said that no one who sees your face will know that you're a dark mage. That true?"

Uncomfortable feelings swirled up inside my chest. The only people who knew that I was a dark mage were my parents and my older sister, but they had been too embarrassed to admit that so they had apparently made up some story that I had moved to Castlebourne instead. And that had been years ago. I had long since become an insignificant footnote in our great family tree. Well, there was one more person who knew. But she would never sell me out.

With a mask of indifference on my face, I replied, "Yes. And you?"

"Same," he said, his features smoothened into a similar passive expression.

"Okay then. So we insert ourselves in their social circles and secure an invitation."

Callan nodded. "We'll need papers to prove that we're legitimate citizens. Preferably from another city. Like Castlebourne. Without that, we won't be able to rent a house or do anything."

"I can take care of that. I know a forger who lives in Eldar. She can make the documents for us." I raised my eyebrows at him. "But first, we'd need to get into the city."

"I can get us in."

"Really? How?"

A smirk spread across his lips. "You'll see when we get there."

I flashed him a smile dripping with poison in return.

Surprise flickered through me. This planning session had gone really well. It was as if Callan could actually keep up with my own scheming mind. Irritation burned through the surprise. Strategizing with my enemy should not be this effortless.

Flicking my hair back over my shoulder, I raised my eyebrows in a taunting challenge. "Well then, we have a plan. Let's get this done as fast as possible so that we can go back to trying to kill each other."

Furniture creaked as Callan pushed up from the couch and closed the distance between us. Dark amusement blew across his face. I considered standing up, but that would make it look like I was getting ready to defend myself, so I remained in my seat.

Discreetly shifting my arms, I moved my palms closer to one another so that I was ready to call up my magic in a matter of moments.

Callan stopped next to me. His muscled form towered over me where I sat at the head of his table. Reaching out, he grabbed the armrest of the chair. I arched a nonchalant eyebrow.

My chair scraped against the wooden floorboards as Callan drew it out from the table until it faced him instead. While keeping his grip on the left armrest, he planted his other hand on the right one, caging me into the chair. His brown eyes glittered as he leaned down over me.

"Well, if you hadn't settled on my territory," he began in a deceptively smooth voice, "we would never have had to start this war between us."

Tilting my head back, I met his gaze. "I didn't settle on *your* territory. And I'm not the one who started this war. If you hadn't attacked me unprovoked and tried to get me to bow down before you, I wouldn't have had to respond with force."

"Unprovoked? I leave for a few months to take care of some business and come back to find that you've built a mansion on *my* lands. Close to *my* home. And you dare to call my reaction unprovoked?"

"It's not your land. What you have in this world is what you can take, and what you can keep. And you could clearly neither take nor keep the lands I settled on, which means that they're *mine*."

He leaned down until I could feel his hot breath on my skin. A vicious smile curled his lips. "Once our temporary truce is over, once we have taken and broken Lance and used him to make the heroes back off, I *will* take back my lands. And I will make you kneel before my feet as you surrender them to me."

Raising my chin, I laughed in his face. "Come try it, pretty boy."

Death gleamed in his eyes while he brushed his fingers over my throat, as if considering whether or not to crush my windpipe. But in the end, he just straightened and jerked his chin towards the doorway.

"Leave, *sweetheart*. While I still let you." He gave me a wicked smile as he strolled away. "We ride out tomorrow."

Pushing up from the chair, I ran my hands down the armored bodice of my dress before turning and striding towards the other doorway.

Tomorrow, Callan Blackwell and I would leave on a mission together to stop those self-righteous heroes from wiping out all the remaining dark mages. This would never work.

How was I supposed to stop myself from killing him every time he opened his mouth?

I didn't possess nearly enough self-restraint for that.

Not even close.

CHAPTER 6

Callan

The endless grasslands were at last broken up by a tall wooden building in the distance. My horse snorted as if it too recognized it. I glanced over at Audrey. The setting sun painted gilded highlights in her dark hair and made her eyes glitter like emeralds. She wore a tight-fitting riding outfit, which drew far less attention than those half-armor dresses she usually wore, but the dark garments still clung to her figure in all the right places. Truth be told, she was rather gorgeous. However, any attraction I might have felt towards her was overshadowed by the monumental desire to cut her heart out.

I didn't stand for challenges to my authority, and Audrey had done nothing but disrespect me since the day she decided to settle on my territory. Our fight had lasted for years and left many dead in its wake. But *she* was somehow still here. It baffled me. And it made me want to crush her even more.

"We stop here for the night," she said, her tone full of command.

It was the voice of someone who was used to people

obeying her every order. It was *not* a voice people usually used with me.

Flexing my fingers, I considered sending a force wall at her to knock her pretty little ass right off her horse. However, if I did that, I would be as good as admitting that she was getting under my skin. And we couldn't have that. So in the end, I just threw her another lazy glance.

"Of course we are," I scoffed. "Where else would we be staying?"

This inn, called The First and Last Stop, was the last one along the Valdan Road between the city-states of Malgrave and Eldar, and from here it was a full day's ride to the walls of Eldar. Audrey and I, along with the other dark mages in this city-state, lived in mansions out in the hills around the city to make sure that the insufferable heroes couldn't reach us all that easily. But the great road that connected all the city-states across the continent of Valda was the least suspicious route to approach the city from, which was why we had opted for it.

"I don't know," Audrey answered, and raised her eyebrows at me while a mocking smile stretched her lips. "Maybe you're one of those who likes sleeping outside in the dirt with the animals."

I matched her smirk. "Ah, so that's the kind of company you usually keep. That explains so much."

While still holding on to the reins, she shifted her palms closer to one another in a move I assumed was supposed to have looked casual. But it was clear that she was preparing to throw that poison magic of hers at me. I let my hands drift closer too. Part of me wanted her to try it. To start that fight. Out here, all alone and with nothing for cover, she didn't stand a chance against me, and I wanted to make her admit that while I pinned her to the ground with a force blade. However, there was a significant risk of someone from the inn seeing us. And as soon as they saw our magical battle, they would know that we were dark mages.

The seconds stretched on.

Then she just clicked her tongue and spurred her horse on. Whether it was because she knew she would lose, or because she didn't want to risk us being made, was unclear, but I liked to think that it was the former.

Several oxen and heavy wagons waited outside the inn when we dismounted, but the stable was empty of horses. A young lad jumped down from a loft inside the stable and hurried over to take our horses as we walked them over. Audrey stalked straight for the door as soon as the reins had left her hand. After handing over my own, I shook my head and strode after her.

Warmth and noise assaulted me as I stepped across the threshold and into the tavern area that covered the whole ground floor. Travelers in dusty clothes talked and laughed loudly at several of the tables while bright candles cast the whole room in yellow light. I elbowed my way through the crowd and approached the pale wooden counter along the back of the room.

"Welcome," said a cheerful man with graying hair and blue eyes. "What can I get you?"

"A place to sleep for the night, and some food," I replied as Audrey stopped next to me.

The innkeeper looked between the two of us. "One room?"

Audrey snorted as if that was the most ridiculous thing she'd ever heard. "Two."

"Alright then," he replied with a small smile. "Please have a seat while I get the rooms ready. I'll be out with food in a minute."

After paying him, I grabbed Audrey by the arm and hauled her over to a table by the wall. She stared daggers at me and tried to yank her arm out of my grip, but I was a lot stronger than her. And short of starting an actual fight, there wasn't anything else she could do, so she clenched her jaw and followed me to the table I had picked out. Pulling out a chair, I shoved her down into it before taking the seat opposite her.

Her eyes flashed as she rolled her shoulder and then met my gaze. "If you ever do something like that again, I'll make you cough up your own lungs until they're lodged in your throat and choke you to death."

"Calm down, sweetheart." I flashed her a sly smile before lowering my voice. "Remember that we can't use our magic in public, or we might as well scream to the whole world that we're dark mages."

"I know that. I'm not an idiot."

"Could've fooled me."

Before she could reply, the blue-eyed innkeeper returned with two bowls of stew and two mugs of what looked like watered-down ale.

"Here you go," he said as he placed them before us. Reaching into his stained apron, he pulled out two more objects. "And here are the keys to your rooms. They're not quite ready yet, but they should be all done by the time you finish your dinner."

I gave him a nod in acknowledgement before he drifted off.

The rather sad-looking stew actually smelled pretty good, so I picked up my spoon and dug in. Meat and potatoes, and some kind of herb. I'd had worse.

"How long will your forger need?" I asked between mouthfuls.

Audrey swirled the ale in her mug before lifting one shoulder in a shrug. "It shouldn't be more than a night's work."

"So we'll need a discreet place to stay in the city for one night before we get the papers."

"Yeah."

Running a hand over my jaw, I considered for a moment before nodding. "I think I can take care of that."

"Good." The chair scraped against the floor as she stood up. "Now, excuse me while I seek out more pleasant company."

My hand shot out. Grabbing her arm across the table, I locked hard eyes on her. "Sit down."

She twisted her wrist and ripped it out of my grip while her green eyes bored into me. "The next time you try to give me orders, I will cut out your tongue."

"Big words for someone who was bent over a table, completely helpless underneath me, only two days ago."

Narrowing her eyes, she stared me down for another few seconds. Then she snatched up her bowl and mug before stalking over to a different table. I huffed out a silent laugh. She was so easy to rile. This was going to be such a fun mission.

I tracked her as she made her way across the pale wooden floor. Instead of going straight to an empty table, she briefly stopped next to an already crowded one. Burly men in dusty clothes took up most of it, but there were a couple of women seated with them as well. Suspicion swirled inside me as Audrey bent down to whisper something in the largest man's ear.

Rage flashed across his face.

Audrey only gave him a solemn nod and then continued to an empty table by the other wall. There was a wicked smirk on her face as she sat down and locked eyes with me from across the room.

A moment later, wood creaked as the muscular traveler pushed to his feet and turned in my direction. I raised my eyebrows in amusement as he clenched his fists and stalked over to my table.

"You're gonna come with me," he said. "And apologize."

Rolling my eyes, I flicked my hand. "Leave. I'm not in the mood."

His hands shot down and he grabbed me by the collar before hauling me halfway out of the chair. Tilting my head back, I met his rage-filled gaze.

"I suggest you take your hands off me," I warned.

"You disrespectful little whelp," he growled down at me. "I'll make you—"

I rammed the heel of my hand into his solar plexus. A strangled noise ripped from his throat as he staggered backwards, his hands disappearing from my collar. Instinct told me to call up my magic, but we were in a crowded public place where I couldn't reveal that I was a force mage. Which was exactly what that damn poisoner had counted on.

As if she could read the thoughts on my face, Audrey lifted her mug in a mocking salute.

A growl rumbled from my chest. I sidestepped right as the traveler recovered enough to swing his fist at me. It sailed uselessly through the air. Twisting back around, I aimed another strike at him, but his other hand caught me in the side before my hit could land. Dull pain pulsed through my ribs.

Changing tactics, I ducked under his next strike and slipped slightly behind him. While he was still trying to turn around, I aimed a hard kick at the back of his knees. A grunt escaped his throat as he crashed down on the ground. Yanking out my knife, I placed it against his throat before he could get to his feet again.

Throughout the room, people looked at us uncertainly while a tense hush spread. The innkeeper stared at me from across the bar, worry evident on his face.

Rage pounded in my veins. But it wasn't directed at the man kneeling in front of me. Blowing out a controlled breath, I leaned down until I could speak directly into the man's ear.

"Whatever she told you is a lie," I said. "She's pissed off that I rejected her and now she's trying to get revenge. That's all it is."

My captive let out a grunt in acknowledgement that he had heard me.

"Now, go sit back down." Taking the blade from his throat, I gave his shoulder a shove from behind. "Before my patience runs out."

While he struggled to his feet again, the rest of the inn breathed a sigh of relief. I swept my gaze around the room. Audrey's table was empty. My eyes darted towards the doorway leading to the staircase and the rooms at the top. Long black hair fluttered around the corner.

I took off across the room.

Her foot had barely even touched the first step when I caught up with her. Wrapping an arm around her waist, I yanked her back down and slammed her up against the wall while pushing the knife I was still holding against her throat.

Green swirls glittered along her forearm as she placed her palm against my chest. With my back to the tavern area beyond, I prevented the rest of the patrons from seeing both her magic and my knife.

"What did you tell him?" I growled in her face as I pushed the blade harder against her skin.

Raising her chin, she flashed me a cocky grin. "I might have told him that you were boasting about how you were going to fuck the two women in their group before the night was over."

"You little—" I began before the voice of the innkeeper interrupted me.

"Is everything alright?"

Audrey's magic disappeared in an instant. After flicking a quick glance at the man over my shoulder, she looked back at me expectantly. Blowing out an irritated breath, I took the knife from her throat.

"Yes, everything is fine," I said as I turned around and shifted the blade in my hand so that the innkeeper couldn't see it.

"Miss?" he said, his blue eyes darting over to Audrey.

She let out a carefree laugh. "Yes, yes, everything is alright. Just a little moment of passion." Reaching up, she gave my cheeks a few pats. "I'll see you in the morning." Her eyes glittered as she held my gaze for a moment. "Make sure to lock your door."

With the innkeeper still standing there, I couldn't do what I really wanted to do to her. So in the end, I just gave her a smile laced with threats and stalked out the front door towards the stables.

CHAPTER 7

Morning sunlight shone down on the empty spot where my horse should have been standing. Anger and disbelief rolled through me as I stared between the saddle hanging on the low wall and the young boy who should have been keeping an eye on my horse while I slept.

"What happened?" I ground out.

The boy's nervous eyes darted towards the person behind me. "H-horse thieves."

"Oh really?"

Hooves thumped against the ground behind my back as a large brown horse moved to stand next to me. Seated atop it was Callan Blackwell, and he was smiling like the villain he was when I dragged my furious gaze to him.

"How unfortunate," he said with a mocking lilt in his voice. "That there were horse thieves out and about right here last night, and that they just happened to steal your horse."

"Yes, how unfortunate. Especially since there were only two horses in this entire stable, and they left yours alone."

"Indeed." He smirked down at me. "Looks like you'll have to walk the rest of the way to Eldar."

Oh I was going to kill him. I was going to poison him and watch as he clawed at his own throat, fighting for breath, while he squirmed on the floor at my feet. I was going to make him suffer if it was the last thing I did.

Keeping the wildfire rage burning in my heart, I spun on my heel and stalked back out of the stable. I grabbed my pack from where I had placed it against the wall and hoisted it before striding towards the road without another word.

The lazy clopping of hooves on stone informed me that Callan followed. On his horse, he quickly overtook me. But he didn't press far ahead. Instead, he moved his horse so that he was riding only a few steps in front of me. As if he was some sort of lord and I his lowly servant trudging after him on foot. I ground my teeth so hard that they almost cracked. Once we had Lance Carmichael, I was going to kill this arrogant bastard.

"We could share," he tossed over his shoulder.

I narrowed my eyes at him. "What was that?"

"I could allow you to ride with me." Twisting slightly in the saddle, he shot me a taunting look. "If you ask nicely."

Biting back a snarl, I whipped my gaze away and stared out at the landscape instead while I stalked forward.

Callan let out a satisfied laugh.

The sound of hooves thudding against the ground filled the air as he kept riding.

Sweat trickled down my back as I continued walking along the road while the sun rose higher in the sky. My shoulders ached from carrying the heavy pack, but I just clenched my jaw and kept moving. Hills and grasslands rolled past on both sides as I walked. And all the while, Callan comfortably rode his horse a few steps in front of me.

Unsticking my tongue from the roof of my mouth, I

swallowed against my parched throat. I really needed to stop and drink some water. But I refused to show Callan any weakness. My gaze seared into his back while I considered how I could stop for a rest without it making me look weak.

"This is taking too long," he suddenly announced, breaking the long silence that had fallen.

"Well, then perhaps *horse thieves* shouldn't have made my horse disappear," I sniped back.

Callan pulled on the reins. His large brown mount trailed to a halt while he turned in his saddle to face me as I walked past next to him. Our eyes met, and I swore that hatred crackled in the air between us.

"Get up on the horse," he ordered.

A disbelieving huff ripped from my throat. Stopping right next to him, I looked up at him and raised my eyebrows. "Over my dead body."

His eyes glinted as a wicked grin curled his lips. "That could be arranged."

My patience ran out. Slamming my palms together, I shot a cloud of poison magic straight at his face. He sucked in a strangled breath right before a force wall hit me in the chest.

I flew backwards, my magic disappearing as I could no longer concentrate enough to keep it up.

Pain shot up my back as I landed awkwardly on the ground with my pack still attached to my shoulders. Slipping out of the straps, I rolled out of it and then pushed myself up on an elbow. A boot appeared on my shoulder. I touched my palms together again while Callan used his foot to shove me back down on the grass before he crouched down, straddling my hips.

Glittering green magic hovered right in front of his face while a force blade rested against my neck.

"This is taking too long," he repeated. "At this pace, we

won't reach the city walls until morning."

"Well, maybe you should've thought about that earlier," I spit back at him.

"Just get on the fucking horse."

I glared up at him through the poisonous mist. He stared back at me.

"Fine," I bit out.

He held my gaze for another few seconds before pushing to his feet. The force blade disappeared from his hand. Struggling upright again, I brushed crushed grass off my clothes and ran my fingers through my hair.

"And drink some water," he said.

Shifting my gaze to him, I raised my eyebrows in annoyance.

"I can tell that you're dehydrated." He strode over to his own pack and pulled out a waterskin. "And you're useless to me if you're unconscious."

After taking a long drink from it himself, he threw it at me. The liquid sloshed inside the bag as I caught it in my left hand. For a moment, I considered pouring it out. But in the end, reason won out and I drank deeply from it while Callan rearranged his pack on the saddle and then attached mine as well.

Once I was done, I stalked over to his massive horse. After shoving the waterskin back into his hands, I swung myself up into the saddle. It was a rather flat and long model, probably made with packing space in mind, so both of us would be able to fit. Though, I would still need to sit almost on top of him.

The horse snorted and shifted its weight as Callan climbed into the saddle too. Grabbing my hips, he adjusted my body until we could both sit relatively comfortably. His firm chest was solid against my back when he at last leaned forward to grab the reins. I held on to the front of the saddle as the horse started forward. While it walked, I let my body shift with the movements.

"Stop that," Callan ordered, his voice gruff.

I frowned. Stop what? I wasn't doing anything to...

Realization dawned.

A wicked grin spread across my lips.

Shifting my position slightly, I ground my ass against his crotch with deliberate precision. His cock hardened in response.

"Audrey." My name rumbled from his throat like a warning.

I rolled my hips. His firm cock pressed into my ass as I continued grinding into him at a steady rhythm. It tore a low groan from deep within his chest.

A gasp ripped from my lips as Callan's hand shot up from the reins to wrap around my throat. His strong fingers dug into my skin as he forced me backwards until my back was pressed hard against his chest. I sucked in a strained breath from under his iron grip.

The firm muscles of his chest and abs shifted against me as he leaned down and placed his lips against my ear. My skin prickled as his hot breath caressed my skin.

"Unless you want me to tie you up and bind you to the packs behind me, I suggest you stop that," he growled in my ear.

Satisfaction sparkled inside me and a smirk curled my lips, but I stopped rolling my hips. Once Callan was certain that I would not start it up again, he released my throat and grabbed the reins with both hands again.

I suppressed a wicked laugh. So, he found me attractive, huh? Now, I knew exactly how to mess with his head.

Smug victory bloomed inside me.

This was going to be a fun mission after all.

CHAPTER 8

Audrey

Night had long since fallen when we at last arrived at the walls of Eldar. I had let Callan ride the rest of the way in relative peace, only rolling my hips against him occasionally to keep him on his toes. While I could almost hear him grit his teeth behind me, he hadn't actually tried to follow through on his previous threat.

"The gate is over there," I pointed out as Callan continued steering the horse away from the Valdan Road and into the darkness.

"You don't say?" he replied with a mocking huff of laughter.

"You said that you could get us through the gate."

"No, I said that I can get us into the city."

Blowing out an exasperated sigh, I shook my head but decided not to argue further as a structure appeared ahead. Squinting against the darkness, I tried to figure out what it was.

"It's a cheap stable," Callan offered. "For those who can't afford to stable their horses inside the walls."

"So we're going to do what? Stable the horse and then climb over the walls?"

"As much as I would have liked an opportunity to push you off the city walls, no... we won't be climbing them."

The brown horse snorted as Callan swung himself down. I did the same.

No candles were lit inside the building, so we approached the door with only moonlight to illuminate the area. I flicked my gaze over the stable. It was a wide one-story building that looked as if it had seen better days. Splinters stuck out from the wooden boards and moss speckled the tiles on the roof.

Dull thuds echoed into the silent night as Callan pounded his fist against the door.

Something clanked from inside. A moment later, light bloomed in the windows. Slight curiosity swirled inside me as I watched a man open the door and peer out at us. He looked to be in his forties, with dark hair and muscular build.

"A bit late to be stabling horses, don't you think?" he grumbled at us.

"You're John, right?" Callan asked.

Suspicion crept into his eyes. "Yeah. What of it?"

"I've been told that you operate a smuggler tunnel out of this stable."

"A smuggler tunnel? If I did something as lucrative as that, I wouldn't have to spend my night out here all alone, now would I?"

"There's a horse out here that needs stabling," Callan continued as if he hadn't spoken. "We also expect there to be three horses waiting for us here when we return. Now, hurry up and open the tunnel for us."

John stabbed a finger into Callan's chest. "Now, you listen here. Who the hell do you think you are? Coming to my stable in the middle of the night and trying to give me orders?"

"Last chance before this gets ugly."

"I'll show you ugly." Drawing his large fist back, John got ready to swing at Callan.

"West Market Street."

John blinked at him, his fist hovering uncertainly in the air. "What?"

"Sixth house on the right."

Mouth falling open, John stumbled a few steps back. Callan advanced on him. Light danced over his cold features as he and I moved into the candlelit stable.

"A lovely little green door," Callan continued as he backed John across the floor. "And white curtains in the windows."

"N-no..."

"Apparently your wife is a beloved librarian. And your two sons are both approaching twenty." Callan touched his palms together before a force blade materialized in his right hand. Death gleamed in his eyes as he cocked his head. "I wonder if they're strong enough to protect her. And themselves."

"Please, please, please," John begged.

I touched my hands together and let poison magic swirl down my arms as well. John's eyes darted to me briefly before returning to the force mage who was still advancing on him.

Desperation shone in his eyes as he abruptly dropped to his knees in front of Callan.

Callan placed the force blade under John's chin and tilted his head back. "I can have your family wiped out in a matter of minutes."

"P-please," he begged once more.

"But... if you do as I say, I might be motivated to spare their lives."

"Anything. I'll do whatever you want."

Dark desire coursed through my body. A grown man, muscled and hardened from dealing with smugglers, groveling at the feet of someone fifteen years his junior. With only a few sentences, Callan had stripped him of his pride and made him beg for mercy. I watched the way John trembled, looking up with pleading eyes. The absolute power that Callan wielded in that moment made my core throb with desire.

Irritation flitted through me and I shoved out those feelings. I would die before I ever let the actions of Callan Blackwell have any sort of effect on me.

"I thought so," Callan said. "Now, let's start again. There's a horse out there that needs stabling and I expect there to be three horses waiting for us when we return."

"Done. It's done."

"Good. Now, where's the tunnel?"

John scrambled to his feet. I let the magic along my arms die out while Callan made his force blade disappear as well. After a glance back at me, he followed after the frightened smuggler.

The smell of hay enveloped me as I walked deeper into the stable. A few horses raised their heads to watch as we passed, but most of them seemed to be sleeping. I adjusted the straps on my pack as I weaved between a few tubs of water.

"Here," John said as he shoved aside a bale of hay at the back wall of the stable. Crouching down, he slid a metal bar to the side before grabbing the handle and lifting the trapdoor that had been hidden underneath the pile of hay. "This will take you into the city."

"We're going to need a place to stay tonight as well," Callan said. "Somewhere discreet where people don't ask too many questions."

"There's a place three streets to the left of where you'll come out. Has a duck painted in yellow on the sign. Go there and tell them that John sent you."

Callan nodded and motioned for me to start down the

ladder. I narrowed my eyes at him but then skirted around him and positioned myself on the first step.

"Oh, and John?" Callan said while I started downwards.

"Yes?" he replied, nerves making his voice shake a little.

"If you breathe a word about this to anyone, I *will* slaughter your whole family. Do you understand?"

"I understand."

"Good."

I jumped the final bit to the ground and craned my neck to look back up. Callan was climbing down the ladder while John held the trapdoor open for a few more moments before gently closing it again.

Darkness fell around us, but it wasn't pitch black. I turned towards the low tunnel behind me as I noticed that there was still some sort of light source nearby. Bending down, I peered into it.

Crystal-like stones that emitted a faint white glow had been set into the walls of the tunnel. They weren't bright enough to fully light up the place, but they at least provided some sort of illumination that would prevent people from losing all sense of direction and crawling right into a wall.

A thud rang out as Callan dropped down from the ladder. The space was incredibly small, and only a single step separated us even though we were standing as far apart as was physically possible. Turning around, Callan looked between the low tunnel and my face before arching a dark eyebrow at me.

"Well," he drawled. "You'd better get down on your knees then."

"You too, pretty boy."

Challenge glittered in his eyes as he motioned towards the entrance that was right behind me. "Ladies first."

Taking a step closer, I erased the small space between us and reached up to draw my fingers along his jaw. A sly smile drifted over my lips. "If you wanted a chance to stare at my ass, you could've just said so."

His strong fingers curled around my wrist, forcing my hand away from his face. "The only thing I want to do with your ass is to beat it."

A mocking chuckle rolled off my tongue as I rose up onto my toes and slanted my lips over his. "Your cock seemed to disagree back on that horse earlier."

The iron grip on my wrist tightened even more. "You really are begging me to crush you into oblivion, aren't you?"

"I'm just pointing out facts."

"Well, here's a fact for you. If I ever were to fuck you, you wouldn't be able to handle it. You would come completely undone underneath me and be reduced to a trembling ball of need begging me for more."

"Oh please, you couldn't even find a woman's clit with a map and a compass."

"Ah, Audrey." He let out a dark chuckle. "I learn more about your sad sex life every day. If you haven't been with a man who actually knows where your clit is, you might as well not have been fucked at all."

Embarrassment flashed through me. How did he always manage to do that? How did he always take my insults and read through the lines until he found some weakness that he could throw back in my face? It was infuriating.

Letting out a derisive snort, I yanked against the hand still keeping my wrist trapped.

Callan didn't let up. Instead, he smirked down at me. "Tell me... When was the last time you had an orgasm?"

"Take your hand off me," I warned, ignoring his question. "Before I cut it off."

Callan's grin only widened. For a few more seconds, he just

continued staring me down as if to really drive the point home that he had won. Then he loosened his grip and released me.

I made a show of rolling my eyes and then turned around. After dropping to my knees, I started into the tunnel.

A smug laugh sounded behind me. "I knew it."

"What?" I growled over my shoulder.

His dark brown eyes gleamed in the faint light from the crystals as a smirk stretched his lips.

"I really do enjoy watching you crawl."

CHAPTER 9

Callan

A tall three-story building made of dark wood rose before us. Scowling, I stared at the closed door. I had lived in Eldar before, and I had my fair share of connections among its secret shady groups, but I'd never been here before. I glanced over at Audrey. We had agreed to stop our attempts to kill each other until we'd finished this mission. However, she was vicious enough that there was still a risk of her leading me into an ambush. I'd have to keep my eyes sharp.

"What is this place?" I asked.

"The Black Emerald," Audrey said as she stepped up to the front door. "It's a thief bar."

Without waiting for me to reply, she pushed down the handle and strode across the threshold as if she owned the place. After flicking a quick glance around the area to check for potential ambushers, I stalked after her into the dark wooden building.

A spacious room met me. Tables and chairs were arranged across the floor, and booths with dark green cushions lined the back wall. There appeared to be a kitchen through the door on the right while a long counter made up the bar. Beyond it was a staircase leading up into the building. Light from the candles fell across the faces of the men and women drinking and eating around the room.

Yeah, this was a thief bar alright.

It was funny. The leaders of Eldar truly believed that everything was perfect in their democratic little city. They had no idea how much resentment actually festered in its underworld. Even though the majority of the population might be happy and content, not everyone bought into the idea of sharing magic equally. There would always be mages who were angry that they had been forced to give up their powerful magic. People who had wanted to become dark mages, but who hadn't been strong or sneaky enough to escape before the graduation ceremony. And they gathered in places like this. Hoping to one day get hired by a real dark mage, and attain their slice of power that way instead.

Eyes tracked us curiously as we moved towards the brown-haired woman behind the bar.

"I'm looking for Paige Turner," Audrey said as she stopped before the counter.

The woman regarded her in silence for a few seconds while she continued wiping down a mug. "I don't know where she is."

A sharp smile spread across Audrey's lips. "Perhaps I wasn't clear..."

"No, I mean," she began before Audrey could finish her threat, "I really don't know where she is. She had to move recently because of... interference." She jerked her chin towards the stairwell. "There's a group up there in the VIP room, though. And I think they know."

Audrey studied her for a moment, as if making sure that she wasn't lying. Then she nodded and started towards the stairs. I followed. Our boots thumped on the wooden steps as we made our way upwards.

"Paige Turner?" I snorted. "Seriously? That's her real name?"

"No. But it's a subtle way to tell the right clientele what she is without drawing the attention of the constables."

"It's a ridiculous name."

She whirled around. Since she was in front of me on the stairs, the extra steps brought her face level with mine. Anger flashed in her eyes as she pressed the knife that she had pulled against my throat.

"Watch your mouth," she said, her voice like smooth poison.

Amusement flickered through me as I raised my eyebrows at her. "Touchy, huh?"

Clenching her jaw, she glared down at me as if it was taking every ounce of her self-control not to slit my throat. It just made me want to bait her even more.

"You done?" I cocked my head while a smirk slid home on my lips. "Then put that knife away before I make you."

"As soon as we have Lance locked up in Peter Essington's warded mansion and this mission is over, I will kill you, you know." Threats dripped from her pretty little mouth as she smiled at me. "And it won't be a quick death."

I snorted in genuine amusement, but before I could reply, she rammed her dagger back in its sheath and stalked up the final steps to the hallway beyond. Her shining black hair rippled down her back as she strode straight for a doorway on the left and yanked it open. I took the remaining steps two at a time and then followed her as she walked inside.

"I'm looking for Paige Turner," she announced without preamble.

An entire room full of people looked up from their tables

and turned to stare at her. When the woman at the bar had said VIP room, I had expected something small. This room was huge. And the group she had mentioned was more like four groups.

They were seated at a mass of round tables, and based on the cards and dice that littered the tabletops, they all appeared to be in the middle of different games. Both men and women occupied the seats around the tables, and all of them had that hungry look in their eyes that marked them as people who had dreamed of becoming dark mages.

"Who's asking?" a muscular man called back.

Audrey had stopped a few strides into the room, and the look of absolute authority on her face as she crossed her arms and arched an eyebrow at him almost made my heart skip a beat. Oh I had never wanted to make anyone submit to me more than I wanted to make her do it at that moment.

"I'll be asking the questions," she said. "Now, tell me where I can find Paige Turner."

"Who the hell do you think you are?" another man spit from a table on our right. "Coming in here and thinking you can give us orders."

"Yeah," the muscular man added as he pushed to his feet. He was almost as tall as me, and he towered over Audrey as he took a few steps closer to her. "If you want answers..." a grin split his face as he looked down at her and palmed his cock through his pants, "you're gonna have to earn them."

Cold fury crackled across Audrey's face. She slammed her hands together before the burly man could take another step, and glittering green mist shot out. It blanketed the whole room in a matter of seconds, forcing its way down everyone's throats.

The panicked cries were quickly cut off as every single person in the room reached up and clawed at their own throat. I swept my gaze over the large room and the mass of people currently choking to death in it. So this was how Audrey Sable had survived to become one of only six dark mages left alive.

I had seen her powers before, of course. But when we had fought one on one, her attacks had always been much more concentrated. And the times when she'd left droves of my people dead, I'd only seen the aftermath, not the actual attack. I slid my gaze back to the poisoner still staring at her choking victims. I was going to have to kill her quickly once this mission was finished.

When several people toppled out of their chairs, their eyes bulging and their desperate breaths only coming in shallow bursts, Audrey pulled back her poison magic. The men and women in the room sucked in deep breaths and coughed as they tried to refill their lungs. Once they had managed to get some air back, they all turned towards her. A hushed silence fell over the room. These people wanted to work for a dark mage, and they had just realized that Audrey was one.

Audrey touched her hands together, and glittering green tendrils snaked around her arms. The crowd flinched.

"Do you want me to spare your miserable lives?" Audrey said, her voice pulsing with cold command. "Then bow down."

Wood clattered as people shot up from their seats, knocking their chairs over in the process, and dropped to a knee on the floor.

Audrey's piercing eyes cut through the room. "Both knees."

Dull thuds sounded as people hurried to do as she said. When they were all kneeling on the dark floorboards, Audrey cocked her head.

"Now beg."

A cacophony of voices filled the room as the bowing men and women begged for their lives. I slid my gaze to Audrey. She just stood there, staring down at them while power pulsed from her body.

My mouth dropped open ever so slightly. What the hell? Blood rushed to my cock, making it strain against my pants. Orchestrating a power play like this just for the pleasure of it was something that I would have done. But I hadn't expected it from Audrey. And why the hell did I find it so hot?

"Enough," she said, her voice slicing through the noise like a blade. "Tell me where Paige Turner is."

Several people started speaking at once. Audrey held up her hand to silence them before pointing at a man in a rumpled blue shirt. I watched the way the expression on his face shifted between embarrassment, fear, and anger while he gave her the directions she wanted. Sweeping my gaze over the rest of the crowd, I found similar expressions in their eyes as well. These were useful people. I marked their faces as I realized that this might be a good place to come back to and recruit from.

"Good," Audrey said once he was finished. "Congratulations. You get to live."

Spinning on her heel, she stalked towards the door while her eyes drifted over my body. Wicked satisfaction blew across her face as she brushed past me. It took me a second to realize why. A low growl of irritation rumbled in my chest as I remembered the treacherous state of my cock.

I whirled around before anyone else in the room could notice it, and then strode after Audrey with powerful steps.

She was dangerous, there was no question about that. And it infuriated me that she was starting to find ways to get under my skin. I had wanted to subjugate Audrey Sable since the first time I saw her arrogant face when she declared that the land she had stolen from me was now hers. But after this power demonstration...

The ruthless authority she had displayed, making people

get down on their knees and beg her for mercy, had me itching to do the same to her.

Dark desire burned in my chest. Now that I knew how powerful and lethal she really was, I wanted even more to make her submit to me. I wanted to make her grovel. I wanted to make her beg and plead, and to know that I was the one who brought her to her knees.

And by all hell, I swore I would make it so.

CHAPTER 10

Audrey

"This is it." I nodded towards the pale stone building ahead. "This is where we'll find the forger."

Callan gave me a curt nod while his dark eyes shifted from the area around us to the house. Oil lamps burned in their glass domes along the street, helping the pale moonlight illuminate the otherwise dark city. We were close to one of the parks, and crickets chirped their nightly songs in the thick green bushes a short distance away. I drew in a calming breath of clear night air and then flicked my gaze towards Callan.

I didn't want him with me when I talked to Paige. Mostly because I didn't want him to know more about me or my contacts than was absolutely necessary. But also because he had laughed at Paige's name, and if he were to mock Paige to her face, I would kill him where he stood. And we still had a mission to finish before I could get to that part.

A wicked plan formed in my mind. *Ah, yes, that'll keep him occupied.*

"Callan." I raised a hand and pointed towards the street

that would take him to the other side of the building. "Go to the back door and make sure she doesn't run. We have a complicated history so I'm not sure how she'll react to seeing me."

For a moment, it looked like he was about to argue, but then he just nodded again and started in the indicated direction. An evil smile spread across my lips. Oh, he was in for a surprise.

I closed the final distance to the door and rapped my knuckles against it in a predetermined pattern. Or at least, that was the pattern it had been last time I'd seen her.

Seconds passed.

Then the door was edged open and a blond woman peered out. Shock pulsed in her blue eyes as she met my gaze.

"Audrey," she pressed out. Before I could reply, she opened the door wider and motioned for me to get inside. "Come in."

I moved into the darkened hallway while she closed the door behind me. There was candlelight coming from a room up ahead, so I started towards it when Paige nudged me forwards.

A cozy study met me as I crossed the threshold. There was a beautifully carved desk and a comfortable-looking chair by the wall, and a couch in front of a small fireplace. Potted plants with thick green leaves dotted the room and a plush carpet covered the stone floor.

Stopping in the middle of the room, I turned around to face Paige.

"You're alive," she said before I could open my mouth.

"Yeah."

"I hoped you were, but I was never sure." Her eyes searched my face. "What's it been? Five years?"

"Six."

"You've grown up."

"So have you."

She held my gaze for another few seconds, her expression neutral. Then a wide smile lit up her face and she closed the distance between us, wrapping me into a hug. Warmth swirled in my chest as I hugged her back. For a moment, we just stood there. Locked in an embrace that was long overdue.

Paige ran her hands down my arms as she released me and stepped back. "I knew that you made it out, but I never knew what happened afterwards."

"Yeah, I'm sorry. I couldn't risk contacting you."

"I know."

"Did you go through with the...?"

"Yeah." When she saw the sadness that blew across my face, she just gave me a small smile and shrugged. "Oh, don't worry about me. This was the path I chose, and I don't regret it for a second."

Paige was a water mage. Or she had been when I escaped Eldar. I had always suspected it, but now I knew for certain that she had stayed at the academy and gone through with the graduation ceremony. So now she was just a mediocre mage with access to a little bit of everything through the Great Current. However, her true skills had always lain elsewhere.

"Your parents used our story, by the way," she continued. "They twisted it so that it sounded like you moved to Castlebourne to start a new life after a serious falling out with your sister."

"Yeah, I heard."

"She has started a school for troubled kids. To help them get back on the right path."

I snorted. "Of course she has."

Paige laughed too. Then she turned serious as she once more searched my face. "But you didn't risk your life coming here just to say hi. You need my help with something. Were you caught? Do you need me to help you get out again?"

Gratitude warmed my wicked heart. Even after all these years, Paige was still ready to help me with my illegal acts. A wistful smile blew across my lips. Dark mages didn't have friends, but I had always considered Paige to be a small exception to that rule. After all, she was the reason I'd even managed to escape Eldar in the first place.

We'd been friends back at the academy. Early on, she had realized that she was really talented at copying people's handwriting. That had later led to her starting up a small side business as a forger while we were still in school. In each other, we had recognized the same need to excel at whatever we did, along with a certain penchant for breaking the rules, so we'd become friends. When I at last made the decision to run, Paige was the one who forged the documents that allowed me to just walk right out the gate. If she hadn't done that, I wasn't sure how I would have escaped.

"I'm in serious trouble," I answered. "In fact, all dark mages are in serious trouble."

"Because of Lance Carmichael and his campaign?"

"Yeah."

She nodded and then held up a hand. "Don't tell me any more than I need to know. It's safer that way. For both of us."

I inclined my head in acknowledgement before saying, "I need two documents of citizenship."

"From which city?"

"Castlebourne, and I need them as fast as possible."

Rubbing her arm, she glanced over at the clock on the mantelpiece before nodding to herself. "Two, you said? I should be able to get that done tonight." She waved a hand towards a notepad on the desk. "Just write down all the information there."

I moved over to the indicated notepad. Paper rustled faintly as I pulled it closer and began writing down all the information that needed to be included in the documents, and also where to deliver them once they were done. When I was finished, I straightened and turned back to Paige.

"Thank you." Reaching into my pocket, I pulled out the stack of cash I had put there before Callan and I stashed our packs at the end of John's smuggler tunnel. I held it out to her. "For this. And for last time."

She let out a light laugh and waved me off. "Nah, you get the friends and family discount."

I kept holding out the rather large pile of money, but she still refused to take it so I placed it on her desk instead. Another huff of amusement escaped her lips as she shook her head at me. Leaving the cash on the smooth tabletop, I closed the distance between us again.

"Thank you for what you did for me back then." I held her gaze. "I'm sorry I couldn't return the favor."

"Don't be." She smiled back at me. "I'm happy with my life just the way it is. I could never have been a dark mage. It's too lonely. And violent."

Tangled emotions blew through my soul. Well, she was right about that. Dark mages always had to fight each other for the limited territory in the hills and grasslands outside Eldar. And because of that, trust was scarce and the most respected currency was power. Dark mages had enemies and people who served them. But not friends. Not lovers. No one who wasn't bound to them by either threat or money. That was how we survived.

"I'm glad you're happy," I answered, and gave her arm a gentle squeeze. "You deserve it."

"So do you," she said as she reached up and squeezed my hand back.

Stepping back, I just smiled at her in response. "By the way, bold move setting up shop in this particular house."

"I know, right?" Mischief glittered in her eyes as she grinned at me. "And that's why it works. The constables don't think anyone would ever be stupid enough to run an illegal business right next to their favorite break area."

"You always were a clever one."

"Well, I won't argue with you on that." She laughed again before turning serious once more. "Good luck, Audrey. With everything."

I nodded back at her.

After one final smile, I turned around and strode towards the door, leaving Paige behind. Clear air enveloped me as I walked back out into the night.

A malicious grin tugged at my lips.

Now, I only had to find a certain force mage and see just how badly I'd managed to screw him over this time.

CHAPTER 11

Callan

Wind ripped at my clothes as I hurtled down the street. Boots thudded against the stones behind me as five constables gave chase.

"Stop!" one of them called. "Burglar!"

Lightning crackled through the air as someone shot a bolt at me. I dodged left and kept on running. More lightning magic sizzled behind me.

If I had used my own powers, I could have killed them before they'd even gotten up from that bench they had sat down on. But there were two problems with that. One was that we were in the middle of a respectable neighborhood, which meant that there was a significant risk of someone spotting me, and if they did, the whole city would know that there was a dark mage here. And that would make our plan to kidnap Lance so much harder. Which brought us to the second problem. Even if no one saw me, killing five *constables* would draw far too much unwanted attention that we couldn't afford. So I was forced to run away instead. As if I was some kind of weak coward.

Using the power of my anger, I pushed myself to go faster as I sprinted towards the park up ahead. Magical attacks made of water, wind, and lightning followed in my wake. But I was still moving too fast for them to get a clear shot.

The low fence that boxed in the park appeared before me. Bracing one hand on the cool metal, I leaped over it and landed in a flowerbed. Bright yellow flowers glared up at me in annoyance as I trampled half of them on my way out.

"He ran into the park!" one of the constables yelled.

Changing direction, I sprinted to the left instead of continuing towards the entrance on the other side. Fire bloomed in the sky above, lighting up the dark rows of bushes and trees. I dove behind the massive rhododendron next to me. Crouched down behind it, I listened for the sound of footsteps.

What were the fucking odds? I had moved over to the back door like Audrey had asked me to, waiting right in front of it to catch the forger if she tried to run. But not a minute later, a group of constables had strolled in and sat down on the bench right across the small courtyard. Since I'd just been standing there very suspiciously, facing the door, they'd thought I was a burglar. I'd had to run right away so that they wouldn't have time to see my face. Hopefully, Audrey had managed to get the forger to do the job anyway. But it bothered me that I hadn't been able to do my part of the plan. Just because fortune had seen fit to send five constables to that spot at that exact time.

"Which way?" someone asked.

The ball of flame moved through the air, casting my surroundings in orange and red light. I kept still.

"I'm not sure."

"Damn. Then spread out. He has to be here somewhere."

Shit. I had banked on them moving past me as a group, so that I could slip back the way I had come.

Boots thudded against grass.

I slid my knife out of its sheath. Maybe I needed to kill one of them after all. If it was just one person dead, and it was clear that it was from a knife wound, maybe it wouldn't draw that much attention. Indecision flitted through me.

The footsteps drew closer.

My gaze drifted to a branch lying on the grass, half buried by the rhododendron's thick leaves. That could work. Sheathing my knife again, I picked up the branch and tested its weight. It was solid enough to do real damage, but not lethal enough to kill. I shifted it to my right hand and then picked up a small stone with my left.

The constable was almost upon me now. Straining my ears, I focused on the sound of his feet and counted down the seconds in my head.

Now.

I threw the stone.

It sailed over the bush and clattered down on the other side. The blond constable who had been about to stumble onto me, turned around right at the same time as he stepped into view. I shot to my feet and smacked the branch into his head.

A *thwack* echoed into the park.

Then the man crumpled to the ground.

As I leaped over his unmoving body and sprinted back towards the fence, I looked down at the branch in my hand. There was blood on one side of it. Maybe I had put too much force behind that strike. As I thought back to the sound it had made on impact, I had a sneaking suspicion that I might have killed him after all. I shrugged. *Oh well.* After dropping the bloody branch in a bush, I vaulted over the metal fence and darted towards the closest street.

I ran in twisting patterns for a while to make sure that I had really lost them. When I had come to the conclusion that the constables were long gone, I turned and got ready to jog back towards the forger's house. But a figure visible between two buildings stopped me.

It was Audrey.

She was moving in the direction of the smuggler's tunnel, where we had hidden our packs. Most likely, she had found me missing and decided to head back there to see if I had returned there too. Brushing a few stray leaves off my clothes, I jogged down another street to cut her off.

She blinked at me as I stepped out of the shadows in front of her.

"How did it go?" I asked before she could speak.

Taking a few steps to the side, she moved into a dark and narrow alley that was well hidden from prying eyes. I followed.

"It went well," she replied as she came to a halt. "We'll have the papers in the morning."

"Good. Then we'll head to that house John mentioned and get some sleep while we wait." I dragged a hand through my hair. "I couldn't guard the back door, but it sounds like it worked out anyway."

"Yeah." She looked up at me curiously. "What happened?"

"Five constables decided to take a break right across the courtyard. They thought I was a burglar, so I had to give them the slip."

"Huh."

"What are the fucking odds of..." I trailed off.

Wicked satisfaction shone in her eyes and a smirk curled her lips. Almost as if she...

Realization dawned.

She knew.

I slammed her up against the wall. Surprise flashed in her eyes and she moved to evade me, but it was already too late.

With one hand keeping her wrist trapped and the other wrapped tightly around her throat, I held her pinned to the stone wall.

"Did you know that there would be constables there?" I growled in her face.

My fingers kept her throat in a death grip. A smile dripping with threats and smug mockery spread across my lips as I held her gaze.

"Oh, I'm sorry," I began in a tone laced with venom while I kept my hand firmly wrapped around her delicate neck, "I'm having a little trouble hearing you. Answer."

I'd had a lot of practice choking people with one hand, so I knew that I had cut off her air supply completely. She couldn't answer even if she wanted to. But she didn't. She didn't even try to speak. Or try to draw breath. There was no fear or panic in her eyes. No pleading look. She just stood there with a fucking smirk on her face, glaring up at me defiantly. As if I didn't hold her life in the palm of my hand. And damn it all to hell, but that actually made me respect her a bit.

When her eyes started to slide in and out of focus, I finally relaxed my grip and allowed her to breathe again.

Her knees buckled and she crashed down on the street before me as I released her throat and wrist. Pressing her palms against the cool stones, she sucked in deep breaths. My cock swelled slightly as I looked down at her. Oh she really did look good on her knees before my feet.

Fiery hatred burned in her eyes as she raised her head and looked up at me. "If we weren't in such a public place, you would be the one on your knees gasping for air right now."

I smirked down at her. "Too bad you're nothing without your magic."

She pushed to her feet, making a very valiant effort to appear unaffected. After brushing her hands down her clothes, she ran her fingers through her long black hair and jerked her chin at me.

"Let's go finish this mission so that we can go back to killing each other as soon as possible."

A huff of amusement escaped my throat. "Fine by me."

Wicked anticipation pulsed inside me. I did look forward to the day when I could devote my full attention to making her surrender to me, but there was still quite some time left before that.

And I was going to spend every day until then finding other ways to torment her.

CHAPTER 12

Audrey

A wooden sign with a duck painted in yellow swung in the gentle night breeze. The rest of the street was empty, so no one noticed us as we continued moving towards it.

We had retrieved our packs from the smuggler's tunnel before heading to the house that John had told us about. Tiredness rolled over me. Due to the detour to Paige's place, we were now far into the night. And I had also walked a good portion of the Valdan Road this morning because of Callan's stunt with the horse.

While running a discreet hand over my neck, I glanced over at him. My throat didn't even hurt. I hated to admit it but the bastard was actually really skilled at choking people. But it pissed me off that he had decided to demonstrate it on me.

I knew that I could have gotten away with it. He hadn't realized that I had sent him there on purpose until I had practically donned the victory like a gleaming mask. But I had wanted him to know that it was me. Narrowing my eyes, I dragged my gaze from him and back to the door we stopped at. And I would get him back for the choking.

Callan lifted his fist and pounded on the door.

For a few moments, nothing happened. Then a light bloomed in the upstairs window. I tracked it through the windows as it moved down towards the front door. Keys rattled. I shifted my palms closer as the door was pushed open.

A man with brown eyes full of suspicion poked his head out. "Yes?"

"We need a place to stay tonight," Callan said.

"Sorry, we're full."

"John sent us."

He paused. Shifting his gaze between the two of us, he sucked his teeth while considering in silence. I raised my eyebrows expectantly.

"We *are* full," he said at last. "Well, almost. We've got one room left."

"We'll take it."

"Come on in then."

Callan slipped the innkeeper some cash while he passed him and walked towards the stairs at the end of the hall. I followed as well. Behind me, the door clicked as the brown-eyed man locked it behind us again.

"Top of the stairs," he said. "Last room on the left."

Giving him a nod over my shoulder, I followed Callan up the stairs. The hallway was dark when we reached the landing, but there was just enough light from the candle downstairs to help us navigate it. I adjusted the straps on my pack as I walked down the corridor. There was a key already waiting in the door when we reached it, so Callan just turned it and then pushed the door open.

Another dark room met us.

While I closed the door and locked it behind us, Callan lit the oil lamp that was waiting on the side table. Light bloomed inside the room. Turning back from the door, I swept my gaze over the sparsely furnished space.

All it contained were the side table with the oil lamp and an empty trunk.

And one bed.

It was a double bed. But still, it was *one* bed. And I sure as hell wouldn't be sharing it with that bastard.

"You can take the floor," I announced as I strode forward. "I'll be taking the bed."

Callan snorted. "Oh I don't think so."

"I am not sharing a bed with you."

"Then *you* take the floor."

Stopping next to the bed, I turned back to face him. He was standing two strides away, his arms crossed and his eyebrows raised in challenge. Light from the oil lamp danced over his annoyingly attractive features.

I raised my chin and flashed him a cold smile, answering his challenge. "Make me."

"Oh I could."

Glittering green magic materialized between my hands as I slammed my palms together.

A ball of force magic took me in the chest. I flew the final two steps to the wall and crashed into it with a loud bang. Landing on my knees, I touched my hands together again and shot a cloud of poison at Callan. He had been advancing across the floor, but the green mist hit him in the face before he could block it. While gasping in a strangled breath, he leveled a force blade at me. I increased the strength of the poison.

Callan went down on one knee, his arm shaking slightly as he pressed the force blade against my neck while he continued choking on my poison. The pressure against my throat grew until I was certain he would draw blood soon. I added even more lethal poison to the cloud.

His other knee hit the floorboards with a thud, but the blade stayed at my throat.

Someone banged their fist against the wall on my right. "Quiet down!"

We stared at each other for another second. Then I let the green mist dissipate at the same time as Callan made his force blade disappear. He sucked in a deep breath while I reached up and rubbed my tender neck.

"Unless you want to wake the whole inn as we battle it out," he began and then raised his eyebrows as he paused, waiting for me to argue. When I didn't say anything, he finished, "We share the bed."

"Fine," I ground out.

Stalking back to the bed, I sat down and began unlacing my boots. My feet throbbed after being trapped inside these shoes for almost a full twenty-four hours that had involved walking a good portion of the Valdan Road. I rolled my ankles while Callan moved towards the other side of the bed. The mattress shifted underneath me as he sat down.

I stood up and walked over to the oil lamp. While he was still unlacing his boots, I extinguished it and then walked back to the bed with only faint moonlight from the window to guide me. Callan growled a curse at me.

With a satisfied smirk on my face, I climbed into bed. Lying on my back, I stared up at the ceiling while Callan finished with his boots. A distressed creak came from the bed as he lay down and repositioned his muscled body across it, making the mattress dip towards the middle. Annoyance rippled through me as I realized that he took up more than half of it.

Pushing it out, I closed my eyes and tried to get comfortable enough to sleep. My body was exhausted, but my mind was still spinning at full speed. How was I supposed to make it all the way to the ball, that was still something like ten days away, when all I wanted to do every second of every day was to cut Callan Blackwell's heart from his chest?

Deep rhythmic breaths came from the force mage.

He's already asleep?

I carefully sat up. The hard lines of Callan's face were smooth and his chest rose and fell steadily.

Very gently, I touched my palms together. Green mist appeared in my palm. For a couple of minutes, I sat there, debating whether or not to kill the bastard right now and just get it over with. I could probably find a way to finish this mission on my own. Especially now that I knew about the smuggler's tunnel.

Indecision flitted through me.

In the end, I just blew out a soft sigh and let my poison magic fade as I lay back down again.

"Good choice."

I whipped my head towards Callan. He cracked open one eye and smirked at me. The damn bastard had been awake?

Turning my gaze back to the ceiling, I clenched my jaw in irritation. I wanted to do something to wipe that smirk off his face and completely throw him off his game. There had to be something that...

A sudden idea struck me. *Oh, of course.*

With a wicked grin on my lips, I reached down and unbuttoned my pants. The mattress shifted as I shimmied out of my dark pants and tossed them to the floor.

"What the hell are you doing?" Callan grumbled next to me.

Instead of answering him, I drew my hands down my stomach and then towards my underwear. Moving the fabric to the side, I trailed my fingers over my clit. A small moan fell from my lips.

"I said, what the hell are you doing?" Callan repeated, but this time there was a dark edge to his voice.

I continued to ignore him. Closing my eyes, I rubbed my clit with practiced moves for a little while longer before pushing a finger inside me. Another moan rolled out of my throat. I added another finger.

While continuing to apply friction to my clit, I started pumping my fingers in and out.

"Audrey," Callan growled, a warning note in his voice.

My eyes were still closed, but it didn't matter because I already knew what his face would look like if I opened them. With a slight smirk tugging at my lips, I continued pleasuring myself.

The mattress dipped next to me. I ignored it. My chest heaved as I kept pumping my fingers and moving my thumb in circles. Tension built inside me. I let out a muffled groan. This was as far as I always got, but I could probably keep up the nice feeling a little while longer. If this didn't throw Callan off his game, I didn't know what would.

Strong fingers wrapped around my wrist and yanked my hand away. I jerked up in shock, but Callan rolled over, straddling me and pinning my other hand underneath his knee while still keeping his grip on the other. His eyes were dark with desire as he leaned down over me.

"If you're going to do it," he began, his voice rough, "at least do it properly."

Releasing my wrist, he scooted backwards and grabbed my thighs. Surprise still rang inside my head, so I just watched as he spread my legs wide and shifted his position so that he knelt between them. I propped myself up on my elbows and frowned at him, but he just leaned forward and planted a hand on my chest. After shoving me back down against the mattress, he reached down and moved aside the thin fabric of my underwear.

A thrill coursed through me as his fingers brushed my sensitive skin.

At this point, I had to admit that I was curious. What could he possibly accomplish with his hands that I couldn't with my own? After all, it was my body. I knew it better than anyone. And besides, it wasn't as if it was the first time a man had tried to replicate the act. None of them ever knew what they were doing.

He drew his fingers down over my clit. I shifted my hips at the friction, but again, there was nothing special about it. Callan removed his hand.

While still lying back against the mattress, I raised my head to look at him. There was a wicked grin on his lips. He touched his palms together. I was just about to question what the hell he thought he was doing, when he moved his right hand back to my center.

A gasp tore from my throat.

Force magic was wrapped around his fingers and he made it vibrate as he pressed his fingers to my clit.

I sucked in a breath. Gripping the sheets hard, I arched my back and tried to shift my hips away. Callan's other hand shot out. Taking my hip in a firm grip, he held me steady against the mattress while his force magic continued vibrating.

I let out a groan from deep within my chest as a wave built inside me. Callan shifted his fingers slightly and I threw my head back, gasping out a desperate moan as the pulsing vibrations hit just the right spot.

Tension kept building inside me to a height I hadn't even

thought was possible. I squirmed against Callan's grip on my hip as my mind threatened to fracture from the building desire. His fingers dug into my skin as he forced my body back against the mattress.

My chest heaved. I clenched and unclenched my hands, gripping the sheets hard, as I was pushed to an impossible edge. The vibrations pulsed against my clit until I thought I would lose my mind. That edge moved closer. A pitiful moan tore from my throat. Callan increased the strength of the vibrations.

I sucked in a shuddering breath as pleasure suddenly exploded inside me. It coursed through my body, making my legs shake and my vision flash white. Pleading groans spilled from my lips as my inner walls trembled. Callan kept the vibrations going, prolonging the wave while I moaned incoherently.

When the last of the tremors had passed, my whole body just slumped down against the mattress while heat radiated from my flushed cheeks. My heart pounded in my chest. I felt lightheaded. Staring up at the ceiling, I tried to piece my scattered brain back together.

What the hell had just happened? That explosion... that tidal wave of pleasure... I had never felt anything like that before in my entire life. It was intoxicating. The final tremors had only just passed, but I already wanted to feel it again.

Callan shifted my underwear back into place before returning to his side of the bed. The wooden frame creaked as he lay back down next to me. Tilting my head, I watched the side of his face.

A smug smile curled his lips.

"I was right." He let out a dark chuckle. "You'd really never had an orgasm before."

If this was what an orgasm felt like, then he was right.

I watched the satisfaction evident on his face.

And now, Callan bloody Blackwell was the first person to ever make me feel something that I desperately wanted to experience again.

Turning my head back, I stared up into the ceiling.

Fuck.

CHAPTER 13

Callan

A warm body was pressed against mine. Still half asleep, I pulled it harder against me while breathing in the scent of hair that smelled faintly of jasmine.

Reality started trickling in.

I cracked open my eyes and took in the sight before me. Hell damn it all. I was spooning Audrey fucking Sable.

My arm lay draped over her side, my forearm nestled between her tits and my palm resting below the base of her throat. Her lean body lay flush against my chest, and her ass, still only in her underwear, was pressed against my crotch. I could feel my morning wood pushing against her.

Biting back an annoyed growl, I released her and rolled over on my back before sitting up. She had tried to get under my skin last night by fingering herself right next to me. Well, that had backfired for her, hadn't it?

I raked my fingers through my hair, combing it back.

But watching her have her first ever orgasm had been... something else.

Another wave of irritation washed over me. Pushing to my

feet, I turned halfway back around and kicked the side of the bed.

"Get up," I snapped at the sleeping poison mage.

She shot up from the bed. Before she'd even landed fully on her feet, she had a cloud of poison swirling between her hands. Whipping her head from side to side, she blinked repeatedly until her eyes landed on me. I had to admit, she had nice reflexes.

My gaze roamed over her body. While she wore the shirt she had slept in, her sculpted legs were completely bare. There were also faint imprints from the pillow on her cheek and her long black hair was disheveled, a few strands sticking to the corner of those luscious lips. That, more than her state of undress, made her look oddly vulnerable.

An evil smile spread across my mouth. "The orgasm I gave you knocked you out good, huh?"

Her eyes flicked briefly to her discarded pants before she returned her attention to me. "It's cute how you think that you somehow got the better of me last night." She dragged a hand through her hair, removing those loose strands from her lips, before her chin rose in a cocky tilt as she matched the smirk on my face. "When I'm the one who manipulated you into it."

"Manipulated me? Nice try, sweetheart."

"So you just decided completely out of the blue that you were going to make me come like that?"

I opened my mouth to respond, but no smart answer came out. It was true that I had only done it because she'd been driving me nuts with her pathetic attempts to get herself off while lying right next to me.

Audrey flicked the rest of her hair back behind her shoulder and let out a mocking laugh. "Men. You're so easy to play that it's barely even entertaining anymore."

Snatching up her pants from the floor, I balled them up and threw them at her. "Get dressed. We leave in five."

She caught them in both hands and then shook them out while that poisonous smile still danced over her lips. Shaking my head, I stalked out the door to relieve myself and get ready. And maybe to find someone whose face I could bash in.

People bustled up and down the street around us. A mother was making small water animals that jumped in the air in front of her three children while an older man a bit farther down on the road used a swirl of wind magic to levitate his hat back onto his head. The bright summer sun shone down on a couple who strolled along with their arms linked.

Disbelief coursed through me as I watched these mediocre men and women go about their mediocre lives. How could they be satisfied with this? A scrap of magic and a city where everyone got a vote. As if they all actually knew how to run a city. And all they did was pass laws and make decisions to please other people. To make sure that everyone around them was happy. Well, I'd had enough of that for several lifetimes over.

"This is it," Audrey said as she trailed to a halt in front of a polished green door. "This is the house renting agency."

I nodded and took a step forward. "I'll do the talking."

"As if." She slid in front of me and placed her hand on the handle before twisting to speak over her shoulder. "Remember the story."

"Yeah, I got it."

Turning back to the door, she pushed it open and sauntered across the threshold. A small bell above the door tinkled into the otherwise silent room as we entered. Drawings of different houses lined the walls in an artful pattern, but the only piece of furniture in the room was a pale wooden counter at the back.

As the door shut behind us, making the bell tinkle again, a woman in her forties appeared from the open doorway behind the counter. She drew her hand over her brown hair which she had tied up in a bun, and gave us a glittering smile.

"Welcome," she said as she nodded towards the packs on our backs. "Travelers, I see. Are you looking for a place to rent?"

"We are," Audrey answered before I could. Moving over to the counter, she handed the woman the forged documents of citizenship that had been delivered to us from Paige Turner this morning. "My husband and I are from Castlebourne and we would love to rent a house for about two weeks. We're thinking about moving here permanently, you see. But we want to get a feel for the city first to see if we like it here."

"Oh of course. Half of our clients are people who do the same."

I stifled a snort. Of course they were. That was why we had picked this cover story.

"You can call me Violet," the woman continued with that wide smile still on her face. "What kind of house were you looking for?"

Audrey browsed the drawings on the wall in a very convincing manner. "Something beautiful. And spacious."

"I see. And the budget?"

A sweet smile graced Audrey's lips as she turned to meet Violet's gaze. "Not an issue."

"Wonderful. Then I think I have just the house for you."

Ducking back through the doorway, she disappeared for a couple of minutes. The clanking of keys filled the air. Audrey and I exchanged a glance.

When Violet returned, she was carrying a ring of keys as well as a whole bunch of documents. That same smile was still plastered to her mouth.

"Please, follow me," she said as she motioned towards the front door.

The morning sun climbed slowly higher as Violet led us towards one of Eldar's fancier districts. Grand houses lined the wide streets, and even though their gardens were small, they were immaculately kept. White marble buildings sat next to houses made of shining dark wood while a few had been painted in pale colors of green or blue. This whole neighborhood practically smelled of money.

I scanned the area with sharp eyes as Violet opened a gate in the low fence and walked up to one of the houses made of white marble. It was a two-story building, with a door painted red.

"The couple who owns this house is renting it out for a month," Violet began as she inserted one of the keys and unlocked the door. "While they are in Malgrave, doing the same as you."

"Malgrave?" Audrey said while following her into the house. "What an odd choice of city."

"Isn't it? But apparently, they have relatives there." Violet came to a halt in the spotless hall and spread her arms. "Anyway, here we are. Please feel free to look around. I'll be in the living room just through that doorway when you're ready."

In truth, a grand house in this district was all we needed for our plan. It didn't really matter what it looked like. However, we needed to keep up appearances in front of Violet, so I strode deeper into the house as if to inspect it.

Rich carpets lined the marble floor and heavy drapes of dark red hung around the tall windows. There was a kitchen next to the living room that Violet had disappeared into, and another large room meant for socializing across the hall. I pretended to be interested in it before making my way up the stairs. Audrey was still checking out the small downstairs bathroom so I left her behind.

Upstairs, there were several bedrooms. One was clearly the master bedroom, with a massive four-poster bed and a cluster of armchairs and sofas arranged around the cold fireplace. The other was a smaller bedroom, though it still housed a comfortable-looking double bed, while the final bedroom was completely empty. I briefly stuck my head into the very luxurious bathroom at the end of the hall before making my way downstairs again.

I met Audrey halfway down the hallway.

"Come on," I said and grabbed her arm on the way past. "Let's sign those papers and get this done."

She yanked her arm out of my grip and glared at me, but still followed me down the stairs and into the living room. It was furnished in the same elegant style as the rest of the house with bookshelves along the walls, several seating arrangements, and another fireplace that was probably connected to the same chimney as the master bedroom above.

"We'll take it," I said.

Violet looked up from where she was sitting at the long dining room table. Documents were spread out before her on the tabletop. "Excellent. Then I just need a few signatures. And then there is of course also the matter of the payment."

"You'll take care of that," Audrey said with a viciously sweet smile as she met my gaze. "Won't you, *husband*?"

Turning so that my back was to Violet, I narrowed my eyes at the damn poisoner. Money wasn't an issue for people like us. But still. This was a deliberate move on her part because she knew that I couldn't argue unless I wanted to risk ruining our cover story. Her pathetic attempts to get back at me were driving me nuts.

I let her see the promise of revenge in my eyes as I answered, "Of course. *Wife*."

She just grinned wider.

Wiping the anger off my face, I turned back around and walked over to the table. Violet pushed several pieces of paper towards me and pointed at the different lines while explaining the terms of the contract.

Once I had signed them all, and given her a rather large pile of cash, she handed me a set of keys and then stood up. Paper rustled faintly as she gathered up all the documents before giving me back our forged proofs of citizenship as well.

"There we are then," she said and gave us a businesslike nod. "If you have any questions, please don't hesitate to reach out. And if you want to stay longer, please just come and see me at any time. Otherwise, I'll see you again in two weeks when the contract is up. Have a wonderful stay."

"Thank you," Audrey said.

Violet smiled and nodded again as we followed her to the door. After a very lovely little wave from my pretend wife, we closed the door and blew out a soft sigh in unison as Violet disappeared down the street.

At last, we had an actual house to live in. With private bathrooms, a spacious kitchen, and comfortable bedrooms. And I knew exactly which room was going to be mine.

I slid my gaze to Audrey. "Come with me. There's something you need to see."

She frowned up at me, but when I turned and strode up the stairs, she actually followed. Once we reached the landing, I continued straight towards the empty bedroom that was opposite the bathroom. Pushing the door open, I strode inside.

"It's empty," Audrey said as she walked into the room as well.

"Yeah, I know. But look at that wall over there."

Her brows creased as she shifted a little closer to the back wall I had pointed at. "What about it?"

While her attention was still fixed on trying to discover the nonexistent thing about the wall, I took two quick steps back out and slammed the door shut. I barely managed to see the look on her face as she whirled around before the door banged closed and I rammed the key into it. But it had been enough. Absolute shock had flashed on her face as she realized what I was doing. But it had been far too late.

I locked the door right before a weight crashed into it from the other side.

"You bastard!" Audrey screamed as she yanked at the handle. "What the hell do you think you're doing?"

A malicious grin stretched my lips as I watched the handle move up and down while the door stayed firmly locked. Banging echoed into the silent house as Audrey no doubt slammed her hand against the door over and over again.

"You open this door right now or I swear I will kill you!"

I let out a chuckle. "Big words for someone who's stuck inside a room."

If it had been me inside that room, I could have just blasted down the door with my force magic and gotten out. But Audrey was a poison mage. She had nothing that could break through solid objects like that.

"Callan," she snarled. "I swear I will..." The door shook as she banged her fists against it again. "Hell damn it! Let me out right now."

"Nah. I think I'll leave you in there for a while. I suggest you use the time to think very carefully about who is actually in charge here."

"You bastard!"

I chuckled to myself as I strolled away from the door. Audrey's curses and angry banging followed me. Amusement swirled inside my chest.

Did she really think she could mess with me without facing any consequences just because we were in the middle of a mission? Oh I couldn't wait for the day when we'd finally gotten Lance Carmichael away from this city. Then, I would really put her on her knees.

But for now, she was going to stay locked up in that room for a few hours while I claimed the master bedroom for myself and took care of some things that needed to be done. And then, I just might let her out.

If she begged prettily enough.

CHAPTER 14

Audrey

Maybe I would bring him to the brink of death, and then allow him one breath to beg for his life... and then kill him anyway. Or I could rein in the poison a little and make him grovel *the whole way* to death's doorstep instead. That might be even better. He'd have to do it all. Kneel, bow, kiss my feet, beg and plead with everything he had. And then, I might dig out a scrap of mercy and allow him the sweet release of death.

Afternoon sunlight played in the pale ceiling while I lay on the floor in the empty bedroom, planning Callan's excruciatingly painful death in my head.

It had been hours since the bastard had locked me in this room, and I still had no idea what he was actually doing out there. I had searched for other ways out, but unfortunately there was only one door, and it was too far to the ground for me to jump out the window. So I'd been forced to stay put, plotting my revenge, while I waited for Callan to deign to let me out again.

The door rattled as someone gave it a light kick from the other side. I shot to my feet.

"So," Callan drawled. "Have you reached a conclusion? About who's in charge here?"

Saying nothing, I left my pack on the floor and snuck over to the wall.

"I might be persuaded to let you out," he continued. "If you beg for it."

I moved so that I stood halfway between the door and the outer wall, before drawing myself up against the smooth marble wall that separated this room from the corridor outside.

"You only get one chance, though. So make it pretty," Callan finished.

Still not replying, I just stood there, pressed against the wall a short distance from the door, while I kept my eyes on the handle.

The wooden door rattled as he kicked it again. "Did you hear me?"

Green mist appeared between my hands as I touched my palms together.

"Audrey. You alive in there?"

I shifted my stance.

"Don't tell me she fucking passed out or something," he grumbled from the other side of the door.

The metallic clinking of keys joined Callan's muttered curses as he unlocked the door. Slowly, the handle was pushed downwards. My muscles tensed. Then the door was shoved open.

Nothing else moved. From my position by the wall, I could only see the open door that hit the marble on the other side. No dark mage. The silence stretched. He was probably standing right outside the door, studying the room without going inside.

His head appeared in the doorway.

I struck.

A flash of glittering green magic shot straight at his face from the side. He whipped towards it, but it was too late.

Gasping in a choked breath, he crumpled to the floor. I kept forcing the poison magic down his throat while I moved away from the wall to stand in front of him. He was going to look me in the eye when he begged for my mercy.

Shock clanged through me as I was thrown off my feet. Slamming down on top of my pack, I rolled across the floor. Hell damn it. He'd already had a force wall ready to throw at me when he stuck his head through the door.

Dull pain pulsed through my shoulder as I tried to right myself again.

Something big sped towards me. Pushing myself into a sitting position, I touched my palms together and shot a poison cloud at it. A blast of force knocked it aside while Callan closed the final distance. I already had another attack ready, and shoved a swirl of poison right into his face.

He crumpled down right before he reached me, and I rolled to the side. But not far enough. Even though he was choking on my magic, he managed to time his fall so that he landed on top of my legs. I added more strength to the poison, but he had already called up a force blade.

While shifting his position so that he straddled my hips, he pressed the vibrating blade over my throat, forcing me down harder against the floor.

Because of my magic, he couldn't speak. But his eyes said it for him. *Pull back the poison or I'll slit your throat.*

For a moment, I considered whether I could get him to die from my poison before he could kill me. But in the end, I did still need him for this mission. Regrettably.

He pushed the vibrating force blade harder against my skin.

I blew out an irritated breath, but then gave him a nod.

While I let my poison cloud dissipate, he released his force blade and let it fade out.

Callan sucked in a deep breath. I raised a hand to check if he had managed to break the skin on my neck, but before I could, strong fingers wrapped around my wrist. Shifting his knees, he rolled me over onto my stomach and twisted my left hand up my back before he settled his weight firmly on my ass instead.

I pressed my other palm against the cold marble floor and used it to try to push myself up. Placing his free hand between my shoulder blades, Callan shoved me back down while forcing my left arm higher up my back.

A small groan of pain ripped from my throat.

"You ever try something like that again," Callan began in a voice dripping with authority, "and I'll tie you up and keep you on a leash while we finish this mission."

"If you try to lock me in a room again, you won't wake up the next morning," I spit back at him.

He leaned down, putting more of his weight on me, and placed his lips next to my ear. "Keep telling yourself that if it helps you sleep at night."

Pushing against the floor with all my strength, I tried to force him off me. He only twisted my arm again, and a treacherous whimper escaped my lips. I slammed my palm into the floor.

"We agreed to pull our magic back," I snarled, my cheek still pressed against the cold marble.

"Yes, we did. And now, you're completely at my mercy. You might be skilled with your poison magic, but never forget that in every other way, you will always be thoroughly outclassed against me."

I curled my fingers into a fist. Callan kept me pinned to the floor for a little while longer, as if to truly rub it in my face. Then he gave me one final shove between the shoulder blades and stood up.

Shooting to my feet, I rolled my aching shoulder while staring daggers at the arrogant force mage. He raised his eyebrows in a silent challenge.

The seconds stretched by.

When I didn't do anything else, he let out a mocking laugh and started towards the door.

"Go unpack," he ordered with a lazy wave of his hand. "I'm going to take a bath."

Narrowing my eyes, I watched him disappear into the hallway. Take a bath, huh? Oh, I knew just how to get my revenge on him for his little power play. He thought he was the one calling the shots, but I knew exactly how to mess with his head. And by all hell, it was so much fun watching that battle behind his eyes.

After grabbing my pack, I slunk into the hallway. One glance was enough to confirm that Callan had claimed the master bedroom, and I didn't feel like fighting him over it. Yet. So I just dumped my things in the second room and then got ready before striding towards the bathroom at the end of the hall. The sound of sloshing water came from the other side of the door. I pushed it open and strode inside.

An incredibly luxurious bathroom met me as I stepped across the threshold. Not only was there a spacious open shower in the corner, but the whole back half of the room was taken up by a massive sunken bath. Since we were on the second floor, there were steps leading up to the bath, which had then been sunk into the raised platform of marble. Two lounge chairs were waiting by the wall and white drapes fluttered slightly in the breeze from the window that Callan had cracked open. The force mage himself turned his head to scowl at me as I sauntered into the room.

His gaze drifted over the towel wrapped around my body before dipping down to my bare legs. Drawing his brows down deeper, he met my eyes again.

"There's a bathroom downstairs," he announced as I came to a halt in the middle of the room.

"I know." I lifted one shoulder in a nonchalant shrug. "But that one doesn't have a bath."

"Then wait your turn."

"Oh darling, don't you know?" A sly smile tugged at my lips as I removed the small piece of string and let my long black hair tumble down my back. "People who wait their turn never get anywhere in life."

Callan opened his mouth to retort, but right before he could, I released my towel and let it flutter to the floor. The words died on his tongue. Before he could recover, I sauntered up the steps to the sunken bath.

When I reached the top, I stopped and drew my fingers through my hair, shaking it out while letting him get a good look at my body. I knew that I was attractive, and I intended to use that to the fullest. Just like I used my magic and my mind and everything else about me.

Warm water lapped around my ankles as I at last moved down the steps on the other side and into the bath. Callan's eyes tracked me.

He was seated on the stone ledge that had been set into the walls of the bath. Since the water only reached waist or chest level, depending on how tall you were, it was meant as a sort of bench where people could sit so that they would be more thoroughly submerged. The top half of Callan's muscular chest was visible above the surface where he sat, but the water was so clear that I could see his body quite well underneath it too.

Damn. I had forgotten how ridiculously hot he looked naked.

"How's your arm?" he asked when I reached the end of the steps.

The warm water skimmed the bottom of my breasts where I stood. Turning slowly, I met Callan's gaze. The lethal smile on his lips informed me that he was referring to the arm he had been forcing up my back not ten minutes ago. I let a thoughtful expression descend on my features.

"I'm not sure." I rolled my shoulder. "I should probably test out the range of movement."

He frowned. That was probably not the reply he had been expecting. While keeping that thoughtful look on my face, I moved my left arm so that I drew my hand over my collarbones. It took all my self-control not to smirk as his eyes widened slightly in surprise. I dragged my hand downwards, kneading my tits before continuing down my stomach.

"What the hell do you think you're doing?" he demanded.

"I already told you. I'm testing the range of movement to make sure nothing is damaged."

He huffed out an irritated breath and looked away. Since I had no plans to let him off the hook that easily, I started towards him while my hand made its way over my breasts again. Water sloshed around my chest. Callan's eyes slid back to me. Indecision flickered in them.

If he moved away from me, he would be as good as telling me that what I was doing was affecting him. But if he stayed...

Keeping my eyes on him, I closed the final distance between us. Where he sat on the marble ledge, his face was almost level with mine. Water rolled against my tits as I moved, and it took him a second to shift his eyes back to mine. He was sitting with his legs spread wide on the bench, and I moved closer until I stood between them, getting in his face as much as I could without our bodies actually touching.

At last, I dropped the innocent and thoughtful look I'd kept on my features and instead let a wicked smile decorate my mouth. Callan remained firmly in his seat, looking back at me with thunder brewing in his eyes.

I drew both of my hands over my stomach. While I let one of them continue down my hip, I ran the other over my tits. Callan's eyes darkened. Holding his gaze, I traced my fingers over my thigh on their way towards my center. I let out a small moan from the back of my throat as I let them skim across my entrance.

Callan clenched his jaw.

While continuing to tease my pussy, I moved my other hand from my breasts and drew it up my throat. Water ran down my skin as my wet hand reached my chin. I released another moan and let my eyes flutter closed as I rolled my clit between my fingers. Tracing my other hand over my lips, I stuck two fingers into my mouth and bit down as if to suppress a groan of pleasure.

My stomach lurched.

I drew in a startled breath and my eyes flew open as I was yanked off my feet. Water slapped against the marble walls of the bath as Callan shot to his feet and grabbed me before spinning me around and slamming me down on the ledge he had been sitting on. The force as my ass met the ledge sent a jolt through my body. Water rippled around me, reaching all the way up to my collarbones. I snapped my gaze up to the dark mage before me.

Callan Blackwell released his grip on my arms, but his hands quickly appeared on my legs instead. His strong fingers dug into my skin as he took my thighs in a firm grip and spread my legs wide. I smirked up at him.

Bracing a knee on the ledge between my legs, he leaned forward until I could feel his hot breath on my skin. His kneecap was pressed against my entrance and his hard cock brushed my hip as he leaned down the final bit. Drops of water ran down his lean muscled chest and lightning flashed in his eyes. When he spoke, his voice was like rumbling thunder.

"I hate you more than I have ever hated anything or anyone in my entire life."

I let out a dark laugh. "You want to fuck me so badly, don't you?"

His hand shot up. Taking my jaw in a punishing grip, he forced my head back against the wall behind me while he stared me down. War raged behind his eyes, and for a moment, I thought he might actually kiss me.

Then he released my jaw with a force that made my head snap to the side. Pushing off from the ledge, he rose to his full formidable height above me. I turned my head back so that I faced him, and found death swirling in his dark eyes. A victorious smile slid across my lips.

Callan let out a low snarl. Whirling around, he stalked out of the bath and down the steps. After wrapping a towel around his hips and the very telling state of his cock, he strode out of the bathroom without a second look back.

A smug laugh bubbled from my throat. Leaning back against the wall, I smiled up at the pale ceiling above me.

If I had known that baiting Callan like this to mess with his head was this much fun, I would have done it ages ago.

And now I had even more weapons to draw from when we started our war back up again.

CHAPTER 15

Callan

My eyes drifted towards Audrey. It bothered me more than I wanted to admit how easily she managed to get under my skin.

There were always a bunch of people who dreamed of hooking up with dark mages, so at any time, I could have women begging at my feet for a single night with me. *I fucked them.* Not the other way around. *I decided if and when and how.* So why was Audrey bloody Sable getting to me like this?

The thought sent a flash of anger, mixed with panic, through me. I'd already spent far too many years following other people's lead and trying to please them, and I had long ago sworn that I would never let anyone push me around ever again.

I knew exactly what Audrey was doing. I knew that she was doing it just to mess with me. But it didn't change the fact that every time she did something like that, it made me want to fuck her until the only thought left inside her head was my name. And I hated it. We had to finish this mission quickly so that I could finally end her infuriating existence and get some damn peace.

"This is the one," Audrey said as she nodded towards a massive house across the street.

Drawing myself up against the wall next to her, I studied the house from where we were standing hidden in a small alley. The sun was dipping lower towards the horizon, making the buildings cast long shadows. But it still wasn't dark enough for people to start lighting candles and oil lamps, so the windows of the house up ahead only reflected the golden light of the sunset.

"The man in there lives for juicy gossip." Her green eyes slid to me. "If anyone knows which families currently belong to the social elite, it's him."

Suspicion crept into my mind as I met her gaze. "How do you know?"

For a moment, she only stared up at me in silence. Then she broke eye contact and went back to watching the house. "I grew up two streets away."

My eyebrows rose. She had grown up *here*? This was a really rich neighborhood.

"Won't he recognize you?" I asked.

"No. I spent most of my time at the academy."

"What about the weekends?"

Instead of answering, she turned back to me and declared, "We knock on his door and go with the same ruse as before. We're a couple from Castlebourne who traveled here to rent a house so that we can figure out if we want to move here permanently. And we want to get a feel for the social life here, which is why we're asking him for help."

"Wouldn't it be easier to just threaten or bribe him into telling us?"

"Didn't you hear me? He's a huge gossip. If we do that, he'll tell other people about us."

"We could just make him disappear."

"Which wouldn't draw attention *at all*." She rolled her eyes at me. "People in this social class are far too well-connected for that kind of heavy-handed bullshit." A vicious glint crept into her eyes as she flicked a glance up and down my body. "But then again, you've got more muscles than brain, so I shouldn't be surprised that you'd make a suggestion like that."

Locking hard eyes on her, I cocked my head while a dangerous smile curled my lips. "Careful now."

She let out a dismissive laugh and brushed past me. "Let's go."

After smothering the impulse to run a force blade through her ribs, I pushed off from the wall and stalked after her. Golden sunlight played in her long dark hair, and her rich green dress shifted around her legs. It wasn't one of those half-armor things she usually wore but instead an elegantly cut dress that fit right in here among these expensive houses. I watched the way she swayed her hips when she walked.

Irritation shot through me when she cast a sudden glance over her shoulder and caught me staring at her ass. A sly smile blew across her lips. I glared back at her. Of course she had been doing it on purpose.

Sunflowers had been planted along the whole path from the fence to the front door, and Audrey gently drew a hand over a few of them as she closed the final distance to the door. Lifting her hand, she gave the polished wood a few brisk knocks. I came to a halt next to her right as the door was opened.

"Yes?" said a thin man as he peered out at us. He had a pair of round glasses perched on his hooked nose.

"Oh, hi!" Audrey said in a light and cheerful voice that I

had never heard from her before. "I'm so sorry to disturb you, but my husband and I were just walking past and I couldn't help but notice your extraordinary sunflowers. And I said to him, *darling, I just have to ask what the secret behind them is. Didn't I?*"

Confusion rippled through me as she looked up at me with those sparkling green eyes. Weren't we supposed to ask about influential people? Why was she talking about sunflowers? It had to be her way of buttering him up before she asked what we really wanted to know, so I pushed the surprise aside and smiled down at her. "You sure did, sweetheart."

"They're simply magnificent." She motioned towards the tall yellow flowers while shifting her gaze back to the man in the doorway. "Could you please share what it is that you do to make them like this? Mine always start to droop when they get this big."

The man's whole face lit up. "Oh, of course. It's so wonderful to find someone else who appreciates sunflowers as much as I do."

Pushing the door open wider, he moved out to stand next to one of the flowerbeds while he enthusiastically started describing what he did with them. I kept a mildly interested look on my face while he and Audrey chatted about the proper way to care for sunflowers. She must have known about his obsession with them before she even walked up to the door. No one could pull this many random questions about flowers out of thin air.

"Oh, thank you so much," Audrey said once his lengthy presentation finally ended. A bright smile shone on her face as she continued looking at him while waving a hand towards me. "You know, my husband and I have just moved here. Well, we're renting a house for two weeks to see if we want to move here. And now I'm starting to feel really good about it."

"I'm glad to hear that," he answered. "Have you met any other people yet?"

"No, in truth, we only moved in this morning." She let out an embarrassed laugh. "Where would we even go to meet new people? It can be so awkward trying to make new friends as an adult."

"Oh, I know what you mean. But what kind of friends would you like to meet?"

Audrey pressed a hand to her chest before fanning her face as if to cool her heated cheeks. "I'm embarrassed to even admit this, but I do like high society."

His eyes lit up and a satisfied smile blew across his face. "Then I know exactly who you should meet. Elise Dawson is the gem of high society right now, and she has a large circle of friends too."

"That's amazing. Where would I go if I wanted to meet her?"

"They usually stroll through the market around midday, so you should find her there."

I studied Audrey while the chatty man described what this Elise person and her friends looked like. It would have been a lot more fun to threaten him into telling us, but I had to admit that this approach was not only incredibly smooth, it also established our ruse even more firmly since this guy would most likely go blabbing to others about the nice newly-arrived couple he had met. Maybe her poison magic wasn't the only reason that Audrey had survived this long.

"Thank you so much," she said and flashed him another brilliant smile. "You've been such a tremendous help."

I nodded a goodbye too as we turned and made our way back out onto the street. The sounds of people chatting and laughing came from around the corner. When we rounded it, we found a group of well-dressed men and women gathering outside someone's door as if they were on their way out. Their colorful clothes shone in the light of the setting sun. Audrey and I gave them a friendly nod as we passed. Keeping our pace to a casual evening stroll, we continued back towards our house.

"What a liar you are," I commented when we were finally out of earshot.

Audrey let out a smug chuckle and swept her hair over her shoulder. "I'll take that as a compliment."

"Who knew that you could be so pleasant and bubbly when you put in some effort. Maybe you should work a little harder on that."

A dark shadow passed across her face. Cutting me a scathing glare, she picked up the pace and stalked ahead. I frowned. What had that been about?

Shaking my head, I shoved out the thought and strode after her. Who cared? We had a name and a location. Now, we just had to go and find this Elise Dawson.

If Audrey was this good at pretending to be civilized, she'd have no problem ensnaring our mark on her own.

Because I was certainly not interested in making any friends.

Real or otherwise.

CHAPTER 16

Audrey

Merry chattering filled the market around us and the intoxicating scent of spicy meat pies and freshly baked bread hung in the air. I slid my arm through Callan's as we strolled between the colorful stalls.

"What are you doing?" he grumbled down at me while keeping his gaze sweeping across the crowd.

"We need to look like a happy couple."

"As opposed to you, I'm not nearly good enough at faking it in order to pull off that massive lie."

While keeping a blissful smile on my lips, I discreetly jabbed a vicious elbow into his side. "Just do as I say."

He didn't even wince at the strike. Instead, he just tightened his grip on my arm until it almost hurt. I shot him a pointed look. After holding my gaze for another few seconds, he relaxed his grip slightly.

A woman with loose blond curls suddenly appeared on the other side of the stall we were passing. She had an entourage of chatting women trailing along after her. Their voices cut through the rest of the murmur and people turned their heads to look at them. Even if I hadn't gotten a description of what she looked like, I would have recognized someone like her from miles away. This was Elise Dawson.

"That's her, isn't it?" Callan said, which was surprisingly perceptive coming from him.

"Yes." I nodded towards the booth with a bright yellow awning on our left. "Quick. Buy us something to drink."

He blew out an amused snort. "I paid for the house. You can pay for the drinks."

Suppressing a snarl, I pulled him with me towards the lemonade stand and bought us one each. While I paid the round-cheeked woman who owned the stall, Callan nudged my back and spoke in a low voice.

"They're coming this way."

I thanked the woman for the lemonade before turning to press one of the cups into his hands, and then briskly moved us away. There was a sharp corner in the path between the market stalls up ahead which would work perfectly for our scheme. We slid in behind a red and white striped cloth wall right as Elise Dawson and her friends rounded the corner at the far end.

Since they were speaking so loudly, we didn't need to peek out from behind the wall to see where they were. We could hear them getting closer.

"Ready?" I whispered when they were almost upon us.

Callan nodded.

We took a confident step around the corner right as Elise Dawson rounded it from the other side. Startled yelps rang out as we bumped right into each other. I made sure to spill my drink all over my stunning dress.

"Oh, by the Current," Elise exclaimed as she stumbled backwards.

While doing the same, I looked up at her with worried eyes. "I'm so sorry. It was completely my fault. I wasn't looking where I was..." My gaze drifted down to my empty cup and then flashed to the big wet stain right across my chest. I let a hint of dread seep into my voice as I finished with a sad, "Oh."

Elise pressed a hand to her mouth as she looked down at the stain while the rest of her group sucked in a gasp. "Oh no."

"It's fine." I waved my hand in front of my face as if to brush off the embarrassment. "I can just... It's fine."

Callan shook his head at me while a very convincing look of concern descended on his face. "But wasn't this the dress you were supposed to wear tonight when we—"

"It's all fine," I interrupted while turning back to Elise. "It was entirely my fault."

"No, not at all," she said. Leaning forward, she ran her fingers over my ruined dress and pulled slightly at the fabric of the skirt. "And it was such a gorgeous dress too. You really have exquisite taste." Her blue eyes met mine. "And you were supposed to wear this to some kind of event tonight?"

"Yes, but I'm sure I can find a dressmaker somewhere to purchase another one."

"Oh, then I absolutely recommend Wendy's boutique."

"I'm sorry, I'm not sure where that is. My husband and I just moved here from Castlebourne."

Elise, along with every woman in her little entourage, turned towards Callan as if truly noticing his presence for the first time. Several pairs of eyes flicked up and down his lean muscled body, and the dark-haired woman behind Elise's left shoulder bit her lip. It made a flash of annoyance shoot through me.

"How lovely," Elise answered, and exchanged a conspiratorial look with her friends before dragging her gaze back to me. A glittering smile spread across her lips. "We could accompany you to Wendy's if you want?"

"I don't want to cause you any inconvenience."

"Not at all." She flicked her gaze to the dark-haired woman. "Lisa was thinking about getting a dress too. Weren't you, Lisa?"

She nodded. "I was."

Elise clapped her hands and made a shooing motion. "Then it's settled. We'll accompany you to Wendy's to make up for spilling your drink all over you."

"How kind of you."

Victory sparkled in my chest as Callan and I fell in beside the chatting group while they led us towards this dressmaker. We had established a connection. Now, we just needed to let it mature a little before we could make our offer.

The smugness inside me was dampened a little as I glanced over at Callan. It annoyed me that his presence had been important for the success of this scheme. Especially when all he had done was stand there and look hot.

A smirk tugged at Callan's lips as he briefly met my gaze. Of course the bastard knew it too.

Cheerful tinkling from a small metal bell filled the air as Elise pushed open the door to a light and airy shop. Excited giggling followed it as the rest of her friends strolled inside after her. Callan motioned for me to follow before he stepped in too and closed the door behind us.

I swept my gaze over the room as we moved farther inside. Gorgeous dresses were displayed on long wooden racks that ran the length of the room. They glittered in the bright sunlight that fell in through the windows.

"Elise," said a woman with graying hair as she appeared from a room at the back. "How good to see you again so soon."

"Wendy," she replied. "I'm not here for me this time. I

accidentally bumped into..." Trailing off, she looked over at me as she realized that she had never bothered to ask for my name.

"Audrey," I filled in.

"Audrey. And..." She turned her blue eyes to Callan.

"Callan," he said.

She smiled at him before turning back to Wendy. "And Audrey spilled her drink all over her dress. Can you help her out? You do have something for her, don't you?"

"Of course." Wendy's kind brown eyes shifted to me as she motioned towards the rooms at the back. "Please, this way."

I followed her. As did everyone else. Lisa hooked her arm through Callan's and led him towards the back rooms as well while Elise started up a conversation with Wendy about which kinds of dresses she thought might look good on me.

Some ushering later, I found myself in a changing room while the rest of them took a seat on the pristine white couches outside. Wendy handed me a stunning evening gown in black and gold before she pulled the pale fabric curtain closed. I looked between the garment and my body.

"I also want to try something on," Lisa's voice said from outside the changing room. "Something in blue, please."

Rippling laughter followed as her friends no doubt encouraged her. I rolled my eyes but began stripping out of my lemonade-stained dress. After draping it over the hanger inside, I straightened and reached for the other dress.

The skin at the back of my neck prickled. I twisted slightly to look behind me. Through the small gap between the white curtain and the wall, Callan was visible where he sat at the edge of the couch. Three beautiful women were squeezed in next to him, but his eyes were locked on my changing room. Locked on the sliver of my body that he could see through the gap.

Smug satisfaction bloomed in my chest. Moving slightly, I made sure that my body was in the perfect position before I bent down to retrieve the other dress. While in that position, I took my time and ran my hands over the dress as if inspecting it. Then I abruptly looked straight out through the gap in the curtain.

Callan blinked in surprise. Drawing down his eyebrows in a scowl, he snapped his gaze away and stared towards the other side of the room. I stifled a laugh.

After shimmying into the black and gold dress, I turned towards the full-length mirror on the wall. It really was a gorgeous piece of clothing. I might actually buy it just because I wanted it and not only to help sell the ruse.

"How is it looking?" Elise called from somewhere outside the curtain.

"I'm not sure," I said, because we still needed to spend a little more time with these people.

"What does the husband think?" someone else called.

That unleashed a wave of giggles. I let out a silent huff of laughter. Oh, I had already seen exactly how he reacted to me in this changing room. But they of course didn't know that.

"Yes, Callan," Elise picked up. "Why don't you go and help your wife decide whether to buy that dress or not?"

Since I had moved away from the small gap, I could no longer see him, but I had no trouble imagining the irritated scowl on his face. He would never agree to that. Especially not after I had already caught him stealing glances at me through the curtain.

Fabric rustled as the white drape was shoved aside to allow a muscled force mage inside. I blinked at him in surprise. The curtain fluttered closed behind him again as he took a step forward, forcing me to press myself against the wall for us both to fit. He raked his eyes up and down my body.

"Well?" I said as I gave him a sly smile.

"It's fine," he answered in a gruff voice, but it was low

enough that I knew none of the others would have heard it from the couch.

"Fine?" I arched a dark eyebrow at him. "I don't do *fine*. I do perfect, or nothing at all."

He opened his mouth, but before he could reply, I reached up and pushed the dress off my shoulder, letting it slip down to reveal more of my skin. The fingers of his right hand curled into a fist.

"Maybe I should try on something else then," I continued as I lifted my hand to slide the dress off my other shoulder as well. I raised my eyebrow in challenge. "What do you think?"

His hand shot out and grabbed my wrist before I could push the dress off my shoulder. Holding it in a firm grip, he closed the final distance between us. He planted his other palm against my collarbones so that he could pin me to the wall. I raised my chin and smirked up at him in challenge while he pressed his honed body into mine and leaned down to place his lips next to my ear. My skin prickled as his hot breath danced over my neck.

"I think you need to stop being so cocky," he whispered against the shell of my ear. "I can make you beg for mercy anytime I want. So unless that is something you're secretly craving, I suggest you stop playing this game with me."

"Oh I suspected that I was getting under your skin." A grin stretched my lips. "But now I know for certain."

"So?" Elise called from outside. "What does the husband think?"

Callan straightened again, but kept his hand against my collarbones, pushing me into the wall. Releasing my wrist, he used his other hand to draw the dress back up over my shoulder while his eyes stayed locked on mine. Even though he hadn't touched his palms together, he must have somehow been using his force magic because a tremor coursed through my body when his fingers brushed against my skin.

A smile that promised sweet revenge curled Callan's lips as he dragged his gaze over my body before finally replying, "The husband thinks it's *perfect*."

I matched the smirk on his face.

Outside the white curtain, Elise and the others laughed and hooted in excitement.

After Callan had disappeared back out again, I tried on a few more pieces of clothing to help sell our scheme before we all finally returned to the front of the shop. Since I had only been able to bring what could fit in my pack, I took the opportunity to actually purchase a few garments.

Once I had paid Wendy, I turned to face Elise Dawson. "Thank you so much for all your help. Please, let me make it up to you by inviting you to dinner." I swept my gaze over the rest of her friends. "You are of course also welcome."

"That would be lovely," she answered.

"How's the day after tomorrow?"

Some of Elise's friends already had previous commitments, but Elise herself, along with Lisa and another blond woman whose name I didn't know, said that they would be happy to come.

"We will bring our husbands too," Elise said with a wink at Callan. "So that you won't be lonely."

"Of course," I said. "Please do."

The small bell tinkled merrily as our whole group walked back out into the bright sunlight. I waved at the group of excited women as they disappeared down the street before I heaved a deep sigh and let the cheerful mask fall from my face.

"Alright, we have our dinner with the social elite," I said as Callan and I started back towards our house.

"Yeah. Now we just need a cook skilled enough to pull off a dinner for eight in two days."

I drew my fingers through my hair, letting it flutter down my back, while I blew out another long breath. "Yes."

Callan glanced down at me for a few seconds before giving me a businesslike nod. "I'll reach out to Violet."

I nodded back.

One step closer to our goal.

CHAPTER 17

Callan

Anger crackled through me as I stalked back and forth across the dining room, trying to work off some of the impatience bouncing around inside my body. I had sent word to Violet to inquire about where to find a skilled chef on such short notice, and she would get back to us in the morning. But that wasn't what was fueling my restlessness.

What the hell had Sam and the others been thinking when they suggested this mission? Audrey and I were like oil and flame. Put us too close together and we'd burn the world down.

It was absolutely infuriating how she seemed to somehow always be one step ahead, knowing exactly when I gave in to the temptation of letting my eyes linger on her a bit longer. She had known that I was watching her through the gap in the curtain and had undressed like that on purpose. Did the damn poisoner have eyes in the back of her head or what?

I was always in control of everything and everyone around me, but she had a way of unsettling me. Of throwing me off balance. And that made her dangerous.

The sound of her footsteps slowly became audible from the corridor beyond the doorway. My hand brushed the hilt of the knife I kept strapped to the small of my back, but instead of drawing it, I stopped my pacing and quickly leaned down over the dining room table as if I was perusing the documents scattered there. I *had been* reading up on the intel we had gotten from Sam earlier, but I had already finished that now. However, I didn't want Audrey to see me pacing like that. It made me look uncertain.

"Violet said she'd get back to us in the morning," I said without turning to look as Audrey's footsteps rounded the open doorway and sounded from inside the room.

"Great," she answered. "We need to make a good impression on them if we're going to get them to invite us to that ball. That means we need to dress the part too. I was thinking I could wear this."

With my back still turned, I rolled my eyes at her obvious attempt to pick up where we had left off in that shop earlier today. But I knew her tricks now. Steeling myself against her gorgeous body in another well-cut dress, I turned around and raised my eyebrows while I let a look of disinterest slide across my features.

I opened my mouth to tell her to wear whatever the hell she wanted, but the words got stuck in my throat as my eyes landed on her.

"Under the dress, I mean," she finished, and flashed me a sly smile.

My gaze flicked up and down her body. The damn poison mage was standing there wearing nothing but a pair of lacy black undergarments. She swayed her hips slightly as she sauntered up to me with that knowing glint in her green eyes.

"I bought a few of these at the shop too," she said. "That Elise Dawson looked like she could spot un-classy people from a mile away, so I figured it's best to go all out for this dinner. And these match that black and gold dress rather well, don't they?"

She moved until she was standing next to me by the long dining room table. I turned so that our eyes met again. There was a cocky tilt to her chin as she looked up at me, and it made me want to dominate her even more.

A lethal smile spread across my lips as I made a decision. *Fine.* If this was the game she wanted to play, then I would show her exactly what I could make her do.

"Maybe," I answered with a nonchalant shrug before jerking my chin at her. "Let me see the back."

Smug satisfaction swirled in her eyes as she turned while I moved a step behind her. She really thought she was winning.

I struck.

Before she had even finished turning fully, I grabbed her wrist to twist her arm up her back and slam her down chest first onto the tabletop. A surprised huff ripped from her throat at the impact, and I used her stunned moment to yank the knife from under my shirt.

It had only taken a matter of moments, but when Audrey finished blinking in shock, she found herself bent over the table with my blade resting against the side of her neck.

"Oh Audrey, if you're that desperate," I mocked, "then let me show you what it really feels like to be at my mercy."

She slid her free hand across the smooth tabletop, as if to grab my wrist and pull the knife aside, so I forced her other arm higher up her back. A low snarl escaped her lips, but she stopped moving her hand. I stepped closer until my knees dug into the back of her legs and my thighs pressed against her ass, keeping her pinned to the tabletop. Then I shifted the grip on my blade.

Keeping the pressure enough to be felt but not enough to

break the skin, I trailed the point of my knife down her neck and towards her shoulder. "You got a glimpse of the way I can make people fall apart underneath me when you showed up unannounced at my mansion. Are you trying to tell me that you want to experience it firsthand?"

"What I saw was an actress faking it for your pleasure," she retorted.

"Whatever you need to tell yourself."

I drew the knife over her shoulder blade and then down towards her side. Pushing my body forward, I forced her hips harder against the table while I traced the edge of her brassiere with the blade. A low moan rolled from her throat, and her eyes fluttered as a shudder coursed through her body.

Shock clanged through me. I had expected her to be angry. To spit insults at me and swear her revenge. Or maybe even scared as she realized that she was completely at my mercy and that I could end her life with one cut of the blade. But she didn't look angry or scared. She looked turned on. Blood rushed to my cock as I stared down at her. She was *enjoying* this.

The spiteful part of me wanted to stop what I was doing, because hell damn it all if I ever did anything that filled Audrey with pleasure. That orgasm she had manipulated me into giving her at the Yellow Duck was already far more than she deserved. But another part of me really wanted to watch her gasp and tremble and come apart underneath me.

Leaning down over her, I ground my hard cock against her ass while tracing the point of the blade over her ribs. She drew in a shuddering breath. I released my grip on the wrist I had been forcing up her back.

She could summon magic now. All she had to do was touch her palms together in front of her and she could throw a cloud of poison at me. But she didn't. Her hands were splayed against the tabletop on either side of her face as she arched her back while I dragged the knife over her hip. I straightened slightly so that I could trace it over her ass. A soft moan came from her chest.

I kicked her legs apart, widening her stance. Then I paused, staring down at her. Waiting for her to say or do anything to indicate that this wasn't something she wanted. I might be planning a violent death for this damn poison mage, but I would never force myself on her sexually. Her or anyone else, for that matter. When I wanted to engage in that particular kind of stress relief, I wanted people who *begged me* to fuck them. Nothing less.

When she only bucked her hips to brush her ass against my crotch, I drew the knife over her hip and down towards her toned leg. After tracing it across the back of her knee, I dragged the blade up the inside of her thigh. A shudder coursed through her body.

Drawing it up to her ass, I slid the blade underneath the black lace fabric and pulled the knife upwards. A faint tearing sound filled the air as I cut her panties off. She sucked in a gasp as they tumbled to the pale marble floor below, leaving her completely exposed to me. But she kept her legs spread in that wide stance I had shifted her into. I lifted my knife hand from her ass and quickly touched my palms together.

Force magic sprung to life around the fingers of my left hand. When Audrey did nothing to push herself off the table, despite the lack of both my hands and my knife, I stepped closer again and brought my fingers to her pussy.

She sucked in another shuddering breath as the vibrations from my magic skimmed her clit. Wicked satisfaction swirled inside me as my fingers brushed her core and found her completely soaked. I increased the intensity of the vibrations while I used my other hand to drag the knife across the small of her back.

A whimper spilled from her lips.

I trailed the point of the blade up along her spine while I continued teasing her with my magic, making her squirm against the tabletop underneath me. Her long black hair rippled as she changed between pressing her forehead and pressing her cheek against the smooth wood. I upped the vibrations again.

She gasped.

With the same efficient moves as before, I slid my knife underneath the black lace of her brassiere and expertly cut the sheer fabric from her trembling body. Using the side of my hand, I brushed the strips off her back, leaving her completely naked and bent over the table before me.

A dark moan tore from her throat as I shifted my fingers while strengthening the vibrations again. She bit her lip and curled her fingers against the tabletop. I did the same thing again. It drew a pitiful whimper from her chest as she squirmed underneath me once more. Sliding the blade along her neck, I positioned the edge against the exposed skin of her throat while she was busy squeezing her eyes shut and pressing her forehead against the table. She stilled.

Her chest heaved as I continued sending pulses of force magic against her clit, but with the blade to her neck, she was forced to keep her body in the same position. She bit her lip again, and I wanted to run my thumb over that luscious mouth of hers. Instead, I heightened the vibrations.

She released a long shuddering breath that transformed into a dark moan halfway through, and then she clenched her fists against the table. I shifted the blade to the front of her throat while she turned her head, allowing her to rest her cheek against the tabletop instead of pressing her forehead into it.

Dark desire swirled in her eyes. I pushed my fingers harder against her wet core. A pleading groan tore from her throat. I kept my magic in place.

Pleasure exploded behind her eyes. A string of unintelligible moans rolled from her mouth and her whole body shook against the table as she came all over my fingers. Leaning forward, I pushed my legs into the back of hers to keep her hips firmly against the tabletop when her knees buckled. She sucked in a desperate breath and arched her back as I continued sending pulsing magic against her throbbing clit, prolonging the wave of pleasure.

When the last of the tremors had left her body, I removed the knife from her throat and let my force magic fade out. Audrey just lay there, slumped against the tabletop. Her chest heaved and her eyes were slightly unfocused. Smug victory burned inside me.

Bracing an arm against the table, I leaned down over her.

"See," I began in a dark whisper. "Every time you play this game with me, you always lose."

She just continued forcing breaths in and out of her lungs. I straightened. Finally, I had reset the power balance to its proper place. She was the one who came apart underneath me, and I was the one who chose whether or not she would be allowed to experience such ecstasy again.

A smirk tugged at my lips as I took a step back from the table so that I could saunter out the door while she was still trying to piece her mind back together.

Green flashed at the corner of my vision. I blinked in surprise as Audrey shot upright, a cloud of poison magic already hovering in front of my face. Her cheeks were flushed and her naked skin practically glowed from the orgasm I had given her, but there was a lethal look in her eyes as she took a step forward.

"It's funny how you think I can't tell how hard you are for me," she said while sweet venom dripped from her smile.

My back connected with the wall as she pushed forward, keeping that poison cloud between us.

She swept her long dark hair over her shoulders so that it tumbled down her back while she came to a halt in front of me. "Now stand there like a good boy and let me show you who really holds the power here."

I could summon a force wall and send her flying across the room if I wanted to, but I had to admit, I was intrigued. So I spread my arms in a cocky gesture and arched my eyebrows at her. With that challenging smirk still on her pretty lips, she let the glittering poison dissipate. For a moment, she only continued staring up at me, as if testing to see what I would do when her magic was gone. I only looked back at her expectantly.

Her tongue skimmed her teeth as her lips curled in a sharp smile.

Closing the distance between us, she rose up on her toes and brushed her lips along my jaw while her hands traced over my stomach. My heart gave a couple of violent beats and blood shot down to my cock as Audrey started unbuttoning my pants. Wickedness glittered in those bright eyes of hers as she let out a dark laugh. Her breath caressed my skin, making it prickle from the soft brush of her lips.

My cock strained against my underwear as she shifted my now unbuttoned pants, creating a space at just the right place. I kept my spine straight and my chin raised in a pose of complete disinterest while she slid the final layer of fabric down, making my already hard length spring free. A small but very treacherous breath ripped from my throat as she wrapped her fingers around my cock.

She released another dark chuckle. "You men might have a

lot of advantages that we don't, but at least you can't hide your arousal the way we can."

"It's—" I began, but she drew her hand up and down, making me inhale another sharp breath.

After tracing her lips over my jaw one final time, she slowly lowered herself to her knees before me.

My heart started thumping hard behind my ribs. Hell damn it all. I had fucked lots of people before. Why was I reacting like a little virgin boy still in his damn teens? Tipping my head back, I rested it against the cool marble wall and blew out a steadying breath. With my resolve back in place like an iron wall, I returned my attention to the poison mage who had now reached the floor. I refused to let her believe that she was capable of affecting me in any way. Apart from making me want to kill her, of course.

She swirled her tongue over my tip and I damn near came right then.

Squeezing my hand into a fist, I clenched my jaw and tried to pull that resolve back as Audrey slid her lips over my cock, taking it into her mouth. My heart stampeded in my chest as she took me deeper before slowly pulling back. Her tongue flicked over my tip again. I ground my teeth so hard they almost cracked. She pushed forward again.

It took all my self-control to keep breathing normally as Audrey worked her lips and that damn tongue of hers until I thought my whole body was going to explode. Clenching and unclenching my fist, I kept blowing out measured breaths while she pushed me closer and closer towards the edge.

Her teeth grazed my skin, making a violent tremor course through my body. My hand shot out and grabbed her hair. Before I could recover, she followed it up with a move that involved both her lips and her tongue that made all of my control snap.

Release exploded through me.

While fisting her hair, I sucked in a gasp as waves of pleasure rolled over my body and my vision flashed. Audrey's lips were still wrapped around my cock, and she took it all. When the last pulses of pleasure had faded, I realized that I was still gripping her hair. I snatched my hand back.

With her head now free to move again, she slid my cock out of her mouth and wiped her bottom lip with her thumb as she rose to her feet again.

Arrogant victory glittered in her eyes. She opened her mouth to say something, but before she could, my hand flashed up and I took her jaw in a punishing grip.

"So, apparently that tongue of yours is good for something other than spitting disrespect in my face," I said in a low and vicious voice as I stared her down.

"Told you." She reached up, but not to wrench my hand off her jaw. Instead, she lifted her palm higher and gave my cheek a couple of brisk pats. "You're not the one in control here, pretty boy."

"Whatever you need to tell yourself, sweetheart."

But that smug satisfaction still shone in her eyes.

I had done this to make her understand that I called the shots here. Not her.

But as I looked down at that wicked smirk on her pretty little lips, I couldn't help but feel that I was in deep shit now.

CHAPTER 18

Audrey

Morning sunlight streamed in through the skylight and illuminated the large indoor market. Though, it was more of a market for services rather than goods. I swept my gaze over the multitude of rows containing tables and the people who were trying to promote their business behind them.

Violet had gotten back to us this morning, telling us that this was where we would most likely find a chef who was both skilled and available on short notice. It was where people, especially young ones who were trying to make a name for themselves, went to get some visibility for their business. Customers who needed something, anything from help fixing a broken pipe to sewing a ballgown, then showed up and browsed the vendors available. But there were a lot of them, and the space wasn't structured into clear subsections with just one type of trade in each.

"We should split up," I announced.

Callan glanced down at me before flicking his gaze over the mass of people and tables again. "Yeah."

"Come find me if you talk to someone who fits the bill," I said, and then stalked away before he could answer.

Searching separately was more efficient, but that wasn't the only reason I had suggested it. I needed some space from Callan.

Cheerful chatter filled the air around me as I strode down one of the long rows of tables, letting the crowd swallow me while I looked for someone who advertised that they were a good cook.

While I walked, my mind kept going back to what had happened in that dining room last night. I didn't like Callan, and love wasn't even on the map. I hated him with every fiber of my being and I still planned to kill him as soon as we had gotten Lance out of Eldar. But what he had made me feel when he bent me over that table was beyond anything I had ever experienced. It was intense and raw and burned like wildfire inside me. I wanted to feel it again. And that terrified me.

I was self-sufficient. If I wanted something, I got it myself. I never relied on anyone else for anything. And now here was Callan Blackwell with something that I wanted. Something that only he could give me.

Straightening my spine, I shook my head. No. What happened last night could never happen again. From now on, it was strictly business until this mission was finished, and then I could finally kill this dangerous enemy of mine that I had let live for far too long.

My gaze snagged on a small wooden sign up ahead. *Chef.* Finally, someone who might be useful. Changing direction, I slunk through the crowd and approached his table. His eyes lit up when he saw me coming, but only a few questions into the conversation, I realized that he was far too inexperienced for this kind of thing. We needed someone who could impress the social elite, and he was not it.

Disappointment bloomed inside me as I detached myself from the conversation and moved on. The next few tables were all full of people advertising for the position of gardener. I strode through them and moved into the next row.

A few more chefs appeared as I made my way through the sunlit indoor market, and one of them actually seemed promising. When I reached the end of yet another row of tables, I paused for a second while considering whether or not I should just go and find Callan so that we could talk to the young dark-haired man who had seemed promising. I glanced down the other side. There was only one row left.

Blowing out a breath, I stalked around the table at the end and moved into it. I might as well check them all.

My blood froze.

Stopping dead in my tracks, I stared at the trio who had suddenly become visible next to a table halfway down. My parents. And my older sister Jenny.

They were standing in front of a small wooden table, speaking to a young woman who had a sign up that said *teacher*. I quickly moved across the now fairly open space so that there was a large group between me and them, but it took me within earshot.

"And how do you feel about working long hours?" Jenny asked.

A voice that I assumed belonged to the young woman on the other side of the table answered quickly, "Oh, that's not a problem."

"Excellent. Teaching is a calling, you know. And only a certain type of person can handle it."

"Y-yes."

"Well, I'll be in touch."

I glanced around the group I used for cover just in time to see my parents and sister move away from the young teacher and towards me. Walking around the big group, I made sure to stay on the opposite side while they rounded it too. Once they reached the side I had originally been on, they stopped. So did I.

"Have you made a decision?" my mother asked.

Pain stabbed into my heart. She sounded exactly the same as she had six years ago when I ran away.

"I'm not sure," Jenny answered. "They're all nice and everything, but they just don't meet the standard for the kind of school I want to run."

"That's completely understandable. After all, they have very big shoes to fill if they are going to take over some of your classes."

"But how am I supposed to expand the school if I can't find any teachers? Am I being too harsh on them?"

"No, not at all."

"I just want this to work."

"It will."

"Your mother and I are so proud of you, Jenny," my father added.

It made a wave of emotions crash over me and I had to close my eyes briefly to stop myself from getting washed away by it.

"You have been a joy to raise," he continued, and I could hear the smile in his voice. "Excelling at everything you take on. And we have no doubt that this school of yours will become a roaring success too."

"Thanks, Dad. I really needed to hear that."

Anger and pain ate away at my heart like acid.

I couldn't be here.

I couldn't listen to this.

It made me feel like I was fourteen years old again and it tore up a storm of emotions that I had spent years getting rid of. Feelings that had no business being in my chest. I was a dark mage now. I made men beg me for mercy with a flick of my wrist. I didn't get my heart ripped open by a casual conversation between family members who I had left behind long ago.

The group I was hiding behind suddenly thanked the builder they had been speaking to, and clothes rustled around me as they got ready to leave. I snapped my gaze between them and my family who were becoming visible behind the dispersing group.

Turning abruptly, I strode straight for the other side of the row.

The teacher my sister had spoken to called out, asking if I was interested in hiring a tutor. I ignored her as I stalked down the alarmingly empty path between the tables as fast as I could without drawing attention. Casting a quick glance over my shoulder, I tried to discreetly make sure that no one in my family had seen me.

Thankfully, they weren't even looking in my direction.

I turned my head back to the path ahead right as I got ready to round the corner.

And slammed straight into Callan's muscled chest.

CHAPTER 19

Callan

A huff ripped from my chest as Audrey barreled right into me. Irritation crackled through my veins, and I shoved her off me, getting ready to tell her to watch where she was going. But the words died on my tongue as my gaze found her face.

Pain swirled in her eyes. Not physical pain, but more like... hurt that came from deep inside her. It looked like someone had just carved open her chest and plunged a dagger into her heart.

I snapped my gaze to the people behind her. Apart from the professionals behind the tables, the only ones left in this row were three people. A man and a woman who looked to be about the same age as my parents, and an attractive woman with dark hair and gray eyes who looked to be roughly our age. The man was resting a hand on the younger woman's shoulder. I frowned.

Audrey, who had straightened again, flicked a glance over her shoulder, and the hurt in her eyes bloomed again.

I looked from her pained face and back to the three strangers.

I'm going to cut their hearts out.

Surprise clanged through me. The thought had shot through my mind so fast that I barely even knew where it came from. Why would I care if they had hurt Audrey? I was planning to kill her myself.

"What's going on?" I asked.

"Nothing," she snapped back. Her usual infuriating arrogance was back on her face as she tried to sidestep me and walk away. "Let's go. I think I've found a cook."

My hand shot out and I grabbed her arm. Holding her trapped next to me, I stared her down. "Answer my question."

"You're making a scene," she snarled at me through clenched teeth while she was trying to make it look to everyone else like we were just engaged in a casual conversation. "And we need to leave before I'm spotted."

"You said no one in this city would recognize you."

"Best not take any chances."

I slid my eyes to the dark-haired trio up ahead. They appeared to have finished whatever they had been doing and were now moving towards the other end.

"Now, take your hand off me," Audrey continued in a voice dripping with cold threats. "Before I make you."

"Don't make threats you can't back up," I answered, but I released her arm.

After cutting me a scathing look, she stalked around the corner.

Remaining where I was, I watched the three strangers disappear on the other side, while marking their faces. If they were able to identify Audrey as a dark mage, we might need to kill them. Yes. That was the reason I had to memorize what they looked like.

Once they were out of sight, I twisted around to see where Audrey had gone. Her dark green dress fluttered around the corner of a table farther down as she strode into one of the rows closer to the middle. Blowing out an annoyed sigh, I stalked after her.

The crowd parted before me as I plowed straight towards where she had disappeared. As I turned the same corner, I found her standing in front of a wooden table halfway down, talking to a young man with curly brown hair. A small sign on the tabletop in front of him read *chef*.

As I weaved through the packed space and approached them, I futilely wished that I had been wearing my leather armor. In this kind of throng, it was easy for an attacker to just stick a knife through someone's ribs without anyone seeing. But unfortunately, wearing armor inside Eldar was out of the question. It would have drawn too much attention, so I had to settle for a pair of normal pants and a dark shirt. Though I supposed it didn't matter. In the noble heart of Eldar, there were no villains who would want to kill anyone. Or so they thought.

I smothered the paranoid instincts that had been ingrained in me after living with only dark mages around me for years, and instead turned scrutinizing eyes on this cook that Audrey had found. I flicked my gaze up and down his scrawny body as I came to a halt next to Audrey.

"Oh, here he is," she said in a bright and cheerful voice that sounded nothing like her usual tone. "So yes, as I was saying, my husband and I are hosting a dinner for Elise Dawson and her friends."

"How exciting," the young man replied, and his brown eyes lit up with hope and endless possibilities.

"Yes, isn't it? Anyway, we're having it tomorrow, so we would need someone who can put together a grand meal in a very short amount of time. What would you prepare if we were to hire you?"

While she continued to quiz the excited-looking cook, I shifted my gaze back to Audrey. I nodded at the appropriate times, but I wasn't really paying much attention to his explanation of how he baked cakes and seasoned meat. I couldn't get that look in Audrey's eyes out of my mind.

Over the years, I had both said and done a lot of awful things to her. But she had always taken it in stride. Giving as good as she got, though I hated to admit that. I had stabbed her a few times, and during our first meeting, I had put a boot to the back of her neck and forced her face down against the floor while trying to get her to beg my forgiveness for settling on my lands. I had choked her, beaten her, cut her, insulted her, and explained to her in excruciating detail exactly how I was going to torture her to death one day. But never, in all the years we had been waging this war on each other, had I seen pain like that in her eyes.

It was so rare for me to see anything but cocky arrogance and spitfire hatred on her face that I couldn't help but wonder who those people had been. And more importantly, what they had said to her to make her hurt like that.

That same stunned surprise clanged through me again. Why did I care? I had been trying to kill Audrey for years. Maybe instead of worrying about her little feelings getting hurt, I should seek out those three strangers and ask them what they had said just so that I could do the same to her. After all, it would give me a huge advantage over her that I could use once we had kidnapped Lance Carmichael and ended his crusade against dark mages.

"Right, husband?" Audrey suddenly said while jabbing an elbow in my ribs.

Jolted out of my thoughts, I scowled down at her. "What?"

Annoyance flickered in her eyes.

While resisting the urge to roll mine, I painted a smile onto my face and instead said, "Right. Yes, sweetheart."

"Fantastic," she said as she turned back to the young chef. "Then it's decided. You'll come by our house first thing tomorrow so that you have all the time you need to prepare the dinner for us."

The young man pressed his hands together in front of his chest. "Thank you so much. You won't regret this."

They finished up the final details while my gaze drifted back to the chattering crowd of people around us, unintentionally looking for those three dark-haired people. I had to ask Audrey who they were when we got back.

After all, they could be enemies who would jeopardize our mission.

And then we'd need to deal with them.

Yes, that was it.

CHAPTER 20

Audrey

I raked my fingers through my hair and forced out a long breath. Warm winds blew in through the open window of my room and brought with them the scent of roses and the sound of chirping birds. Stalking over to the windowsill, I dropped down onto it and stared out at the small garden outside.

Seeing my family like that had sent me crashing into the past and I'd suddenly felt all the emotions that my teenage self had been carrying around all those years. It bothered me more than I wanted to admit. Bothered me how easy it had been. That listening to one casual conversation could make me feel like I was fifteen again.

Restlessness crackled through me. I pushed to my feet and began pacing back and forth across the carpet while the birds continued singing outside the window as if nothing was wrong. Drawing my fingers through my hair again, I shook my head.

It didn't even make sense. I had fought against powerful dark mages. I had been stabbed and beaten and almost killed more times than I cared to admit. And I had also done far worse to others. I had blackmailed and tortured and killed countless people. I should have been beyond those kinds of emotions. Beyond feeling like that. But no. One little conversation between people I had left behind years ago had sent me spiraling back into that place again.

The mattress bounced underneath me as I stopped my pacing and instead threw myself down on top of my bed. Staring up at the ceiling, I once more dragged a hand through my hair and blew out another deep sigh. I had to do something to get these feelings out of my chest again. To get my head back on straight. To return to the place where I was now and not the place I had been in all those years ago.

My eyes drifted to the closed door. Maybe I should give killing Callan another shot. If nothing else, it would give me a chance to unleash some of the pent-up irritation in my soul. However, that was dependent on whether I ended up getting the upper hand or not. If he did, it would just piss me off more.

Another wave of anger roared through me. Letting out a snarl, I glared up into the ceiling. I couldn't afford to get distracted like this right now.

The door banged open.

I shot up from the bed and slammed my palms together. Glittering poison magic swirled around my forearms as I landed on the other side of the bed and got ready to kill the intruder.

Callan Blackwell arched a dark eyebrow at me while striding into my room like he owned the damn place. "Who was that back there?"

"When the door is closed, I expect you to knock before entering," I said in a low and vicious voice.

"And when I ask a question, I expect you to answer it."

The already burning irritation inside me flared up as I

stared back at him. There was a cocky tilt to his chin, and power and authority seemed to pulse from his muscled body when he gave me an expectant look as if waiting for me to obey. It made me want to kill him even more. The green swirls around my arms snaked down to my hands.

Indecision flitted through me for a second before I huffed out a silent laugh. *Fuck it.*

I threw the poison magic at him.

He dove aside. Slamming his palms together, he rolled forward across the floor before leaping to his feet. Another cloud of poison was already speeding towards him, but he knocked it aside with a small force wall. I had to get out from the restricted position I was currently occupying between the wall and the bed, so I used his moment of inattention to leap onto the mattress.

Before I could make it to the other side, a blast of force took me in the legs. It swept them right out from underneath me and sent me crashing down on top of the mattress, making the bedframe creak in alarm. Rolling over, I tried to get into a better position.

A hand wrapped around my ankle.

My stomach lurched as Callan yanked me towards him along the bed. I raised my free leg and kicked at him. A soft groan escaped his throat as my foot collided with his stomach, and the grip on my ankle loosened. Kicking out with my other leg, I swung around to break the grip completely right as I skidded across the edge of the bed.

The move worked and Callan lost his grip on me, but the force of his pull sent me crashing to my knees on the floor in front of the bed instead.

Steel glinted in the light falling in from the open window and a large hand appeared on my shoulder, forcing my knees harder against the floor. I clapped my palms together while the knife Callan had drawn closed in on my neck.

Right before he could position it across my throat, I shoved a cloud of poison up into his face. He had to leap back to avoid it. It bought me enough time to scramble to my feet and touch my palms together. Whirling around, I turned to face him, but a force wall hit me in the chest before I could straighten.

I slammed down back first across the bed, my legs hanging over the edge and one of my arms pinned underneath me.

The mattress creaked as Callan braced a knee next to my hip and leaned over me before I could get my wits about me again. Placing a hand against my chest, he shoved me back down onto the bed while he placed the blade against my throat. I tried to move my arms, but as soon as I did, he shifted his hand from my chest to my throat. His strong fingers dug into my skin, making it clear what he was going to do if I moved my arms again.

"Now, I will ask again," he began in a hard voice. "Who was that back there?"

I glared up at him while trying to shift my hand the final bit without him noticing. The pressure on my throat increased, and he drew the knife along my cheek and rested the tip below my left eye.

"What's it to you?" I ground out instead.

"If it was someone who will jeopardize our mission, I need to know."

"It wasn't."

"I'll be the judge of that." Pure dominance pulsed in his eyes as he stared me down. "Who was it?"

Rolling my eyes, I huffed out a dismissive breath.

His fingers slid up to my jaw, gripping it firmly and keeping my head locked against the mattress, while he shifted his knife. Keeping his commanding eyes locked on me, he traced the tip of the blade around my lips. "I know how talented you are with that tongue. I would suggest you use it to answer my questions, before I decide to cut it out."

With his eyes staring down into my face, I at last managed to move my hand the final bit and release the poison magic attack that I had called up before his force wall hit me. A slim streak of glittering green shot straight from my hand and into his mouth.

Alarm flashed in Callan's eyes as I shoved the poison down his throat.

Releasing me, he staggered back from the bed. I increased the strength of the poison before he could recover, and he abruptly dropped down on one knee. After pushing myself off the bed, I straightened before him and stared down at him where he was fighting a battle that he couldn't win.

His arms hung uselessly by his sides and his muscled chest convulsed as I increased the poison even more. I took a step closer and plucked the knife from his slack grip. Straightening again, I placed the flat of the blade underneath his chin and tilted his head back so that his dark brown eyes met mine.

"You do not threaten me." My voice was cold and hard, and I spoke slowly even though death gripped Callan's heart tighter with every second. "You will know only what I want you to know. Nothing more. Nothing less. Do you understand?"

Hate pulsed in his eyes as he glared up at me. I increased the strength of my magic, making him double over. After shifting the knife out of the way, I leaned down and grabbed the front of his shirt. Gripping his collar hard, I yanked him back up into a kneeling position. His eyes were sliding in and out of focus and involuntary twitches racked his body.

I leaned down until he could feel my breath on his skin. "I said, do you understand?"

For another few seconds, he only continued glaring up at me with such hatred that it could have set the world on fire. Then he jerked his chin down in a nod.

Power and control flooded my soul, making me feel more like myself again.

Callan's limbs twitched uncontrollably and his eyes were quickly losing all focus, but the expression on his face remained the same. Rage and hatred and a promise of revenge. No fear. No panic. No silent pleas for mercy. I hated to admit it, but I was impressed by that.

Holding his failing gaze, I kept my magic up for another few seconds. Just to make sure that he truly understood that I held his life in the palm of my hand right now, and that I could choose to end him right here if I wanted to. Then I pulled it back and let the glittering green tendril dissipate while I released his collar and straightened.

Dull thuds echoed into the dead silent room as Callan toppled forward, bracing his palms on the floor in front of him. His chest expanded as he sucked in a desperate breath. I backed a couple of steps away but continued to watch him while he forced oxygen back into his lungs again. When the death that had been hovering over his shoulder was at last gone, he dragged a hand through his black hair and pushed back to his feet. Hatred still flashed in his eyes when he finally looked back at me.

For a moment, nothing happened. We only stood there, staring at each other. Then he slowly touched his palms together.

The steel gray of his magic formed into a sword that he gripped in his right hand.

I held his gaze, my eyes burning with just as much rage as his. "Come at me with that force blade right now and only one of us walks out of this room. Mission be damned."

Slow seconds ticked by. Callan clenched his jaw and flexed his fingers on the hilt of the vibrating half-translucent blade as if he was fighting the desire to attack and end this war between us once and for all.

Then he let out a derisive huff and looked away. The force blade disappeared into thin air. I continued studying him for another few seconds before allowing the tension to leave my body as well.

Callan slid his gaze back to me and crossed his arms while raising his eyebrows expectantly. "Well?"

I almost hit him with another cloud of poison magic. Oh he really wasn't going to let it go, was he?

Staring back at him, I lifted one shoulder in a nonchalant shrug. "It was my family."

"Ah."

He said it with such casual understanding that all the fight just bled right out of me. When the burning rage and hatred was gone, I felt hollow, and I just slumped down on the bed and blew out a long sigh. My long black hair fell across my face as I stared down at the deep red carpet for a while.

The mattress dipped to the right.

Heaving another sigh, I reached up and hooked my hair back behind my ear before turning towards Callan. He had taken a seat a short distance from me on the bed, but he was watching the pale wooden cabinet across the room.

"They're the reason you became a dark mage." It was half statement, half question.

"Yeah," I replied.

Silence fell.

Outside the window, the small birds started up their merry chirping again now that the noise of battle had died down. Another warm wind blew into the room, making the thin red drapes flutter and bringing with it the scent of roses.

I glanced over at Callan. He just sat there, looking straight ahead at the cabinet. Releasing another long breath, I tipped my head back and drew my fingers through my hair. Callan said nothing. And maybe that was why I told him. Because he didn't push. Because he didn't demand it. Or maybe I just wanted to put my own thoughts into words so that I could leave those emotions that had swirled up where they belonged. In the past.

"They're actually decent people," I began. "And that was what made it so difficult."

"To leave?" Callan asked, his eyes still resting on the pale wooden furniture.

"No. To realize that they were the reason that I was destroying myself."

He said nothing, as if giving me time to collect my thoughts.

"My sister Jenny," I began at last. "She's only two years older than me, and she's... practically a genius. She's just effortlessly good at everything. Magic. Music. Art. Athletics. Math. Philosophy. She excelled at everything in school. And because we're so close in age, my parents always compared us. I don't think they did it on purpose. It just turned out that way. So whenever Jenny mastered some new skill with her wind magic, my parents always looked to me and asked what I had accomplished."

"Sounds like a lot of pressure."

"Yeah." I was silent for a while before continuing. "I don't think they meant it that way, but yeah, that was what it was like for me. I'm not as effortlessly good at things as she is, so instead I had to work my ass off. I always made sure to be kind and pleasant and perfect, but I could never compete with her on every skill she was good at. So I picked one. Magic. Because that was what I was best at. And then I just trained and studied and trained and studied until my mind and body almost gave out. So that I could show them that I was also worth..."

When I trailed off and drew in a deep breath, Callan just remained sitting there. Waiting to see if I would go on. Eventually, I did.

"They were so happy and proud that Jenny was so good at everything, and I just wanted them to be proud of me too. I sacrificed everything. My free time. My health. Most of my social life. So that I could train and get better with my magic. And I did. I was top of my class in magical abilities. And my parents were happy and proud of me and they praised me right alongside my sister, and I thought I was finally where I wanted to be. But then I suddenly turned nineteen."

"And the graduation ceremony drew closer."

"Yeah. And that's when I realized that I didn't want to give it up. I had worked so hard and sacrificed so much to prove that I was just as good as Jenny. Throughout all my teenage years, I always believed that my parents' love depended on how well I performed. How good I was at things. How perfect I was. And then when I finally had something that I excelled at so that I could earn their love, why would I give it up?"

"And did it? Their love. Did it depend on that?"

"I don't know. Probably not. But it always felt like it did." I drew in a deep breath and shook my head. "I couldn't breathe. All those years, I was constantly trying to be perfect all the time so that I could prove that I was worth loving too. And after all of that, giving up all my magic and becoming ordinary again was completely unacceptable. I had worked too hard for that. Sacrificed too much. So I schemed together a plan and then I escaped." Glancing over at Callan, I shrugged. "My family was so embarrassed about it that they convinced everyone that I had moved to Castlebourne. Even if I were to run into any of my old teachers and they were to recognize me, none of them would think that I was a dark mage. So, to answer your question... No, our mission is not in danger."

At last, Callan turned to face me. And for the first time, I couldn't quite tell what he was thinking when he looked at me. Usually it was either hatred, rage, or lately, lust. But now, I wasn't sure what emotions were swirling behind his eyes.

"Thank you," he finally said. "For answering my question."

That was the first time that Callan had thanked me for anything. Ever. And it threw me off my game enough that I only replied with, "Sure."

As I studied the way the light made his dark brown eyes glow a little golden, I wondered what in the world had made me share all of that with Callan Blackwell, of all people. Only a few minutes ago, I had brought him to the brink of death with my poison magic, and now I was suddenly telling him the reason why I had decided to become a dark mage. Not that it mattered. There was nothing in that story that he could use against me when we started our war back up again.

Brushing my hands down my legs, I rose to my feet and pushed my pensive mood aside.

Regardless of the reason that I had done it, speaking my thoughts out loud like that had helped sweep away those old feelings and resettle myself in the present. Turning back around, I faced Callan once more.

We had a dinner to prepare for.

CHAPTER 21

Callan

The whole dining room shone with candlelight, and the scent of perfectly seasoned meat hung in the air. I had to admit, this cook that Audrey had found really did know what he was doing. While cleaving an herb-roasted potato, I looked over at the poison mage.

Nothing remained of the hurt I had seen in her eyes yesterday. It was as if telling me about it had somehow helped return all those emotions to her past. I didn't really know what she must have felt growing up that way, because my parents hadn't been anything like that. But I also had my own reasons for deciding to become a dark mage, so I still understood her in a way that the rest of the people around this table did not. I narrowed my eyes slightly. I was still going to make her pay dearly for that stunt she had pulled with her poison magic, though.

"So, tell me," Elise Dawson began while she sipped some more wine where she sat next to me. Her blue eyes were practically glittering with the promise of gossip. "How did you two meet?"

Audrey and I exchanged a quick glance, but since there was no way to discuss anything with six other people watching us, I decided to go with something that was close to the truth.

"We were neighbors," I answered. "She moved in next door."

"Aw, that's so sweet," Lisa cut in. She tried to catch her husband's eye. "Isn't it?"

The husband, Roald, who looked to be at least fifteen years older than her, only speared another piece of asparagus and continued eating.

"Not at all, actually," Audrey said. A secretive smile played over her lips as she looked around the table, meeting each of their gazes in turn. "I'll tell you a secret. He didn't even like me at first."

Elise's husband, who was occupying the chair between us, raised his eyebrows at her. "Really?"

"Yes. But I won him over in the end." Audrey leaned forward to wink at me. "Didn't I, husband?"

I held her gaze while letting a slow smile spread across my lips. "You sure did, sweetheart."

Elise laughed. "How marvelous." She looked over at her husband before turning back to give me a look that I couldn't quite interpret. "For Carl and me, it was love at first sight. We knew from the first moment we met that we were destined for each other. Both of us enjoy the same kinds of... freedom."

"Indeed." Carl nodded to his wife before turning to Audrey. "How dull life would be without it."

From the other side of the table, Lisa nodded emphatically at Carl's words. As did Jane, the blond friend that Elise had brought, and her husband where they sat on either side of Lisa. Roald only continued eating his asparagus.

A slight frown creased my brows at their odd behavior, but

I quickly smoothened it out and instead raised my utensils to cut another strip of meat.

"What about you, Audrey?" Carl said as he leaned closer to her.

She smiled pleasantly. "What about me?"

"Do you think that some people are destined only for each other?"

"I don't think there is such a thing as destiny. I think people make choices. They choose who they want to be with."

"Well said."

I glanced up from my plate to find Carl leaning even closer. There was a smile on his face and a gleam in his eyes, or the one that I could see from this side at least, and I was pretty sure it wasn't just from the candlelight. With that interested expression still on his face, he reached out and placed his hand on Audrey's forearm.

My elbow slammed into him from the other side.

He let out a yelp as the hit sent him shooting sideways in his seat, and he threw out his arms to stabilize himself. Clanging filled the room as Carl accidentally knocked over one of the candleholders in his hurry to catch himself. The candle was pushed into one of the plates, extinguishing the flame, before it rolled across the smooth tabletop while the golden candlestick was left lying across the empty asparagus platter.

"Oh, Carl, so sorry about that," I said as I grabbed his arm to help him sit up straight again. "My knife slipped while I was cutting into the meat. I didn't mean to hit you like that."

Carl brushed his hands down his white shirt before running them through his brown hair a couple of times. Then his gaze slid to me. "No worries at all. It just caught me a bit off guard."

"Yes, how very clumsy of you, *husband*." Audrey shot me a

sharp look before she placed a hand on Carl's shoulder. "Are you sure you're alright?"

He gave her a smile. "Yes, I'm sure. Thank you."

After returning the smile, she reached out and righted the toppled candleholder. Standing up from the chair, she picked up the escaped candle and put it back. Then she paused. With a frown on her face, she lifted the golden holder so that she could light the wick on one of the already burning candles.

Lisa chuckled and brought her hands together. "Why don't you just...?"

With a flick of her wrist, a small flame appeared on the wick, lighting the candle. Worry washed over me like cold water. Lighting candles and summoning water to a glass or picking up items with a small gust of wind was something everyone in Eldar did like it was nothing. Because they were connected to the Great Current and could use all different kinds of magic. But we couldn't do those things, and if they found that out, they would know that we were dark mages.

"How kind of you, Lisa," Audrey said with a smile that even I had trouble spotting the venom in. "But Callan and I are actually having a magic-free month. We want to try to live the way we would have done if there had been no Great Current. As a way to give thanks and show our appreciation for the sacrifices that all the mages make for us."

Man, I had to admit, she was an excellent liar.

At last, Roald looked up from his asparagus. A frown creased his graying brows as he peered through his glasses at Audrey. "Sacrifices? What sacrifices?"

"For giving up their magic to share it with everyone."

"They're only doing what's right. What everyone should do in that kind of situation."

Lisa patted her husband on the arm. "I agree. It would be so unfair if only some people had magic. After all, it's just luck that determines who is born with it and who is born without it. Sharing it equally between everyone is the best way to solve the problem."

It took great effort to stop myself from rolling my eyes. Based on the look on Audrey's face, she was fighting a similar urge.

"Yes," Jane agreed from Lisa's other side. She gave her friend a serious nod before brushing her straight blond hair back behind her shoulder. "I still remember when both of my younger brothers manifested their magic. I was so heartbroken that they had been born with magic and that I hadn't. I ran to our mother and cried until she told me about the Great Current. It was such a relief to hear that I would be getting magic too."

"I think most people feel that way," Carl added. "I was born a fire mage, but almost all of my friends back when I was a child didn't have magic. I saw how badly they wanted it too, so that's why I didn't hesitate to share my magic with the Great Current. I truly felt that I did something good for the world when I completed the graduation ceremony."

Elise leaned forward to smile at her husband. "You really did, darling."

"I don't understand how anyone can think that keeping it all for yourself is the right thing to do." Disgust curled Lisa's mouth. "Those *dark mages*. How selfish can you get?"

"I know, right?" Jane said. "But think of it this way. They pick power over love. And then they have to spend the rest of their lives alone out in the countryside." She gave her husband a warm smile. "And power doesn't keep you warm at night. It doesn't fill your heart with happiness. Sharing what you have with other people is what gives you friends and a life of love and joy."

Roald nodded sagely. "Indeed. Selflessness is always the path to true happiness."

"Yes, I think you're right." Elise Dawson smiled as she looked around the table at all of us. "I'm proud to call myself a citizen of Eldar. Our fair and democratic city truly is one of the gems of Valda. It is such a great city to put down roots in. To have children in. To make friends in." Her calculating blue eyes shifted to me. "I do hope that you will consider making it your permanent home."

I held her gaze and returned the smile. "Oh, I can assure you that we are. Especially now that we have met such kind people."

Elise let out a satisfied laugh and nodded. Returning my attention to my plate, I stabbed my fork into the final piece of meat and popped it in my mouth. The taste of thyme and garlic melted over my tongue. Swallowing the delicious bite, I had to once again admit that Audrey had been right about this cook.

Clinking utensils and soft chatter filled our splendid dining room as the rest of the dinner thankfully progressed without further discussions about sharing magic or anything else that we didn't want to get into.

When we at last followed the party of six to the door, I was confident that we had made a good impression. Now, we just needed to secure a promise.

"It was so lovely to have you over," Audrey said as we faced the six of them where they stood before the front door. "And thank you again for helping me with the dress shopping."

Elise smiled back at her. "It was my pleasure."

Carl's eyes flicked up and down the stunning black and gold dress that Audrey wore. "It does look great on you."

Wrapping my arm around Audrey's back, I pulled her closer. "Yes, it does."

She stiffened in surprise for a second before leaning into me and then looking back at Elise and Carl. "You are both far too kind."

The Dawsons exchanged a brief look. Then Elise turned back to us with an even brighter smile on her face.

"You simply must let us return the favor," she said, her eyes glittering. "We're having a little... soirée at our place this weekend. We would love it if you could make it too."

"We would be absolutely delighted," Audrey replied.

"Wonderful. We'll see you in a few days then."

Smug victory swirled inside me as we waved them goodbye while they poured out the door and disappeared into the darkened evening outside.

This had gone perfectly. We had them right were we wanted them, and now all we needed was one final push.

Then, we would have our invitations to the ball.

CHAPTER 22

Callan

My eyes drifted over Audrey's body as she pushed the black and golden fabric of her skirt aside and dropped down on the couch. Stretching out her bare legs along the length of the dark red couch, she crossed her ankles and leaned back against the armrest while picking up her glass of wine from the low table. Light from the multitude of candles throughout the dining room refracted in the glass as Audrey lifted it to her lips and took a sip.

"Well, that was a success," she announced.

After pouring myself another glass of wine as well, I dropped down in the armchair opposite her and propped my feet up on the table. "Yeah. Given how desperate Carl is to get into your panties, scoring an invite next time won't be a problem."

She huffed out a laugh. "I was just about to say the same thing to you about Elise and Lisa and... that other blond one."

"Jane," I filled in.

"Whatever. They've been drooling over you since the moment they saw you. So we just play into that during this soirée we were invited to, and we'll have those invitations to the ball in no time."

"I wonder what their deal is."

"The Dawsons?"

"Yeah. They're married but both of them seem to be interested in fucking other people."

Audrey shrugged and drank some more wine. "Who cares? Anyway, we have a few days before their soirée. We should take some time to scout out the parliament building so we have a plan for how and where to take Lance Carmichael."

"I agree. Let's do that tomorrow."

She nodded.

Silence fell as we both raised our glasses and downed some more of the rich red wine. The cook that Audrey had hired had already finished up and gone home, leaving us alone in the big empty house. All the other rooms were dark, but the now once more pristine dining room was still filled with lit candles. The light filled the space with a golden glow and made Audrey's eyes glitter like emeralds. I watched the way she brushed her thumb over her lips after taking another sip of wine. She might be the most infuriating, arrogant, and disrespectful person I had ever met, but I still preferred her company to that of those equality-loving weaklings.

Leaning back against the dark red backrest, I let out a contented sigh. "I can't wait to get my hands on this Lance Carmichael so that I can show him that pretty words have no chance against true power."

Audrey huffed out a dark chuckle and slid her gaze back to me. "You thought about that too, huh?"

"*Selflessness is the true path to happiness,*" I mimicked, and then snorted. "How naïve can you be?"

"Very, apparently."

"Giving everything you have and everything you are to

other people doesn't make you happy. It makes you an idiot, because all that does is leave *you* empty and drained."

"I know, right?" She shook her head in annoyance. "I will never understand why anyone would willingly spend their life being a mediocre nobody just like everyone else…"

"When they could have everything and be anything they wanted," I finished.

She drew back a little and blinked at me. "Exactly."

Raising my glass, I gave her a small salute and then drained the rest of my wine. When I stood up to refill it, Audrey held out her glass too. I considered ignoring it just out of pure spite, but then poured more wine into her glass before filling mine as well. The plush armchair groaned faintly as I dropped back down into my seat.

"What pisses me off the most is the hypocrisy." I swirled the red wine in my glass and then drank a mouthful before meeting Audrey's gaze again. "Why should magic be distributed equally? Nothing else is. Some people are born rich and some are born poor. But the heroes of Eldar don't make sure that everyone has the exact same amount of money. So why do it with magic?"

"I've been thinking about that too. As far as I know, their reasoning is that money is something you can earn while magic is something you can only be born with."

"And that's supposed to justify it?"

"Apparently. But it's such bullshit because it doesn't work out across all areas anyway. Some people are born beautiful and some people are born ugly. And it's no secret that beautiful people, regardless of whatever else they've got going for them, always have advantages in life that those who are ugly will never have. But no one shares their beauty."

"That's a good point."

"What you're born with is what you have. It's what's yours.

Be it a beautiful face or gorgeous hair or an incredible singing voice. And no one is expected to share that with anyone else. So why should magic be any different?"

"It shouldn't. Our magic is as much a part of us as our face or our voice."

"Right? And besides, why should I spend *a decade* working hard to improve my magic and then just give it to someone who has done nothing to deserve it?" Anger flickered in her eyes as she forced out an irritated huff. "While they were out doing other things with their life, I spent my years developing my powers. And then I'm just supposed to give it away? Like hell."

With that anger still flashing across her face, she downed the rest of her wine and then shot to her feet. Grabbing the decanter, she filled it up again. Annoyance seeped into her movements and made her pour the wine so fast that it almost sloshed over the edge. Leaning down, she slurped some of the wine from the top so that she would be able to move the glass without spilling anything. It was such a strangely innocent and casual thing to do that I lost my train of thought and just stared at her instead.

When she was done, she shifted the decanter to my glass and topped that up too before sitting down on the couch. Curling up against the armrest, she drew her legs up underneath her. Candles fluttered slightly in the draft she had created when sitting down, and they cast shifting light over her beautiful face as she raised her eyes to me. For a while, she didn't say anything. She just sat there with that ridiculously full wine glass in her hand while her eyes searched my face.

"Can I ask you something?" she said at last.

I wasn't sure if it was due to the amount of wine she had drunk, but that had to be the politest thing she had said to me. Ever. And it threw me off a little, so I just answered, "Sure."

"What made you decide to become a dark mage?"

Leaning back in the armchair, I released a long sigh. "I guess I was just tired of trying to please other people."

The leaves on the bushes outside the window rustled as a strong night wind swept through the neighborhood. When Audrey didn't reply, I tipped my head back down and looked over at her from across the low table. Her eyes were locked on me. But she didn't say anything, as if waiting to see whether I would go on. I'm not entirely sure why, but I did.

"When I was a kid, I had really shitty friends. So then when I turned ten and entered the academy, I thought things would be different. That I would finally be able to start over and find my people. I worked so hard to become part of a group." A mirthless huff of laughter escaped my throat. "I was such a nice person back then. I was always there for everyone and helped them with everything I could. Sacrificing my own needs to make sure that they were happy. And do you know what that got me?"

Understanding swirled in her eyes as she looked back at me. "Nothing."

"Exactly. Nothing. I was still always the least favorite friend. The one they kept around so that they could use me when they needed something, but not the one they would choose to spend their time with if they had other alternatives. The one who wasn't invited unless I specifically asked them." I shrugged. "Eventually, I decided that I'd had enough. I'd had enough of being selfless and pleasing others and doing everything they asked just so that they would like me. So I left."

"How old were you?"

"Fourteen."

Her eyes widened. "You've been a dark mage since you were *fourteen*?"

"Yeah."

"Huh."

The armchair groaned faintly as I shifted my weight and shrugged again. "It was a long time ago, my parents have nine kids, and none of my friends paid much attention to whether I was there or not... So no one who knew me back then would recognize me now, which is why no one knows that I'm a dark mage."

"I see."

A wicked smile spread across my lips. "Becoming a dark mage was the best choice I ever made. That whole *selflessness is the true path to happiness* notion is such horseshit. It's just a weapon people use so that they can take advantage of others. The moment I decided to start living for myself and doing whatever made me happy was the moment I finally realized what true happiness really is."

Audrey sat up straighter. Holding out her glass, she leaned forward across the table and clinked it against mine. An equally wicked smile played over her own lips as she met my gaze. "For the first time ever, I think I actually agree with you completely."

Amusement flickered through me as I raised my glass in acknowledgement.

I wasn't sure why I had told Audrey all of that. Maybe it was because I had drunk so much wine. Or maybe it was because for once in her life, the infuriating poisoner had actually asked nicely.

Whatever the reason, as I leaned back in my armchair and watched Audrey from across the table, I realized that it really was rather nice to know that there was someone else who shared my views on life.

CHAPTER 23

Audrey

The white parliament building shone like a jewel in the sunlight as we ascended the pale steps and approached the wide double doors. Well-dressed men and women walked briskly in and out, as if they were on some very important errands, but there were also a few people who looked more like us. A bit more uncertain. I kept an open and curious expression on my face as we approached the doors.

This was where the whole parliament of Eldar worked, but it was also open for visitors. There were areas that resembled a museum where people could learn more about Eldar's glorious history, as well as the famous Rose Hall, which was where the ball would be held. We needed to map out the layout so that we could find the perfect spot to make our move, and also an escape route so that we wouldn't have to haul an abducted Lance Carmichael out through an entire ballroom packed with people.

Callan slid his arm around mine and then spoke quietly through a smile. "You're frowning."

Realizing that he was right, I smoothened my creased

brows and painted that curious smile back on my face. But in my chest, my heart was thumping. Were we really going to do this? Walk right into the heart of democracy? The heroes' stronghold? If something went wrong while we were in there, the odds of us getting out undetected were dishearteningly low. And if that happened, our chance of stopping Lance Carmichael and his band of self-righteous idiots from wiping out all the dark mages would be gone completely.

I drew in a calming breath as we at last stepped across the threshold.

A grand hallway made of white marble met us. The domed ceiling made the murmur of people speaking softly to each other swirl through the air and fill the whole space. I swept my gaze over the portraits on the walls. They no doubt depicted old members of parliament who had done something good for Eldar, or perhaps previous Chancellors, but they looked very stern and imposing in their paintings. Our steps were muffled by a dark blue carpet that ran the length of the hallway. I read the small golden plaques above the different doors while we walked.

"Are you looking for something?" a voice suddenly said.

Callan and I stopped and turned towards it. A woman with gray hair pulled into a neat bun looked back at us with eyebrows raised expectantly.

"The area up ahead is not open to civilians," she went on.

"Oh, I'm sorry," I said and let out an embarrassed laugh that was pure calculation. "We're from Castlebourne and everyone has been telling us that we just have to see the Rose Hall."

Her expression softened. "And they're quite right. It is magnificent." With a smile on her face, she raised a hand to point towards a pair of double doors. "It's down there."

"Thank you so much. That's so kind of you."

Our arms were still linked so I pulled Callan with me as I started towards the indicated doors. He followed, but when I looked up at him, there was a smirk tugging at his lips.

"How come you never speak to me like that?" he asked, and arched a dark brow in amusement. "Saying thank you and please with proper respect?"

"I would rather have my throat slit."

His smile turned lethal. "That can be arranged."

Before I could answer, we reached the massive doors made of polished oak. I glanced around to see if we needed to alert anyone before going inside, but when no attendant appeared, I pushed down the handle and edged the door open. Callan slid his arm from mine as we slipped inside and closed the door behind us again.

"Wow." The word rolled off my tongue before I could stop it.

But Callan's eyes were locked on the incredible room before us as well, and all he said was, "Yeah."

The Rose Hall was a massive ballroom with a rectangular shape and a high ceiling. Private seating arrangements occupied the entire right wall while the outer wall held tall stained-glass windows. Sunlight fell in through their artful patterns and painted colorful shapes across the shining white marble floor. There was a raised podium at the front of the room while a space that looked to be reserved for an orchestra was located on the ballroom's other short side.

Tilting my head back, I looked up at the ceiling. Glittering chandeliers hung along the entire length of the room, both above the dance floor and the seating area, but that wasn't the only impressive thing above our heads. The entire ceiling had been painted with stunning scenes that depicted the city of Eldar and the hills and grasslands around it.

"Impressive," Callan said. "Let's look around a little bit."

I turned back to him and was just about to question his uncharacteristically polite tone when I noticed another couple at the far end of the room. They were walking slowly, staring up at the paintings in the ceiling while moving in the direction of the door. Annoyance rippled through me. We would have to wait until they left before we got started on our real investigation.

Sliding my gaze back to Callan, I gave him a nod and then motioned towards the back of the room where the space for the orchestra was set up. "I want to look at the windows over there."

"I want to see what the ceiling looks like up at the front," he answered.

We shared another look and then drifted towards opposite sides of the room.

The seating area had been marked as off limits with a thick red velvet rope that ran between short golden poles along the entire length of the room. I ran scrutinizing eyes over the space before moving towards the opposite wall so that I could pretend to study the windows. The booths at the very back of the seating area seemed private enough to discreetly knock someone out, but the problem would be getting the body out of the ballroom without anyone noticing.

I glanced towards the wall on the short side while I came to a halt halfway to the stained-glass windows. There were several doors set into it. They were also roped off, but if that couple would just leave, I could investigate them anyway.

Cocking my head, I pretended to study the glass motifs on the window while I waited for them to do just that. On the other side of the room, Callan did the same. The couple was moving at a pace that would have made a limping snail groan in frustration and complain about their slowness, but at least they were heading towards the exit.

While I waited, my mind kept drifting back to the conversation we'd had after the guests had left yesterday.

I had a very hard time picturing Callan as an uncertain boy who did whatever people said just to please them and make them like him. From the very first time I had met him, his entire muscular body had always exuded power and authority. Always in control. Always giving others orders. Hell knew he had done nothing but try to boss me around since that day. To think of him as a scrawny thirteen-year-old who said 'yes, please, and thank you' was incredibly odd. But I supposed that was the thing about growing up. It wasn't about getting older. It was about shedding the false masks you had worn and becoming the person you wanted to be.

And as much as I hated to admit it, I had been impressed when he told me that he left to become a dark mage at fourteen. Most people who escaped the academy did so when they were around nineteen and were getting close to the graduation ceremony so that their magic was at its strongest. Both because it was troublesome to even get out of Eldar, but also because once you left the city, you had to fight all the other dark mages for a place in the hills. If Callan had managed to do all that when he was only fourteen, it certainly explained why he had managed to become one of the six dark mages still left standing. I would have to find a way to neutralize him quickly once this was over.

The large double doors clicked shut, informing me that the couple had finally reached them and left.

From across the massive room, Callan and I turned to look at each other. We nodded in unison. There were doors at the other end too, and he turned towards them while I snuck over to the ones on my side.

Hiking up my dress, I stepped over the velvet rope and edged the door open.

For a moment, I only stood there, peering into it to see if there was anyone else already inside. When nothing moved, I slipped in through the gap.

It looked almost like a small library. A pair of dark leather armchairs were positioned by one wall, and a side table with an oil lamp on top of it waited between them. Every wall except the outer one was covered in dark wooden bookshelves. Gold-foiled titles glinted in the light streaming in through the windows, and not a speck of dust covered the spines.

I moved over to the window. Reaching up, I placed a hand on it and gently edged it open. It moved silently.

Warm winds smelling of grass and summer flowers washed over me. I peered down. There was a lovely garden full of roses and well-trimmed hedges outside. The drop was too steep to jump, but I had to admit that it led to a perfectly remote location. I drummed my fingers against the windowsill while considering.

Deciding to see what Callan had found on the other side, I gently closed the window again and snuck back out. Thankfully, no one else had entered the Rose Hall while I'd been inside the small library, so I could walk back into the ballroom without issue.

After lifting up my dress and stepping back over the red velvet rope, I started towards the other side of the room. It was so large that it took me a while to cross it, even when walking at a brisk pace. My pulse thrummed inside me, but I made it across the whole ballroom without any other unwelcome visitors or nosey attendants poking their head through the double doors.

I repeated the process of maneuvering over the thick rope before opening the door that I had seen Callan move towards earlier. Just like the room I had investigated, it was the door closest to the outer wall. The other rooms might be good places to knock Lance out, but just as with the private booths in the seating area, the problem of how to get him out still remained. If we were lucky, there was an easy way out in the rooms closest to the windows. That way, we would be able to get around the problem of hauling Lance's body through an entire ballroom full of people.

After edging the door open, I slipped inside the room.

Surprise shot up my spine.

Blinking in stunned shock, I watched as Callan withdrew his force blade from some random guy's chest.

CHAPTER 24

Callan

"What are you doing?" Audrey hissed at me as she quickly closed the door behind her.

The man I had stabbed let out a groan and collapsed to the ground as I removed my force blade from his heart and released his shoulder. Dull thuds echoed into the room as his limp body hit the marble floor.

"He's some kind of gardener's assistant and he saw me messing with the side door," I answered while letting my force blade disappear.

As if on cue, the dying man twitched below me.

Audrey's sharp eyes flicked from his body to my face and then towards the side door that I had found. Irritation flashed across her features as she shifted her attention back to me.

"You didn't have to kill him! You could have just made up some bullshit excuse about being lost or something."

I rolled my eyes. "Oh I'm sorry, is your conscience bothering you?"

"That's not what I meant," she snapped, and flicked a dismissive hand at the now very deceased man at my feet. "I don't care that he's dead. He's nothing to me. I care that we now have a dead body. In the parliament building!"

My gaze drifted to the corpse and the small pool of blood that had spread on the floor. I supposed she did have a point.

Whirling around, she cracked the door open and peered out. A soft snarl ripped from her lips as she closed it again. "There are people out there now."

"So? What were you going to do? Drag the corpse out through the front doors?" I motioned towards the side door while holding her furious gaze. "We just carry him out into the garden and bury him there."

"In broad daylight? The building and the gardens and this whole damn hill are crawling with people who work here."

"Good point."

She forced out a sharp breath between her teeth and crossed her arms over her chest while glaring at me. "We can't just leave him here. They'll know something is wrong and it will ruin our element of surprise at the ball."

"Fine. We wait for nightfall and then bury him in the garden. I've already messed with the lock on that door so that we can get in and out whenever we want."

"Wait? Wait where?" She stabbed a hand towards the man's corpse. "We can't just sit here with a dead body on the floor and wait for someone to blunder in and find us."

"Of course not. We need to hide while we wait for nightfall. But I didn't think I had to actually specify something that obvious."

She clenched her jaw in anger before grinding out, "Where?"

I just jerked my chin towards the two closet doors on my left.

The room was bare apart from the twin storage closets set into the inner wall. If I had to make an educated guess, I would say that this room was only used as an emergency exit in case of a fire or something similar. My little unplanned murder aside, I'd say that this investigation had revealed the perfect spot for us to use when abducting Lance Carmichael.

While shaking her head in annoyance, Audrey stalked over to the closets and yanked open the doors. Two empty, but very narrow, spaces stared back at her.

"Let's get to it then," she snapped as she strode back to me. Wrapping her hands around the dead guy's ankles, she lifted his legs up and then arched her eyebrows expectantly at me. "Grab his shoulders."

That had sounded an awful lot like an order, but I would get her back for that later, so I just bent down and hooked my arms underneath his armpits. Walking backwards, I started towards the closet. Audrey stepped around the pool of blood that had formed on the floor and then followed me. Her eyes still flashed with anger, so I shot her a smirk to make it even worse. She narrowed her eyes at me but said nothing.

After backing into the closet, I dropped the dead man on the floor. Once Audrey had released his legs, I stepped over him and turned so that I could pull him up and lean him against the back wall. He wasn't really helping the effort by being dead and unwieldy, but I managed to get him into position eventually.

The sound of ripping fabric came from behind me.

Frowning, I turned around and stepped out of the closet to find Audrey tearing off large swathes of her skirt.

"The hell are you doing?" I asked.

Instead of answering, she just shot me a death glare and then dropped to her knees. Realization, and a hint of approval, blew through my mind.

Using the strips of fabric, she mopped up the blood until the marble floor looked at least passably clean again.

When she was done, she gathered up the pile of bloodied

cloth and pushed to her feet. Her dress now ended in a ragged line at her mid-thighs, and it swung around her as she stalked over and threw the scraps of her skirt into the closet with the dead body. The wet fabric sailed through the air before landing in the deceased gardener's lap.

Turning back to me, she jutted out her chin and raised her eyebrows expectantly. "You can share his closet. I'm taking the other one. This is your mess after all."

I moved towards her and the doorway as if I was about to follow her ridiculous command. When I reached the spot in front of her, I stopped and let a condescending smirk stretch my lips. "I don't think so."

"I'm not—"

Grabbing her by the throat, I yanked her body sideways and then shoved her into the empty closet. While she stumbled backwards into the wall, I slammed the other closet door closed, leaving the dead guy to his lonely hiding place.

"Don't you dare—"

Before she could finish, I strode into the closet she was in and then closed the door behind me.

Darkness enveloped us. I blinked a few times while my eyes adjusted to the gloom. A small stream of light seeped in from the gap underneath the door, which helped me make out my surroundings once my eyes had gotten used to the poor lighting. What I found was a furious poison mage.

"If you ever do something like that again..." she began in a voice dripping with threats.

I snorted. "You'll do what exactly?"

The storage closet was barely big enough for us to stand opposite each other, and it certainly wasn't wide enough to allow her to get past me to the door. My shoulders brushed the sides of the closet, leaving me blocking her way out.

Glittering green light suddenly swirled around her arms. "Or I will finish what I started back in my room."

I shifted my hand slightly, bringing the force blade I had summoned the final bit forward so that it pressed against her ribs. Her eyes shot down to it for a second, but she didn't flinch. That both annoyed me and impressed me.

Grinning down at her, I raised my eyebrows in silent challenge.

She huffed out a mirthless laugh and then let the poison magic dissipate. My force blade disappeared a second later. We would have to settle this when we were back in the privacy of our house instead.

Satisfied that she wasn't going to start a fight right now, I leaned back against the closed door and then slid down it until I sat on the floor. Kicking Audrey's legs apart, I stretched mine out as far as they would go, which wasn't much. I still had to bend my knees as I rested my boots on the back wall, but it was more comfortable than standing up.

"Sit down," I ordered. "This is going to be a long wait."

Audrey was standing with her feet on either side of my knees, and she didn't look at all inclined to sit down. When I locked eyes with her, she only clicked her tongue and flicked a dismissive hand, telling me that she wasn't going to be taking any orders from me. Oh, we'd see about that.

"I said, sit down," I repeated while grabbing the back of her knees and yanking them forward.

A yelp slipped her lips as her legs buckled and she crashed down on top of me. Since my knees were bent, my legs created a slope, and she slid forward until her chest slammed into mine. With her knees resting on the floor, she straddled my hips while her tits pressed into my chest. I had to admit, I quite liked her in that position.

"You fucking—" she snapped.

"What was that?" Grabbing her chin, I forced her head back so that she met my gaze. "Are you asking me to fuck you?"

She reached up and smacked my hand away. I let her. Lowering my arm again, I rested my hand on the floor next to me instead.

Audrey placed her palms against my shoulders and pushed herself backwards. It didn't work. Because of the steep angle of my legs, she just slid right back down again.

A low snarl ripped from her throat.

Even though it was useless, she tried the same thing several more times. The result was always the same. Once she had come to that conclusion too, she crossed her arms and glared up at me where she sat right on top of my cock.

"You can always stand for eight hours while we wait for nightfall," I offered.

For a moment, it looked like she might actually do that out of pure spite, but then she forced out a sharp breath. "The minute the light disappears from under the door, we get the hell out of here and bury that guy in the gardens outside."

"Deal."

She stared up at me for a few seconds before continuing. "So, this is the room we'll use to kidnap Lance Carmichael."

"Unless you found something better on your side?"

"No. There was a private library kind of thing, but there was no door. And the ground slopes downwards that way so the drop from the windows is too high to jump."

"Alright. Then this is the room we'll use."

Silence fell.

For quite a while, we just sat there. Waiting for the hours to pass so that we could bury the damn guy who had seen me from the gardens while I fiddled with the lock on the side door that I had opened for like ten seconds. Ten seconds of bad luck had led to eight hours of boredom. In a closet. With Audrey fucking Sable.

She was staring at the wall above my shoulder as if making a point out of not looking at me, and that arrogance and anger she usually directed at me still lined her cheekbones. But despite all of her insults and her rage, she had still stayed. When she saw that I had killed that gardener, she could have just walked out and left me to deal with it. Instead, she had carried a corpse into a closet, ripped apart her dress to wipe up the blood, and then agreed to spend eight hours with me in a cramped closet so that we could then haul the dead guy out the side door and into the gardens, find a couple of shovels, dig a deep hole, and then bury the bastard in it. Not a lot of people would have agreed to do that. And certainly not for an enemy.

It worried me that I didn't hate her as much anymore. I might even go so far as saying that I found her tolerable from time to time. And that was unacceptable. I had to do something to reset the power balance between us.

My eyes drifted down her body.

A wicked plan formed in my mind. This was the perfect opportunity to get back at her for that stunt she had pulled when we shared the horse on the way here.

While watching her face intently, I rolled my hips.

Her mouth dropped open and a small jolt passed through her body.

I did the same thing again.

She jolted slightly once more. A lethal smirk curled my lips as she turned her head to face me while narrowing her eyes. I rolled my hips again, making her suck in a sharp breath.

"Callan," she said in a low and vicious voice.

"What?" I taunted.

Since she had ripped off part of her dress to wipe up the blood, there wasn't enough skirt left to cover her legs, which meant that the only fabric between her pussy and my cock was her panties. And my pants, of course. But the friction was a lot closer for her than it was for me.

I rolled my hips once more, making my cock shift against her entrance yet again.

Closing her eyes, she clenched her jaw as another small tremor passed through her body. While she still had her eyes shut, I placed my hands on her hips and forced her body harder down against mine. She snapped her gaze back to me, but before she could say anything, I moved my cock against her pussy again.

The words died on her tongue, and she sucked in a shuddering breath instead.

"Tell me to stop," I challenged while I continued the motion over and over again.

Her hands shot to my shoulders. I paused briefly as she dug her fingers into them, but when she remained silent, I started back up again. Pleasure washed over her face and her eyes fluttered closed once more. It made blood rush to my cock, and it strained against my pants.

Still keeping her hips in a firm grip, I rubbed my hard length against her entrance again.

A soft moan made it past her gritted teeth.

I continued teasing her, building up the pleasure inside her, while she kept her eyes stubbornly closed and squeezed my shoulders hard. Another dark moan escaped her. I kept grinding against her.

When I could tell that she had almost reached the edge, I stopped abruptly.

Her eyes shot open.

There was a slightly dazed expression on her face as she blinked a few times and then looked up at me. I cocked my head and arched an eyebrow at her.

"Do you want me to make you come?" I asked while a wicked smile slid home on my lips.

She opened her mouth slightly, and for a moment, it looked like she was about to say something. But she didn't.

When no answer was forthcoming, I drew a hand up her neck and brushed it over her jaw before taking her chin in a firm grip. Leaning forward, I slanted my lips over hers in an almost kiss before pulling back slightly and locking eyes with her instead.

"Then beg me for it," I finished.

Rage flashed in her eyes. Blowing out an angry breath, she knocked my hand aside and then crossed her arms over her chest while pointedly staring at the wall next to us instead of my face. I let out a dark laugh.

Oh, I wasn't worried.

I knew that I would make her beg and submit to me completely in the end.

CHAPTER 25

My muscles trembled with exhaustion. Since I used poison magic for all of my attacks, and I had people who managed my estate, I wasn't used to this much physical labor. Burying a dead body was a lot harder than I had thought it would be. Normally, I didn't care if anyone found the corpses I left in my wake, so I had never had to dig holes and haul dead people around a garden at night. Why did they weigh so much when they were dead anyway?

Tiredness mixed with irritation washed over me as I stalked up the steps to the second floor of our house. I was covered in dirt and blood, and all I wanted to do was to throw Callan out of a window, take a shower, and then get some sleep.

After grabbing a change of clothes from my room, I headed straight for the bathroom. But as I yanked open the door, I found that Callan had managed to get there first and was already stripping out of his clothes. The door banged as I stalked in anyway and slammed it closed behind me.

"You do not get to use the shower first. This whole mess

was your fault, so you can go out and wait in the corridor until I'm done."

He snorted dismissively as he tossed his shirt on the floor and got started on his pants. "How is it my fault that some damn gardener's assistant just happened to walk past right at that time?"

"You didn't have to run a force blade through his chest." I shook my head at him in disbelief. "By all hell, have you always been this stupid? How are you still alive when you are clearly entirely incapable of being sneaky?"

Callan stopped unbuttoning his pants and instead closed the distance between us. Taking my jaw in a punishing grip, he forced my head back and locked eyes with me. "Watch that tone."

"Or what?" I didn't have the strength left to lift my arms, so I just glared up at him. "You'll stab a force blade through my chest too? Seeing how that's the way you always solve your problems."

"Oh I can't wait until we've dealt with Lance Carmichael. Because then, I will do just that. And so much more."

Before I could reply, he released my jaw, making me snap my head to the side as he did so. I just slowly turned my head back and stared at him as he finished undressing. Blood and dirt caked his dark pants, but he simply dropped them, along with his underwear, on top of his shirt and stepped into the shower.

The sound of splashing water filled the room as he turned it on. It was an open shower, and the water came from a wide square in the ceiling, so I had an unobstructed view from where I still stood halfway between it and the door.

Water ran down his body, washing away the dirt and the blood.

For quite a while, I just stood there watching his muscular

back as he scrubbed away the evidence of his latest crime. I knew that I should be doing something. Leave, tell him to hurry up, or even just insult him. But I was so exhausted. It had taken hours to dig a hole deep enough and then bury the body without anyone seeing. My arms and back ached, and I just couldn't find the strength to do anything other than watch as Callan showered. Besides, it was a nice view.

Callan was hot. There was no point in trying to deny that. And as I studied the way his lean muscles shifted, I couldn't help but wonder what his naked body would feel like pressed against mine. An image popped up in my mind. That expression of pure bliss on that woman's face when I had walked in on her and Callan back in his mansion. He probably *was* good at it. But the problem was that I couldn't fuck someone like him. I couldn't put myself into such a vulnerable position with someone who was a threat to me.

"Enjoying the view?" Callan said, smug amusement lacing his voice.

When I forced my mind back to the present, I found that Callan had turned around and was now watching me. His lethal body looked even better from the front. But I would die before I ever told him that. So instead, I dragged my gaze up and down his body with deliberate slowness.

A mocking smirk played over my lips. "I've seen better."

He let out a dark chuckle and strode over to the towel rack. While he grabbed one and wrapped it around his hips, I reached up to undo the laces at the back of my ruined dress.

My muscles screamed at me.

After letting my arms drop down by my sides, I tried to shake out the muscles a little before reaching up behind my back once more. They just fell back down again.

A low growl ripped from my throat. It made Callan look over. Embarrassment flushed my cheeks and I snapped my gaze towards the other wall while I reached towards the laces once more. This time, I managed to grab a hold of the bottom ones. My arm muscles trembled as I tried to undo the knot. Before I could get it open, my fingers slipped and my arms dropped down to my sides yet again.

Callan advanced on me while I tried to get my muscles to obey me. I rolled my shoulders so that I could try again, but before I could reach up, Callan slapped my arms away and grabbed the end of the long ribbons.

"I don't need your help," I snapped.

"You can't lift your arms for more than two seconds and your hands are shaking."

I looked down at my hands. They *were* shaking slightly. Swallowing another snarky reply, I kept my mouth shut and just stood there as he started unlacing my dress.

A muttered curse came from his throat. "Seriously?"

"What?"

"Who even designed this bloody dress?" He yanked angrily at the loops and long ribbons that twisted back and forth. "The Chastity Association of Impenetrable Clothes?"

I laughed. Not a mocking or vicious laugh. But an actual laugh of genuine amusement. It shocked me that Callan had managed to draw such a sound out of me, so I twisted my head to stare at him over my shoulder. But Callan wasn't looking at me. He was studying the ruined remains of my ripped-up skirt as if he was considering something.

Then he abruptly looked up.

His hands dropped from my back to my hips before spinning me around so that I faced him instead.

"What are you doing?" I asked as he lifted his arms again.

"The dress is beyond saving anyway."

Using both hands, he took a firm grip on my collar.

And then he ripped my dress open.

A jolt shot through my body and my heart pounded hard against my ribs as I stared up at him with my mouth slightly open. Heat flooded my core. Before I could press out a single word, Callan released the dress and let it flutter down to the floor around my feet. My skin prickled at the exposure as I suddenly found myself standing there in only a pair of lace panties.

"There you go," Callan said and gave my shoulder a soft push towards the shower that was still running. "Now get in the shower."

I was still so stunned from what I had felt when Callan had ripped my dress open, that I just stripped out of my underwear and did what he said without arguing. My back was to him so I couldn't tell for certain, but I was sure that there was a satisfied smirk on his lips right about now. I would have to deal with that later.

Warm water washed over me as I staggered into the shower. After the night we'd had, it was a heavenly feeling to just have that warmth soaking into my aching body. The water ran red and brown as it swirled down the drain. I still couldn't lift my arms for more than a couple of seconds at a time, so I just stood there, hoping that all the blood and dirt would be washed away on its own.

"You've gotta scrub it off," Callan said from somewhere behind me, informing me that he was apparently still in the room.

"Yes, well..." I didn't know how to finish that sentence so I just trailed off.

Only the sound of water splashing against the marble floor broke the silence for about half a minute. Then Callan cursed loudly.

"For fuck's sake, Audrey."

I slowly turned around.

Yanking off the towel from around his hips, he stalked into the shower with me. It took me by surprise, so I just stumbled a step back towards the wall. Water ran down his body and soaked his hair once more while he closed the final distance between us and stopped in front of me.

Exasperation flashed across his face as he reached over my shoulder and grabbed the soap from the small rack set into the wall. Running it between his hands, he worked up a lather.

"What the hell do you think you're..." I began while taking a small step forward.

He just planted his palm on my collarbones and pushed me back against the wall before raising my arm with his other hand. I stared back at him in disbelief as he ran his palm up and down my arm, washing off the dirt and blood that still clung to my skin.

When he was done, he moved on to my other arm and did the same thing. I studied his face, trying to figure out why the hell he was doing this for me. But his eyes were focused on his own hands, making sure that he got all the blood off me.

Picking up the soap, he worked up more lather before crouching down to scrub the dirt from my legs. A jolt shot through my body when his rough hands made their way up my calf and towards my knee. Water poured down his neck and back, and made his black hair fall into his eyes as he looked down at my leg. My heart did that weird thing again where it pounded hard a couple of times before returning to its normal rhythm.

Callan drew his hands up my thigh.

Desire flooded my core and a shudder of pleasure coursed through my body as his fingers skimmed the inside of my thigh close to my entrance. Tilting my head back, I closed my eyes and let the water run down my face. Callan kneaded my skin for another few seconds before his calloused hands moved to my other leg.

As he reached the same spot on that thigh as well, I failed to suppress another shiver of pleasure. Dark desire rolled through me as Callan drew his hand back and forth across my skin.

By all hell, the bastard did know how to work his fingers. And I had to admit, I didn't hate the way his hands felt on me.

He stood up.

I quickly wiped the expression off my face as I opened my eyes to look at him. For a moment, he looked down at my chest and stomach, as if considering whether to put his hands there too even though those areas were free of blood and dirt. Since I realized that I wanted to know the answer to that too, I just stood there watching him while water splashed down over us.

His gaze flicked to the long dark tresses that now lay plastered to my skin.

Taking a firm grip on my hips, he abruptly spun me around and shoved me chest first into the wall. I let out a hiss and tried to step back, but he just planted a hand between my shoulder blades and pushed me up against the wall again.

"You still have mud in your hair," he announced as if that excused his manhandling.

My arms were still trembling with exertion, so I didn't have the strength to push myself away from the wall. Even if I hadn't been exhausted from digging a grave all night, I doubted I would have been able to win a strength contest against Callan Blackwell. But as he began massaging my scalp while he rubbed the shampoo into my hair, I realized that I didn't think I wanted to fight him on this right now.

With my body pressed against the wall, I rested my cheek against the smooth marble as I let my mortal enemy wash my hair and get all the blood and mud out of it. The cool stone against my naked body helped dampen some of the heat that seemed to pulse from my skin.

"There," Callan said at last.

Instead of answering, I just drew in a few more deep breaths. I hadn't even realized that my chest was heaving.

The splashing noise stopped as Callan turned off the shower. Silence that suddenly felt deafening filled the bathroom. For a while, nothing else happened.

Then Callan reached over my shoulder and wrapped his hand around my throat. Still standing behind me, he hauled me away from the wall until my back was pressed against his chest. When he leaned down to place his lips next to my ear, his cock brushed against my back.

"Aren't you going to say thank you?" he whispered, his hot breath dancing over my wet skin and making another treacherous shudder course through my body.

There was not a chance in hell that I was thanking him for anything, ever, so instead I replied, "I didn't ask you to do that."

Keeping his grip on my throat, he moved me away from his chest and swung me around so that I faced him instead. He took a step forward, forcing my back up against the wall. But before he could answer, I blurted out the question I had been turning over in my head since the moment he stepped into the shower with me.

"Why did you do it?"

He paused. There was a seriousness on his face that I hadn't really seen before. For a few seconds he said nothing, as if he was pondering the answer to that himself. Eventually, he opened his mouth as if to reply, but then he closed it again. Another couple of seconds passed. Then he shook off the seriousness and a cocky smirk slid home on his lips instead.

"I wanted to test a theory."

I narrowed my eyes at him. "What theory?"

"That I can make you do what I want."

A dark laugh slipped my lips. "Once again, you show how clueless you really are. I just got you to wash my body for me, and you think *you're* the one in control?" I let out another mocking laugh and raised my eyebrows in challenge. "You really are so easy to manipulate."

His fingers tightened around my throat as he leaned closer to my face. "Oh the things I could do to you. I could make you beg for mercy."

"I have never begged for mercy in my entire life."

"Then maybe it's high time someone made you experience that."

I shifted my hips so that my body brushed against his cock. It hardened, pressing into my skin. Running my tongue over my teeth, I smirked up at the frustrated-looking force mage. "Keep dreaming, pretty boy."

His eyes seared into mine for another few seconds. Then he flashed me a lethal smile and released my throat.

Without another word, he turned around and walked over to his discarded towel. After wrapping it around his hips again, he strode out of the bathroom, leaving me standing there in the shower. Alone. And wet in more ways than one.

As I watched his half-naked body disappear out the door, I couldn't stop the insane and absolutely ridiculous thoughts that swept through my mind.

No, I had never begged for mercy in my life.

But right now, I kind of wanted him to try.

CHAPTER 26

Callan

The overcast sky blocked out most of the light from the moon and cast the whole street in darkness. In this part of the city, the street lamps were few and far between. But the shop owners here preferred it that way. The items that were sold here were not ones that were meant for the bright light of day and the curious glances that came with it.

I walked up to a nondescript door and placed my hand on the handle before turning to jerk my chin at Audrey. "In here."

She scrunched up her dark brows as she assessed the building. "Seriously?"

There was no sign above the door, and the windows were hidden behind wooden shutters. It looked like a simple residential house. But it was not.

"They don't need to advertise. The people who know about this place already know about it."

"As always, words of wisdom just drip from your mouth like honey," she said, her own mouth dripping with sweet poison.

I considered throwing a force wall at her, but managed to

suppress the urge. Instead, I just pushed down the handle and swung the door open.

Not bothering to hold it open for Audrey, I simply stepped across the threshold and moved inside. A small huff from behind informed me that the door had hit Audrey on the way back, and I could feel her glare burning holes in my neck. At least she had followed.

Light from several oil lamps illuminated the small room and made the products on display gleam. I ran my eyes over the shelves and racks while I approached the counter at the back. They were covered with metal items. Handcuffs and manacles and chains and steel rods and contraptions that even I didn't know the name of. This small shop basically carried everything a person might need to restrain someone.

"Welcome," said a tall but very skinny man with brown hair as he appeared from the back room. "Looking for something specific or just browsing?"

"I need a pair of stiff handcuffs," I replied.

"Just regular ones?"

"Yeah."

"I think we might be sold out." He scratched his jaw. "But give me a few minutes and I'll have a look in the back."

I gave him a nod in acknowledgement before he disappeared through the doorway again. If he was sold out, we would be in trouble.

Knocking Lance out with Audrey's magic was one thing, but we couldn't just leave him unrestrained. He was a Binder, after all. If he woke up and we didn't notice, he could seal away our magic and then it would be all over. Just tying him up was out of the question, because as long as he could touch his palms together, he could still do magic. So we needed a real pair of handcuffs. Ones that had a stiff metal rod that kept a prisoner from being able to put his hands together. I had several pairs back in my mansion, but we'd only had limited space in our packs and I had assumed that there would be tons to buy here. If they were out, I would be seriously pissed off.

"So, how do *you* know about this place?" Audrey asked from somewhere behind me.

Turning around, I found her drifting up and down the aisles, inspecting the items with those sharp green eyes of hers.

"This is where I get all of my own supplies from," I answered.

"Is that so?"

"Yeah. It's been years since I was here in person, though."

She stopped in front of a narrow bucket that contained long metal rods with a cuff at each end. Picking one up, she ran her eyes down its length before frowning. "What do you even need stuff like this for? I've been a dark mage for six years and I've never had to use things like this to incapacitate people. If they have something I want, I just torture them with my magic until they give it up. And if they're of no use to me, I just kill them and move on."

A hint of amusement swirled inside me at how casually she said things like that. I cast a glance over my shoulder to see if the shopkeeper was returning anytime soon, but metallic clanking came from the back room as if he was still searching through his storage spaces. Returning my attention to the poison mage, I closed the distance between us and grabbed the spreader bar she was still holding.

She released it as I twisted it in my hand until it was positioned horizontally in the air. Shifting it slightly downwards, I held it out before me as if I was measuring the distance between her ankles. I looked up again and met her gaze.

"Keeping prisoners isn't the only thing I use it for."

For a second, she only scowled back at me. Then

understanding flickered in her eyes. Clicking her tongue, she snatched the rod back and rammed it into the stand. "Do you ever think about anything other than sex?"

I took a step forward, forcing her to back up against the shelves behind her, before I lifted my hand and brushed my fingers over her cheek in an almost loving gesture. "I'm also thinking about excruciatingly painful and humiliating ways to kill you."

Rolling her eyes, she tried to slap my hand away.

It did nothing to actually push it off, so I rubbed that in by taking her chin in a firm grip. Leaning down, I whispered my next words against her lips so that the shopkeeper wouldn't overhear. "But luckily for you, I still need you for this mission. Otherwise, keeping Lance knocked out while transporting him out of the city is going to be a real pain in the ass. So until this mission is done, you are safe in my hands."

A shiver coursed through her body. Given everything I knew about her, it hadn't been from fear but rather from... something else. Something darker. Something unthinkable. And it made a sharp smile drift across my lips.

The clanking that had been coming from the back room had stopped.

Releasing Audrey's jaw, I straightened just as the tall shopkeeper reappeared behind the counter.

He pushed one hand through his shoulder-length brown hair and then raised his head to smile at me. "I found a whole stack of them in my latest shipment. You sure you just want one pair? Nothing else?"

I glanced over at Audrey. Challenge glittered in her eyes as she stared back at me.

Turning back to the shopkeeper, I flashed him a wolfish smile.

"Actually, I think I might pick up a few other things too."

CHAPTER 27

Audrey

M etal clanked as Callan dumped his newly purchased stack of restraints on one of the chairs in the master bedroom. I studied him from outside in the corridor while he sorted through the items. Light from the oil lamps cast gilded streaks in his black hair, and his muscles shifted underneath his shirt as he lifted a long steel rod and leaned it against the chair instead.

Until this mission is done, you are safe in my hands.

The most infuriating part of that statement was that I knew, without a doubt, that it was true. We both needed each other for this mission. He needed me to make sure that Lance stayed knocked out until we were far away from the city, and I needed him to actually haul the unconscious hero out past the gates since I couldn't very well carry his entire weight on my own. So we couldn't do anything to permanently harm each other until this was over.

Drumming my fingers against my thigh, I kept watching Callan from the doorway while I considered my options.

All of this meant that now was the only time I could act on

the infuriating feelings inside me. By all hell, I still hated him with every fiber of my being. But damn he was hot. And at this point I was curious enough that I wanted to know what it would be like to fuck him.

Indecision swirled inside my chest.

While we were still in the middle of this mission, Callan was not a threat to me. Which meant that I could sleep with him without putting my life at risk. So the only question that really remained was, did I want to?

I stalked across the threshold. "Then do it."

A frown creased Callan's brows as he straightened and turned to face me. "Do what?"

Raising my eyebrows, I strode across the floor until I was standing in front of him. Confusion still lined his face. I crossed my arms and looked up at him expectantly.

"You've been bragging about your abilities in the bedroom for quite some time now." A challenging grin blew across my lips as I raised my chin. "So go ahead. Fuck me. Try to make me beg for mercy."

Silence descended on the room.

For a moment, Callan did nothing. He didn't move. Didn't speak. He just stood there, looking down at me like a statue carved from marble.

Just when I thought I had interpreted everything all wrong, a wicked smile slid home on his mouth.

A dark laugh spilled from his lips as he took a step closer. "Are you sure you know what you're signing up for?"

"I've spent every day for the past week and a half with you, I know exactly what I'm signing up for."

"I need you to say it. Out loud."

"Fine." I spread my arms wide and raised my chin. "I give you permission to do whatever you want to me until I beg you for mercy."

His eyes shone with something I had never seen before. It seemed to burn from all the way inside his soul. He took another step forward, backing me up against one of the carved wooden poles of the four-poster bed. Placing a hand on my collarbones, he pinned me against the wood and then closed the final distance.

I grabbed the collar of his shirt and pulled his face closer to mine. "This doesn't change anything. I still hate you and I'm still going to kill you once this mission is over."

"Oh trust me." He brushed his lips over mine, just shy of touching. "The feeling is mutual."

"Good. So, no feelings. Just pure sex because we might find each other a little bit attractive."

"Just a little bit."

"And when you fail to make me beg for mercy, all we will have done is prove that you really aren't anywhere near as good as you think you are."

He laughed against my lips. "So cocky. I can't wait to turn you into a trembling ball of need."

I yanked him down the final bit. His mouth crashed against mine as I claimed his lips before he could make the first move. Stepping closer, he pushed his body harder against mine while returning the furious kiss. There was nothing sweet about it. Nothing romantic. It was rage and frustration and pent-up desire.

The round wooden pole dug into my back as Callan pressed forward again while his mouth continued to ravage mine. I sucked in a gasp as he bit my bottom lip. He stole that breath from me before his tongue pushed into my mouth.

His hands slid across my skin until he reached the collar of my dress. This one was much simpler, and laced up in the front, so he deftly undid the fastenings and then pushed the fabric off my shoulders while he continued stealing savage kisses from my lips.

A shudder of pleasure coursed through me as his fingers brushed down my bare arms. I reached out and grabbed the hem of his shirt. With quick movements, I pulled it up his chest.

He let out a low growl from deep within his chest, but then broke the kiss and took a step back so that he could yank the shirt over his head. I used the opportunity to fully step out of my dress. It barely had time to flutter to the floor before Callan closed the distance between us.

After drawing his hands up my back, he undid the fastenings on my brassiere and pulled it off me. My nipples hardened at the sudden exposure. While tossing the flimsy garment to the floor with one hand, Callan used the other to yank me away from the bedpost and position me before the mattress instead. Metallic rattling filled the room as he bent down and threw a long chain under the bed. I was just about to open my mouth when he snapped his gaze back to me.

Pure command pulsed from his whole body as he jerked his chin. "Get on the bed."

"Make me." I flashed him a smug smirk and raised my eyebrows in challenge. "If you want to hear me beg, you're going to have to work for it."

A lethal glint crept into his dark eyes.

Before I could react, he slammed his palms together and shot a small force wall at my chest. The hit sent me crashing down on top of the mattress. While trying to push my hair out of my face, I rolled over on my side so that I would be able to see where he was.

His knees smacked down on either side of me. My roll came to an abrupt halt as he put a hand on my shoulder and forced me down onto my back again. While still straddling my chest, he reached towards the side of the bed. I finally got my hands out from underneath him and pushed the curtain of hair out of my face right as metallic rattling filled the room once again.

Callan's strong fingers snaked around my wrist. With a firm grip on it, he moved my arm towards the edge of the bed. Then the cold kiss of steel appeared against my skin.

After locking my wrist into the cuff, he grabbed my other hand and did the same. Then he sat back on top of my chest again.

I yanked my arms. Chains rattled somewhere under the bed. My arms were spread wide towards either side of the bed and my wrists were locked in the handcuffs at the ends of the chain, keeping my hands firmly trapped against the mattress. I pulled against them again, but they didn't budge.

A sudden intense thrill rushed through my body and made my heart pound in my chest. It was followed by dark and throbbing desire.

Callan swung his leg over me, climbing off my chest and positioning himself next to my hip instead. Then he paused, his eyes searing into mine. "We can stop this right now."

But I didn't want to. If I had been curious before, I was enthralled now. I had to see where this was heading and how it all ended.

"I don't want to."

"Good." A sly smile drifted across his lips. "Then I will only stop once you've begged me for mercy."

Lightning crackled over my skin as he curled his fingers over the top of my panties and started sliding them downwards. The lacy material brushed my skin as he took his time drawing them down my legs. I shifted my hips, as if that would speed up the process. My heart was thumping in my chest. I wanted him to start already.

At last, he slid them over my feet, leaving me completely naked.

Callan rolled off the bed. After dropping my panties on the floor, he picked up the metal bar that was leaning against the chair.

My heart skipped a beat.

He trailed one end of it lightly on the floor as he sauntered back to me before stopping at the foot of the bed. Bracing one knee on the mattress, he grabbed my ankle. I sucked in a gasp.

Callan smiled like the villain he was as he locked my ankle into the cuff at the end of the bar. Cold metal pressed against my skin. After grabbing my other ankle, he did the same with that one.

I tried to move my legs, but Callan just grabbed the bar, holding it steady against the mattress. With my ankles locked at the ends of it, the wicked contraption forced me to keep my legs spread wide, leaving my pussy completely exposed to the smirking force mage.

After raking his gaze up and down my body, he climbed up onto the bed and positioned himself so that he straddled my right thigh. His weight prevented me from raising my legs, keeping them both spread wide and pinned to the mattress.

He brushed his knuckles against my center. I sucked in another shuddering breath and shifted my hips.

A smug laugh dripped from Callan's lips. "Oh you really are enjoying this, aren't you?"

There was no hiding how wet I was.

Bracing one hand against the bed next to me, he leaned forward until his face was level with mine. Satisfaction swirled in his eyes. "Do you like it when I dominate you?"

"Dominate me?" I scoffed. "Don't flatter yourself, pretty boy. You said that you'd make me beg for mercy." With my arms spread wide, I managed a strained shrug. "Do you see me begging?"

Instead of answering, he drew his other hand down my soaked pussy. A tremor passed through me as his fingers brushed my clit. Locking eyes with me, he started tracing his thumb over it. Another shudder coursed through my body, and my eyes fluttered closed.

The weight of his arm on the mattress next to me disappeared as Callan straightened and instead placed that hand around my chin.

"Eyes on me," he ordered.

I was just about to spit back a retort when he rolled my clit between his fingers, and a gasp escaped me instead. When I blinked before opening my eyes again, I found him staring me down with an expression that pulsed with authority.

Once he was satisfied that I was looking at him, he briefly moved the hand from my chin and down towards his other one before he leaned forward once more and braced his hand against the mattress again. While his thumb continued circling, he stared down at me from only a few breaths away.

"If this is the best you've got, you—"

I sucked in a sharp breath, my taunt getting cut off halfway through, as Callan's fingers started vibrating with force magic. A moan tore from my throat. Shifting my hips, I tried to remember what I'd been about to say.

The thought flew straight out of my head as Callan pushed two fingers inside me while his magic continued pulsing against my clit. My eyes fluttered again as he started sliding his fingers in and out at a slow pace. Blinking them back into focus, I found Callan smiling down at me like a fiend.

In an attempt to relieve some of the building tension, I tried to pull my legs up so that I could push my knees together and trap his hand between my thighs.

Callan let out an amused huff.

Then the mattress below me shifted as he sat back again, straddling my thigh and putting his whole weight on top of it. My leg was trapped firmly underneath him, and since my other ankle was locked to it as well, I couldn't raise that leg either.

His fingers continued sliding in and out of my soaked pussy while his force magic vibrated against my clit. Pleasure built inside me again. But it never reached all the way to push me over the edge.

I arched my back to get his fingers to a better spot.

Callan just chuckled again and grabbed my hip with his free hand. His fingers dug into my skin as he forced me back down against the bed. I yanked against the chains keeping my arms spread wide.

The vibrations continued at the same intensity while his fingers moved at the same unhurried pace.

Frustration swelled inside my chest. It mixed with the pleasure from the pulsing force magic and made me both angry and horny at the same time. I tried discreetly to buck my hips again so that I could press my clit harder against his fingers.

Callan's hand tightened around my hip bone, pushing me back down. A soft snarl ripped from my throat. Pulling hard against my restraints, I tried to free my hands so that I could force him to give me what I wanted, but the chain only rattled under the bed.

My heart was pounding against my ribs and pressure built inside my chest until I thought it was going to explode. The wave of pleasure was so close, but it never came. I squirmed against the mattress.

A villainous laugh rolled off Callan's tongue. He kept his vibrations low. Just enough to continuously push me to the edge, but not strong enough to actually make me come.

Desperation pulsed through me and a pitiful noise escaped

my lips. I tried to press my legs together, but the bar kept them mercilessly spread for the cruel force mage as he continued edging me until I could feel my mind starting to unravel.

An animalistic whine tore from my throat. I yanked against the handcuffs keeping my wrists locked to the bed, and jerked my body back and forth underneath Callan's weight. His fingers slid in and out while his magic pulsed against the exact right spot, but still not with enough intensity.

My mind was splintering into a thousand different pieces as the pressure built but the release never came. I needed it. I needed that release like I needed air. Thrashing against my restraints, I let out a sob that was pure desperation. My brain was going to shatter. I couldn't breathe. I needed air. I needed release.

"Alright," I gasped out. "Alright."

Callan leaned forward over me again. Using his free hand, he took my jaw in a firm grip and forced me to look at him. "Say it."

"Please."

Power and control pulsed from his body as he held my gaze. "The exact word, Audrey."

My mind was quickly unraveling and I was having trouble focusing my eyes.

Callan's grip on my jaw tightened. "Say it."

Sucking in a shuddering breath, I pressed out, "Mercy."

His smile as he looked down at my pleading eyes was pure victory.

"Please, mercy," I begged as my pride slipped right through my fingers and I found myself surrendering to my worst enemy. "Callan. Please. I'm begging you."

The vibrations increased. I dragged in a shuddering breath as the pulsing force magic finally reached the intensity I needed. Pleasure built inside me exponentially. Callan pumped his fingers harder and then curled them slightly on the way out.

Stars exploded behind my eyes.

My legs shook violently as that sweet, sweet release finally crashed down over me and swept my whole mind right out of my head. I threw my head back and moaned incoherently as Callan kept the vibrations going while my inner walls trembled.

It was the most intense feeling that I had ever experienced.

The chains rattled as I pulled against the handcuffs and gasped out another desperate breath.

After being denied release for so long, the orgasm crackled through my body like a lightning storm. And the thought that Callan controlled it all sent a rush of dark desire shooting through me. I needed more.

While I was still trying to piece my mind back together, Callan unlocked my wrists and ankles and then stripped out of his own pants. I pushed myself up on my elbows as he returned to the bed. Wrapping my legs around his waist, I yanked his body closer. I needed more. I needed...

His calloused hands trailed up my thighs and then hooked around them, spreading my legs wide before him again. I reached up and snaked a hand around the back of his neck. With a firm pull, I drew his mouth down to mine while his hard cock brushed against my entrance.

Callan kissed me savagely while sliding one arm under my back. After lifting my body slightly from the mattress, he pushed inside me.

I moaned into his mouth as his massive length slid into me. He moved slowly in and out a few times to help me adjust, but I didn't want slow. I wanted hard and fast and rough. There was wildfire in my chest and I wanted to feed the flames.

"Harder," I growled against his lips.

He shoved into me all the way to the hilt.

Throwing my head back, I gasped in pleasure at the feeling of his cock filling me completely. I raked my fingers down his back as he pulled out and then slammed into me again. His arm around my back tightened as I arched into him, pressing my tits against his chest. He stole the breath from my lungs as he claimed my mouth with another rough kiss before his lips made their way down my throat.

My body slumped back towards the bed again as a tremor racked my body.

Callan drove into me again. I dragged my hands over the side of his ribs and then up his chiseled abs and chest. While kissing his way down my throat, he kept up his merciless pace.

Pleasure built inside me again.

His teeth grazed my skin as he reached the side of my neck and then started his way back up again. Just as his lips reached that sensitive spot below my ear, his cock hit the perfect spot inside me.

Release crashed over me once more. My inner walls clenched tight around his thick length. Callan kept driving his cock in and out, riding the orgasm with me, until a groan tore from his chest.

He tightened his arm around my back and pressed his forehead against mine as he came as well. My heart slammed against my ribs and light flickered behind my eyes as waves of pleasure washed over the both of us.

When the last of it had drained from our limbs, Callan pulled out and collapsed onto the bed next to me. The mattress swayed underneath my exhausted body as his weight landed on the bed.

"Fuck," we gasped out in unison.

Turning my head, I rested my cheek against the soft sheet and stared at the enemy beside me.

His chest heaved, and there was a disbelieving look in his eyes that made him seem completely dazed. That same disbelief swirled inside me too. I raised a hand and placed it over my own heart, feeling it pound against my palm.

This damn force mage had made me feel things that I had never felt before. Things I didn't even think were possible to feel.

"Fuck," I pressed out again.

Tilting my head back, I stared up at the pale ceiling above.

I was in so much trouble.

CHAPTER 28

Callan

Light flickered in the windows and the sounds of a party drifted out into the night. I scowled at the small building before me. This was not what I had planned. I had assumed that the guy would be on his own. Maybe even sleeping. But I needed to do this tonight, because tomorrow evening, Audrey and I were going to that soirée that Elise Dawson had invited us to.

I snuck closer to the back of the house. Audrey and I had split up to complete two missions tonight because we had to finish our preparations quickly since the ball in the Rose Hall was only a few days away. Or that was the reason I gave when I proposed this, at least. In truth, I also needed some space. From her.

When she had told me to fuck her, I'd thought that I could finally return the power balance between us to its proper place where it leaned in my favor. But it had affected me too, and I was pretty sure that she'd been able to tell.

Anger burned inside my chest as I grabbed the edge of the open window and pulled it farther out before climbing up on the windowsill. The sounds of people talking and laughing came from deeper inside the house. Maybe it was good that the guy had some friends over for a party. I needed to blow off some steam.

After lowering myself silently to the floor inside, I pulled the window shut behind me. For what I was about to do, it was better if the neighbors didn't hear.

I slunk out of the deserted kitchen and moved towards the room that the voices were coming from. Candlelight lit up the pale walls in the room up ahead, and dark shadows shifted against them. Drawing myself up by the wall next to the doorframe, I cast a glance around the corner.

I narrowed my eyes as I studied the living room on the other side. Maybe I had been a bit generous in calling it a party. There were five guys in the room, including my target. They all looked to be around my age, or maybe a few years younger, and as far as I could tell, none of them would pose any threat to me.

When I had set out to do this, I'd had a different approach in mind. After all, this was a normal worker's neighborhood rather than the shady part of town. But I needed to vent my frustration on someone.

Touching my palms together, I called up my magic and then stepped into the living room. None of the young men noticed me. My target was the skinny blond guy seated in a patched-up armchair next to the cold hearth. His four friends were sprawled across the two brown couches on the other side of the low table, and tankards and empty bottles of alcohol littered the scratched tabletop.

I decided on the blue-eyed fellow on the far right and threw a force arc at him. The attack sped through the air and cleaved him in two from the shoulder and all the way down to his lower ribs.

Now, they noticed me.

Terrified screaming erupted as the other four people shot up from their seats. Three of them whipped towards me while the one who had been sitting next to the dead guy just stared in mute horror at the blood and bones visible in his friend's chest.

A man with long brown hair touched his hands together and threw a lightning bolt at me. I knocked it aside with a force wall before hurling a spear of magic at the one who was still staring at his dead friend. It carved a hole right through his chest, making him topple face first onto the couch before he could even turn to see who had killed him.

The three remaining men scrambled back behind the table and started throwing magic at me while screaming battle cries as if that would help the strikes hit better. The funny thing was that if they had just taken a breath and coordinated their attacks instead of throwing everything at me in a wild panic, it would have been much more difficult for me to get through. But now, they were shooting a jumble of wind and water and lightning without thinking about what they were doing, so their attacks slammed into each other's magic more often than not. The ones that made it through, I either dodged or shoved aside with a force shield.

Panic and fear shone in their eyes as I advanced on them. Fueled by their terror, they increased the wildness of their attacks. It was starting to piss me off so I dropped the force shield and instead threw an entire wall at them.

It caught them right in the chest and sent them flying backwards across the room. Three loud bangs echoed into the otherwise suddenly silent house as they hit the wooden wall before crashing down on the floor. Stepping onto the low table, I strode right across it before jumping down on the other side and landing in front of the three young men who had struggled to their feet.

Before they could get their wits about them, I summoned a

force blade and rammed it through the guy on my right. My target, on the left, let out a cry of fear and sorrow, but the dark-haired one in the middle raised his palms as if to attack while my force blade was otherwise occupied. I yanked out my real knife from the holster at the small of my back and stabbed him in the side of the neck. His eyes widened and his hands fell down by his sides again.

Wet gurgling filled the room as I withdrew both the knife and the force blade. The two unfortunate men collapsed to the floor. I turned towards the final person in the room.

His gray eyes were wide and terrified as he tried to back away, but he hit the wall behind him after only two steps.

"You're going to be working as a waiter at the ball in the Rose Hall in three days, correct?"

"You're a dark mage," he pressed out, his gaze flicking to the force blade I still held in my right hand.

"Yes. Now, answer my question. You're going to be working as a waiter at the ball in the Rose Hall in three days, correct?"

"I... I," he stammered, eyes still on the vibrating blade.

Spinning the force blade in my hand, I took a step forward and leveled it at his chest. He sucked in a gasp and snapped his frightened gaze to my face. I cocked my head.

"Don't make me repeat myself a third time."

"Yes," he finally answered. "Yes, I am."

I already knew that, of course. Under the guise of wanting to hire more kitchen staff, I had managed to discreetly get some information out of Violet regarding which company would be supplying the ball with waiters. After that, I had just posed as a potential client and gotten a look at their roster. This guy was apparently the newest addition, which meant that he had the least loyalty towards the company. And the least experience.

"Of course you are," I said and then raised the force blade

until it was pressed firmly against the side of his neck.

Fear flooded his eyes. "No, wait. Wait. I can... I can quit if you want. If you want the spot."

"Are you saying I look like a servant?"

"No!" Horror washed over his face when he thought that he had offended me.

"Then what are you saying?"

"I..." His legs buckled and he dropped to his knees right before my feet. Staring at my boots, he drew in a shuddering breath and then pressed out a pitiful, "Please."

For a few seconds, I just let the silence stretch. I needed him terrified and obedient, and nothing instilled dread in people like the fear of uncertainty. The fear of knowing that their life was hanging in the balance and that they could do nothing but wait for someone else to decide their fate.

"I need someone at the ball who can make sure that a certain person gets to a certain place at a certain time," I said at last.

He jerked his head up and a glimmer of hope shone in his eyes. "What do I have to do?"

"At the ball, I will tell you the name of a person and a place. Then, all you have to do is walk up to that person, give them some bullshit excuse, and lead them to the room. Alone."

"You're going to kill someone."

I just gave him a wolfish smile in reply.

"What happens to me?" He swallowed while looking up at me with pleading eyes. "If I lead this person into the room, what happens to me? Will you let me live? Because if that's the case, I'll do it. I'll do whatever you want."

"Yes, if you get this person into the room I specify, I will let you live. You're no one to me. So there would be no point in killing you."

"Then I'll do it."

"Smart choice."

While letting my force blade fade out, I wiped my knife on the toppled armchair and then sheathed it at my back again. The unlucky waiter tracked my every move with wary eyes. Once I was done, I leaned down and took a firm grip on his collar. With a hard yank, I hauled him to his feet and slammed him up against the wall instead.

Keeping my grip on his collar, I locked hard eyes on him. "But know this... If you fail to hold up your end of this bargain, you are going to wish that I had done something as kind as to simply kill you."

"Y-yes. I understand."

"Good." I arched an expectant eyebrow at him. "Aren't you going to thank me for showing you mercy?"

"Thank you," he blurted out, his words almost tripping over his tongue.

I let out a dark laugh as I finally released his collar. He collapsed to the ground with a thud. Turning my back on him, I started back towards the door.

"Wait..." he called after me. "What do I... tell people?"

Casting a glance over my shoulder, I found him motioning towards the room full of dead people. "Until the ball is over, you tell them that your friends took a spontaneous trip somewhere." I flicked my wrist dismissively as I turned back to the corridor ahead and strode across the threshold. "After that, you can tell them whatever the hell you like."

A small sob followed me as I left the blackmailed waiter and the collateral damage behind while I strode back out of the building.

We had our bait so that we could lure Lance into the room with the side door. Now, we just needed a distraction.

Time to go and see what that damn poison mage had accomplished tonight.

CHAPTER 29

Audrey

An entire room full of criminals turned to watch me as I strode through the door. There had been a murmur of voices hanging over the tavern when I had opened the door, but as I closed it, the wide space fell completely silent.

The men and women sitting at the mass of tables took one look at my face and the dress I was wearing, and then chuckled.

"I think you're in the wrong place, love."

The voice had come from a muscular man with tattoos along both arms. He sat at a table towards the back where he had a full view of the entire room as well as the door. I flicked my gaze up and down his body in a calculated move before letting out a huff of amusement.

"No, I'm exactly where I want to be, Henrick," I said.

A ripple went through the crowd. Several people touched their hands together, making small balls of fire appear in their palms. The added magic brightened the otherwise gloomy room and cast dancing shadows over the dark wooden walls. Steel glinted in the firelight as a few people drew their knives.

Henrick remained leaning back in his seat, his hands resting casually on the table full of half-empty mugs of ale. "You know who I am?"

"Yes. You're the leader of this gang, and you all specialize in particularly noisy attacks."

"And you are?"

"Someone who has a job for you."

He huffed out a laugh. "I don't think so."

"I haven't even told you what the job is."

"You don't need to." He raked his gaze up and down my expensive and well-tailored dress before giving me a pointed look. "I can tell just by looking at you that you're from a social class that I don't wanna get mixed up in."

"Really?"

"Yeah. So whatever the job is, the answer's no."

A sharp smile slid across my lips.

Several people shot to their feet at the sight of it, but before they could do anything else, I slammed my palms together and threw a massive cloud of poison across the whole room. Cries of surprise were abruptly cut off as my magic forced its way down the gang members' throats. I kept the strength of the poison high enough that they couldn't do anything other than sit there and choke, but low enough to make sure they didn't lose consciousness or die.

Henrick tried to push himself up from his chair so I increased the intensity for him. A strangled noise came from his throat and he staggered into the table before collapsing back into his seat.

"No matter what the job is, the answer is no, huh?" I said.

Only the sound of people choking and clawing at the tables in front of them answered me. I locked eyes with Henrick. He had one hand hanging uselessly down his side while the other gripped the edge of the table so hard that his knuckles turned white.

Holding his gaze, I raised a hand to point at a man with dark red hair a few tables away. The redhead sucked in one last gasp and then toppled from his seat. Lifeless eyes stared up into the dark wooden ceiling.

The pointing was for dramatic effect rather than necessity since I could increase the strength of my poison at will. I wanted Henrick to actually see his people die.

I pointed towards a woman with curly brown hair, and a second later, her lifeless body hit the floor next to the chair. My hand moved to a man with a scar down through his eyebrow. His forehead banged into the table in front of him as he died too.

Panic and fear pulsed in Henrick's brown eyes.

While still holding his gaze, I killed another handful of his people. He opened his mouth as if trying to speak, but only strangled gurgling came out. I poisoned a few more people before finally staying my hand.

Cocking my head, I raised my eyebrows expectantly at the tattooed gang leader. "Care to reconsider?"

He nodded desperately. I let them all choke for another few seconds before pulling back my twisting cloud of poison.

The whole room sucked in a collective breath. It was followed by coughs and then gasps of air.

After inhaling deeply a couple of times, Henrick met my gaze again. "What do you want us to do?"

I explained what I wanted them to do and then tossed some money on the floor. "Your usual rate, I'm told."

No one moved to pick up the money. They all just watched me with wary eyes.

"If you fail me in this, I will pay you all another visit." I flicked a lazy hand towards the dead gang members around the room. "And that time, I'll just send in a cloud of poison through the window and kill you all instantly without even bothering to walk through the door. Am I making myself clear?"

"Yes," Henrick answered.

"Good. Remember what I said. Wait for the signal."

Before he could reply, I spun on my heel and strode back out the door.

That had gone more or less as I'd predicted. I had killed a few more people than I had originally planned, but I was still angry that Callan had succeeded in making me beg for mercy last night. It was so ridiculously embarrassing and it made me hate him even more. And at the same time, I also desperately wanted to fuck him again because by all hell, that had been unlike anything I had ever experienced.

All of those contradictory feelings messed with my head and made more rage than usual burn in my chest. So to deal with that, I had killed a few more people just so that I could feel powerful and in control again. And I had to admit, it did work.

I had only made it to the next cross street when the person responsible for my little killing spree appeared.

Callan Blackwell crossed his arms as he came to a halt in the middle of the street. "How did it go?"

"We have our distraction."

"Good."

After closing the distance between us, I stopped as well and raised my eyebrows at him. "And yours?"

"It's done. We have the waiter." His dark gaze slid in the direction of the tavern around the corner. "How did you get him to take the job?"

"I started killing his friends until he agreed. You?"

Callan's eyes shot back to my face. For a moment, he only stared down at me. Then he answered, "Same."

A huff of laughter escaped my chest. "Great mi—" I cut myself off before I could finish saying 'great minds think alike' because there was nothing alike about us. Instead, I cleared my throat and just repeated, "Great."

Boots thudded against the stone behind me. I turned around so that I faced the street I had just come from right as a tall man with white blond hair and icy blue eyes barreled around the corner.

He jerked back in surprise and skidded to a halt when he found us just standing there in the middle of the street. Recovering, he cleared his throat and drew himself up to his full height.

"We will not be taking the job," he announced.

I arched an eyebrow at him. "Excuse me?"

"Henrick is weak and too soft at heart, but I refuse to let our gang be bullied into doing anything."

A snarl ripped from my throat as I stalked towards him. Callan followed. The blond man was a lot taller than me, so I had to crane my neck to look up at him as I stopped a single stride away.

Poison dripped from my voice as I pointed in the direction of the tavern. "You did see me kill a dozen of your friends back there, didn't you?"

"Yes, but I'm not afraid of you."

I touched my palms together. Glittering green magic snaked down my arms a second later. "You should be."

He slapped me.

The force of the strike was enough to snap my head sideways, but it was the surprise rather than the hit that made me stumble a step back and lose the grasp on my magic. Shock clanged through me. He had slapped me. Actually slapped me across the face. I couldn't even remember the last time someone had dared to do something like that to me.

Lightning crackled in front of me. I turned my head back towards him, but my stunned bewilderment had cost me precious seconds. No one slapped a dark mage. It was such a ridiculously absurd thing to do, which was of course exactly why he had done it. Because it had bought him the time he needed to launch his real attack. While I finished twisting my head back, his other hand shot up as he prepared to discharge a lightning bolt straight into my chest at point blank range.

He sucked in a gasp, and the white bolt of lightning in his palm fizzled out.

I blinked at the scene before me as that palm seemed to be dropping lower towards the ground than should be possible.

A thud sounded.

For a few seconds, all I could do was stand there and stare at the severed hand on the ground. Blood leaked out and painted the pale stone beneath it red.

Then an ear-splitting scream pierced my stupor and I snapped my gaze up. The blond guy was clutching his arm while more blood dripped down onto the street from his severed wrist. Callan still stood next to me, but he had taken a step closer to the screaming man, and a force blade vibrated in his grip.

I glanced down at the hand that the guy had used when he slapped me. Callan had cut it off.

Before that thought had finished ricocheting through my brain, Callan grabbed my attacker's collar and hauled him closer while shortening the force blade into a knife. I just watched in complete confusion as Callan shoved the vibrating half-translucent blade into the man's chest and carved his heart out.

The screams were replaced by a wet squelching sound as

Callan ripped the heart out of the hole he had cut into the guy's chest. Releasing his collar, Callan let the man's body topple backwards and crash down onto the street.

Blood coated his hand as he looked down at the heart he still squeezed in his fist. Then his dark brown eyes snapped up to mine. Something flickered in them, too fast for me to decipher.

I opened my mouth to say... something, but I never found out what because Callan jerked his chin at me and stalked towards the tavern I had just left.

"Come on," he growled.

"Uhm," I said, because I really wasn't sure what to say at this point.

Had he cut a man's hand off and carved his heart out just because he had slapped me? It went against everything I knew about Callan Blackwell. And if it were true, I wouldn't even know what to do with that information.

Thankfully, I received my answer and was proven wrong when Callan spoke up again.

"Let's show them what happens to people who don't follow orders."

CHAPTER 30

Callan

A large house made of white stone rose above us as we walked through the gate and across the small patch of grass that separated the building from the street. Light shone from every window, and music and laughter drifted out into the warm evening air. I scowled at the Dawsons' pale blue door as we came to a halt outside it. For people who preached about equality, they sure owned a fancy house.

"Only bring up the ball if it fits with the rest of the conversation," Audrey said from next to me. "Otherwise, they'll see through it right away." She narrowed her eyes as she looked up at me. "And be polite."

Annoyance blew through me. "I know how to be sneaky."

"Could've fooled me."

"You—"

"The ball is in two days. We need to get this invitation *tonight*, or we'll have to go with our back-up plan."

"The back-up plan sucks."

"I know. So be polite and sneaky."

Shaking my head, I grabbed the metal knocker and rapped it against the door. "Let's just get this over with."

She had started getting under my skin more often lately, and it made me even more restless and irritated. Just being in her presence made me want to kill someone. Preferably her.

The door was flung open, flooding the porch with golden light from the candles inside. Two very excited faces met us on the other side of the threshold. Elise and Carl Dawson flashed us bright smiles.

"Callan, Audrey," Elise began as she clapped her hands together. "You made it!"

"Of course," I answered and gave her a calculated sly smile in return. "We wouldn't miss it for the world."

Carl motioned for us to move into the hallway. "Please, come inside."

Placing a hand against Audrey's back, I guided her across the threshold before following as well and closing the door behind me.

The sounds of people talking and laughing came from the rooms down the hall as well as upstairs. Someone was also playing the piano close by. I swept my gaze over the Dawsons. Carl was wearing a white dress shirt which was appropriate for all kinds of events, but Elise had donned a low-cut red dress that clung to her figure and showed off her ass and tits. It wasn't at all what people in Eldar usually wore to dinner parties, which was what I had assumed this would be.

"Come," Elise said as she slid her arm through mine. "Let us show you around."

I glanced over at Audrey and found that Carl had done the same to her, so I let the blond socialite lead me deeper into the house.

An arched doorway opened up in the wall on our left, leading into what looked like a living room. Men and women were sprawled across the blue and golden furniture inside, drinking and chatting and... flirting? It took great effort to keep a scowl from my face as I surveyed the room. Most of the people in there seemed to be making advances on each other. As I watched, one man with pale blue eyes appeared to get rejected by a woman with long red hair, but instead of looking put out by it, he just moved on to someone else.

What kind of soirée had they actually invited us to?

"I imagine you must be a bit confused at this point," Elise said as she studied the expression on my face before flicking a glance to Audrey as well.

"Yes, a little bit," Audrey replied. There was an innocent and curious smile on her lips as she looked between Carl and Elise. "We were under the impression that this would be a dinner party."

"Ah, yes. We kept the details vague on purpose because we didn't want to scare you off."

"What do you mean?"

Elise looked over at her husband. "Carl darling, would you take Audrey for a little tour while you explain it to her? And I'll do the same to Callan."

"Of course." He nodded back at her before turning to Audrey and lifting a hand to motion towards the staircase farther down the hall. "Shall we?"

Audrey and I exchanged a brief glance, and I swore I could hear her damn voice in my head. *Be polite and sneaky.*

Then she broke eye contact and turned to flash Carl a bright smile. "Lead the way."

Before I could say anything else, Carl disappeared towards the staircase with Audrey while Elise pulled me into the living room.

Several people looked up as we entered, and excitement shone on their faces as they ran their eyes up and down my body. I suddenly felt as though I was a bull being led through a meat market. Even though I had to admit that I liked it when people looked at me with lust and hunger in their eyes, this somehow felt different. Since I was apparently the newest addition to this group, it branded me with an air of inexperience and a lack of control. And I hated when I wasn't in control of things.

"You're being very mysterious, Elise," I said as she led me towards a spot by the wall. "What is this?"

She released my arm and swept a hand to indicate the room as we took up position by the marble wall. "This is our group of friends. Everyone here shares a certain yearning for freedom and adventure."

"Of what kind?"

"Couples can easily lose that burning spark after a few years of marriage." She placed a hand on my arm and looked up at me with blue eyes that gleamed in the candlelight. "But if you add a little bit of spice to it, the marriage will be long and healthy and full of burning passion even after many years."

I shifted my gaze between her face and the mass of flirting people around the room. "You switch partners, don't you?"

"Yes. Though not for any extended periods of time. Just for a night or two, to help keep that sense of freedom and adventure alive."

My eyes shot towards the doorway and the staircase beyond where Carl had disappeared with Audrey. "And tonight is...?"

She let out a light laugh and patted my arm. "Oh, don't worry. Tonight is just a meeting place. I host them every few weeks to bring everyone together, and then we can all just chat with each other and see if we would like to schedule a more private meeting with someone."

"I see."

"So, what do you think?"

I think you need to tell your husband to get his hands off my wife. The thought had shot through my mind before I even realized it. Shaking my head, I shoved the ridiculous notion out. Audrey wasn't even really my wife. And besides, we were here to get an invitation to the ball, which meant that I had to play along.

Letting a sly smile drift across my lips, I looked down at the hopeful expression on Elise's face. "I think I'm intrigued."

Relief flooded her eyes. "I'm so glad to hear that. When I saw you and Audrey, I knew from the very first moment that I wanted to introduce you to our world. I just hoped that you would be open to it."

"I have to admit, I've never heard of anything like this before. If it's okay, I'd like to take a little time to get a feel for the whole thing."

"Of course, of course." She took her hand from my arm and made a gesture to indicate the whole house. "Please, take a look around. I'll be down here if you have any questions."

"Thank you."

After giving her a nod, I moved towards the doorway we had come from and the staircase beyond. I knew that I should be cozying up to Elise and getting her to extend that invitation, but I found myself unable to concentrate on anything while Audrey was away with Carl. I just had to make sure that she wasn't doing anything stupid. Then, I could get back to the mission.

Taking the steps two at a time, I made my way upstairs. Dark wooden floorboards covered the hallways and the other rooms upstairs while the same white marble walls made up the rest of the structure. I ran my gaze over the expensive furniture as I scanned the area for any sign of Audrey. She was an explosion waiting to happen. If someone so much as looked at her the wrong way, she might decide to poison them all. Yes.

That had to be the reason why I was worried. Why I had to check up on her.

A woman was playing the piano in the next room I glanced into, and there were several other people in there as well, but none of them were Audrey.

My shoes thumped against the floor as I strode into the final room at the end of the hallway.

There was a group of men playing some kind of card game at the round table in the middle while two other people sat on the couch next to one of the bookshelves. My gaze snapped to the couple.

Audrey laughed and swatted Carl's chest where she sat next to him. He leaned a little closer to whisper something else into her ear while he rested his hand on her thigh. I had to suppress a sudden urge to bash his head against the wall.

Stalking into the room, I closed the distance to them with long strides.

"Audrey," I said, my voice coming out in more of a growl than I had intended. Clearing my throat, I smoothened out my scowl and instead turned to the leech sitting next to her. "Carl, could I have a moment with my wife, please?"

Anger flashed in Audrey's green eyes as she turned to look at me, but Carl just stood up and brushed his hands down his shirt.

"Of course," he replied in a smooth voice. Then he glanced back at Audrey. "I'll be downstairs."

"I'll join you shortly," she said and flashed him a smile that made rage crackle through my soul.

As soon as Carl had disappeared out the door, Audrey shot to her feet and gave my chest a shove. It did nothing to actually push me back, so she tried again. I just grabbed her wrist and raised my eyebrows at her.

"What the hell was that for?" I growled down at her in a low voice.

The men around the card table were still playing, but a few of them cast curious glances at us. From over there, they at least wouldn't be able to hear what we were saying.

"What was that for?" she repeated, her voice equally low but also dripping with poison. "What do you think? I was making progress! Why the hell did you interrupt?"

"Did he explain what this soirée is for?"

"Yes. I was playing into that to get him to invite us. Which is what you should be doing with Elise right now. Why aren't you?"

"Because I had to make sure you weren't about to do anything stupid."

"You're worried about *me* doing something stupid?"

"Yes. Because you're a vicious ball of rage who might decide to poison an entire room just because they looked at you the wrong way."

"*I'm* violent and unpredictable?" She stabbed her free hand against my chest. "You're the one who carved someone's heart out yesterday."

"Yeah, well, he... I don't tolerate when people disobey my orders." Releasing her wrist, I jerked my chin towards the door. "So do as you're fucking told and go get us that invitation without poisoning the whole building."

For a moment, it looked like she was going to summon her magic and poison *me* instead, but then she flicked her gaze to the men still playing cards. Grinding her teeth, she glared up at me for a few seconds before she just stalked off without another word. I ran a hand over my face.

A whole tangle of infuriating emotions snaked through my chest, and once more, I felt an overwhelming urge to kill someone. Preferably Audrey fucking Sable.

"Wow." One of the men at the table let out a low whistle. "Anyone know her name?"

"No, I've never seen her here before," someone else answered.

"After this game, I'm gonna go and find out." He let out a dark chuckle. "She's feisty."

"Yeah."

"If she's like this normally, can you imagine what she's like in bed? And I love me a challenge. I bet I could find a way to tame her."

I snapped my head towards them. "What the hell did you just say?"

Fury burned through my whole soul as I stared at the five men. They must have been able to see it through my eyes, because the one who had spoken about Audrey raised his hands in an appeasing gesture.

"I'm not looking for a fight," he said. "You know her, I take it?"

"She's my wife," I growled at him.

"Ah, sorry, mate. I meant no disrespect. But I would love to talk to her and arrange a meeting later."

It took all of my self-control not to sever his miserable head from his pathetic shoulders. Before I could say anything that would compromise our ruse, I just spun on my heel and stalked out of the room.

This mission was starting to get on my nerves. We had to finish it soon so that I could kill Audrey once and for all and finally be done with her infuriating presence in my life.

Anger rolled off my body as I stalked down the stairs, but once I reached the bottom, I had wiped all traces of it from my face. We really needed that invitation so that we could get to Lance Carmichael, because regardless of how much I hated Audrey, Lance was still a threat that needed to be dealt with first. So when I returned to the living room and found Audrey sitting next to Carl while she laughed and spoke quietly into his ear, I just sauntered over to the couch opposite them and dropped down next to Elise instead.

Draping an arm over her shoulders, I turned my full attention to her instead and flashed her a sly smile. "You know, I think I'm really starting to warm up to this."

"I knew you would." Elise laughed. "I recognize an adventurous spirit when I see one."

From across the low table, I could feel Audrey's eyes drifting to me, but I kept my gaze locked on Elise's gorgeous face as I started discreetly steering the conversation towards the ball. It took a few tries to get the topic where I wanted it, but eventually I was at a point where I could casually say that hearing about the upcoming ball made me realize how much I missed attending grand social events in Castlebourne.

"Oh, social events in Castlebourne have nothing on the official balls in Eldar," Elise said with a light laugh. Then she sat up straight as if she had just had a great idea. Whipping her head between me and Audrey, she slapped a hand on my arm in excitement. "You should totally come to the ball with us. Let us show you why you should really make Eldar your permanent home."

Carl absentmindedly ran a hand up and down Audrey's thigh. "What a great idea, honey. It will be such a wonderful event."

"But don't we need invitations to attend?" Audrey asked in a small and sad voice that even I believed. "We naturally haven't received one, and it's only two days away so I don't expect there to be any left."

A satisfied smile blew across Elise's lips. "There are always invitations available for the Dawsons."

"Indeed," Carl said, matching her grin.

"We will have two invitations to the ball sent to your house first thing in the morning."

Audrey looked between Elise and Carl with big green eyes. "You would really do that for us?"

"Of course." Elise waved a hand as if it was no big deal. Then her eyes took on a serious glint as she locked them on me. "We always take care of our friends."

"You're far too kind," I said, before giving her a suggestive smile. "I think the four of us are going to have a lot of fun together."

Both Elise and Carl laughed. While they exchanged a satisfied look, Audrey and I did the same, but for an entirely different reason.

At last, we had what we needed.

Our ticket into the heroes' ball and access to the Binder who threatened to wipe out every dark mage once he began his crusade.

Everything was ready. And with two days to spare.

We had a way in, we had a way to restrain Lance Carmichael, and we had a way to get him and us out of both the ball and the city once the deed was done. Now, all that was left was to rest up for two days while making the final arrangements.

Then, it was finally time to end this threat to our way of life.

Once and for all.

CHAPTER 31

Audrey

I slammed the door to Callan's bedroom closed behind me as I stalked inside. He looked up from the drawer he had been pulling something out of and turned to scowl at me.

"The hell are you so pissed off for?" he demanded. "We got our way into the ball."

"You almost blew it," I snapped back.

"*I'm* the one who got us the invitation."

"Yeah, after you completely ruined my careful manipulation of Carl by storming in like a jealous lover!"

A sharp smile stretched his lips. "How would you know what a jealous lover looks like when you've clearly never even had a real lover before?"

"Says the guy who pants after me like a horny teenage virgin," I threw back as I stopped right in front of him.

Lightning flashed in his eyes. Before I had even completely stopped moving, he grabbed my wrist and spun me around. My back hit the wall with a thud. While pinning my right hand against the wall next to my head, he positioned his forearm across my collarbones and used it to push me harder against the wall. But I had gone in there expecting a confrontation.

The moment he grabbed my wrist, I had used my other hand to pull the knife I had strapped to my thigh as soon as we returned home from the soirée. Yanking my hand up, I pressed the edge of the blade against Callan's throat. With him using one hand to pin one of mine to the wall, neither of us could do magic right now. Which meant that my knife to his throat currently gave me the upper hand.

"Take your hands off me," I warned in a low voice. When he only stared me down and continued pushing me into the wall, I drew the blade upwards, forcing it higher up under his chin. "Now."

Fury burned in his eyes, but he slowly released his grip on my wrist and then took his forearm from my chest, but he didn't back off. When his hands drifted closer to one another, I pushed the knife higher, forcing him to tilt his head back.

"Keep your hands wide," I ordered.

A mocking laugh rolled off his tongue, but he stopped moving his hands.

I drew the knife downwards again so that it was positioned across the middle of his throat, allowing him to tip his head back down to meet my gaze once more. There was a lethal smile on his lips, and the promise of revenge shone like dark flames behind his eyes.

"Now you listen here, and you listen well." I held his gaze with hard eyes while keeping the blade firmly against his skin. "I might allow you to live despite your constant displays of disrespect because I still need you to get Lance out of this city, but the moment we finish this mission, I will come at you with everything I have. You keep talking about getting your lands back, but as soon as this is over, I am going to take *your* lands from you. I am going to take everything you have and then I am going to make you bow down before me and grovel and beg me for mercy. And once I have destroyed your reputation and everything you have ever touched, then, and only then, am I going to allow you to die at my feet."

His smile sharpened with every word I spoke, and something dark and forbidden pulsed in his eyes. He raised a hand towards my face. I pressed the blade harder against his skin, but he kept moving anyway as his fingers brushed my chin. Taking my jaw in a firm grip, he held it steady and leaned down until I could feel his hot breath on my skin.

"You vicious little poisoner. Every time you open that pretty mouth of yours, I can't decide whether I want to fuck you or kill you."

A thrill raced down my spine. It was followed by dark desire that made my core throb. I stared up at him. "I hate you so much."

"I hate you too."

"Take your shirt off."

His wicked smile widened. Releasing my jaw, he moved his hands back towards his chest. I kept the knife pressed to his throat while he unbuttoned his dark shirt. The smooth fabric fluttered as Callan pushed his shirt off his broad shoulders and shrugged out of it, making it fall to the floor behind him.

I raked my eyes over his muscular chest and down to the V disappearing below his pants. Desire pooled inside me. I wanted to run my fingers all over his lethal body. And I wanted his hands all over mine. It was insane, I knew that. I didn't love him. I didn't even like him. But as I took in the way the candlelight danced over his powerful body and his handsome face, I was forced to admit that he made me feel other things. Things I had never felt before. So just because we would go back to killing each other once this mission was over, it didn't mean that I couldn't take what I wanted from our temporary truce right now.

Keeping the blade to his throat, I dragged my gaze up to his and then raised my eyebrows expectantly. "Now, take off my dress."

His eyes glinted dangerously, but he reached up and started to gently undo the fastenings on my dress. It laced up in the front, so he only had to pull at a few of them before it was loose enough to get out of. Once it was open, Callan widened the collar and drew his hands up my chest and towards my shoulders while pushing the dress off me. Lightning crackled through me as his fingers brushed my naked skin.

I slid my right arm out of the dress as it fell towards the floor, but my left hand was still holding the knife to Callan's throat. After shifting it to my other hand, I slipped out of the dress fully and let the dark green fabric pool around my ankles. My skin prickled at the exposure.

Callan's eyes darkened as he ran them up and down my body. But he said nothing. Only watched me intently, waiting to see what I would do next.

"Now, my underwear too," I ordered.

When he reached towards my body again, I made a split-second decision and intercepted his hand. Wrapping my fingers around his wrist, I stopped his hand mid-air. Callan arched an eyebrow at me in silent question.

My heart was pounding in my chest, but I hadn't forgotten what had happened in the living room that time we had gotten back from the dressmaker. And I wanted to feel the thrill of that again.

Taking the knife from his throat, I twisted it around and then pressed it hilt first into Callan's waiting hand. "Use this."

His eyes widened. Then a sly smile curled his lips and he flexed his fingers on the hilt. Placing his other palm against my collarbones, he pushed me back against the wall. "You're gonna have to stay very still for this."

I nodded.

While keeping his hand against my chest, he positioned the tip of the blade against my wrist and then started slowly drawing it upwards. A shiver coursed through my body, making it shake slightly, as Callan dragged the knife up my arm. Stopping the blade's path, he slid his other hand from my chest and wrapped it around my throat instead.

He cocked his head at me. "What did I just tell you?"

"Don't move."

"Exactly."

For a moment, he just held my gaze as if to truly drive the instruction home. Then he began tracing the knife along my skin again.

The cold metal scraped against my upper arm and over my shoulder, hard enough to be felt but not enough to leave any marks.

I sucked in a shuddering breath as Callan drew the blade over my collarbone. Releasing his grip on my throat, he instead placed the tip of the knife right below it while keeping his eyes locked on me. I bit my lip.

His eyes darkened further as they dipped to my mouth for a second. Then he met my gaze again and began trailing the blade down the middle of my chest.

My heart was slamming against my ribs and it took everything I had to stop a shudder of pleasure from racking my body.

Callan placed his other hand against my side and then drew it over the fabric of my brassiere until his large hand cupped my breast. My eyes fluttered as he kneaded it while also continuing to move the knife closer to it. I inhaled deeply to try to calm my thrumming pulse as Callan's fingers curled around the edge of the brassiere and lifted it slightly off my skin.

With his eyes locked on mine, Callan yanked the knife down and cut through the sheer fabric in the middle of the brassiere.

I sucked in a gasp.

My nipples hardened as Callan drew his free hand up my chest and pushed the ruined garment off my shoulders while still keeping the point of the blade resting above my heart. I shrugged out of the straps when they slid down my arms.

Callan drew his hand back down my chest while moving the knife towards one of my exposed tits. A low moan escaped my throat as he traced the point of the knife in a wide circle around my nipple while his empty hand slid across my other breast. His fingers dug into my skin as he kneaded it. The blade continued circling closer.

Throwing my head back, I rested it against the cool marble wall while my heart beat so hard in my chest that I thought Callan could surely hear it. Desire pulsed inside me, making my clit throb with need.

His fingers sped over my skin and took my nipple in a firm grip. Right as the blade reached its target on my other tit, Callan twisted his hand, and my nipple with it.

I gasped in a shuddering breath as both pain and pleasure crackled through my body. Throwing out my hand, I splayed it against the wall behind me to stop myself from falling over.

Callan released his punishing grip on my nipple and massaged my breast instead while he drew the knife back towards the center of my chest. Another shiver coursed through me as he trailed the sharp point down my stomach.

His lips brushed my jaw.

Pleasure washed over me and I sucked in another shuddering breath and arched my back as he kissed his way down my throat and across my chest. He jerked down his other hand. Taking my hip in a firm grip, he held me steady while he trailed the blade across the skin above my panties. I let out a moan from deep within my chest.

He withdrew his lips right before they reached my tit, and instead stood up straighter. The knife moved down over my hip. With that firm grip still in place, he slid the blade underneath the thin fabric of my undergarments. Then he paused.

"Eyes on me," he ordered.

I blinked my eyes back into focus as I raised my gaze to his face. When I at last looked into his dark brown eyes, I found insatiable hunger burning behind them.

"Stay very still," he commanded.

I nodded.

He yanked the knife up, shredding the fabric. My skin prickled as the last of my clothing fell away, leaving me entirely exposed to my lethal and dangerously attractive enemy.

When my torn panties had at last landed on the floor around my feet, Callan drew the point of the knife over my pussy. Shifting his grip on the hilt, he twisted it and then positioned the flat of the blade against my throbbing entrance. I drew in a soft gasp. Power and control pulsed from Callan's body as he slowly raised his hand, using the knife he pressed to my pussy to force me up onto my toes.

It took all my willpower to keep perfectly still in that position while a thrill of pleasure shot through my body and my heart skipped a beat. The whole situation just stole the breath from my lungs and made my thoughts all jumbled up. I was standing there naked, pinned to a wall by Callan Blackwell, while he rested a knife against the sensitive skin of my pussy. I should have been terrified. But all I could think about was that I wanted more.

He kept me like that for a few more seconds while he studied every twitch of my muscles, every flicker in my eyes, and every expression on my face. Then he slowly removed the knife and held it up before my face. Both of us glanced at the slick blade.

"So wet already." Callan let out a dark chuckle. "You really do like it when I—"

Before he could finish his taunt, I ripped the knife from his grip and dropped it on top of my dress while my other hand snaked around the back of his neck and yanked his mouth down to mine. I wanted *more*.

His lips crashed against mine. I stole angry kisses from them while my hands found his belt. Raking his fingers through my hair, he held my head between his palms and returned the furious kisses while I worked to get his pants off.

When they at last slid down his thighs, he released me and helped shove both his pants and his underwear all the way down his legs before stepping out of them. He grabbed his belt and my sliced brassiere on the way up. Before he had even finished straightening again, I gripped the back of his neck and pulled him towards me once more.

His hands slid down to cup my ass. I wrapped my legs around his waist as he lifted me off the floor. The leather belt and my brassiere were still wrapped around his right hand. Bracing his left hand under my ass and wrapping the other around my back, he carried me towards the bed while I continued stealing the breath from his lungs. His muscled body shifted against my naked skin as he walked, making me press myself harder against him. I wanted to feel it all.

Soft sheets appeared under my back as Callan knelt on the mattress before placing me down on it and moving into position above me.

His hard cock brushed my entrance.

A groan of pent-up desire tore from my throat. I locked my fingers behind his neck and yanked him down against me. My tongue tangled with his as I claimed his mouth and dragged my hands down his back while he pushed inside me.

I moaned into his mouth as his thick length slid into me, but he pulled back again too soon. Arching my back, I pressed my hips against his. He pushed his cock inside me again, a little farther this time.

"I want it all," I panted against his lips. "Now."

He shoved his cock into me, all the way to the hilt. I gasped and dragged my fingers down his muscled back as he pulled out and then pounded into me again, his massive length filling me completely. My hands slid down the side of his ribs and then over his abs. Pleasure built inside me as I raked my hands over his powerful body while he thrust his hips. He kissed me savagely, biting my lower lip and claiming the inside of my mouth with his tongue.

"More," I growled into his mouth. "I want more. I want it rough."

His lips disappeared from mine and he pulled out of me. Reaching up, he grabbed my wrist and then forced my arm towards the bedpost. The leather belt appeared against my skin as he used that to tie my hand to the wooden pole. My heart thundered in my chest as he took my other wrist in a firm grip and used what was left of my brassiere to tie my other hand to one of the decorative wooden rods set into the headboard. I pulled against the restraints, but they held fast, keeping my arms spread and trapped above my head.

Shifting back into position, Callan touched his palms together while he shoved his cock into me again. A grunt of pleasure tore from my throat. When he drew his hands apart, force magic sprang to life on the fingers of his left hand. He slid it downwards while his right hand moved in the other direction. Another shudder of desire coursed through me as he brushed his knuckles over my collarbones before wrapping his large hand around my throat.

Right as he closed his grip, his other hand reached my pussy.

Force magic pulsed against my clit as he positioned his fingers between our bodies while he continued pounding into me.

I sucked in a gasp.

Callan tightened his grip on my throat in response, cutting off my airways and freezing the breath in my lungs.

His dark eyes were locked on mine as he thrust deep into me while his vibrating force magic made my clit throb. Pleasure built inside me like a tidal wave. With my mouth slightly open from the gasp that Callan had trapped inside me, I looked up at the beautiful enemy above me.

Light from the candles glittered in his eyes and painted his hair with gold. His lethal body moved against mine as he brought me closer to the edge with every thrust and every pulse of his magic while his hand stayed locked around my throat. And with my hands tied like that, there was no way for me to summon any of my own magic right now. No way for me to loosen the strong fingers around my neck.

I pulled at my restraints, but they kept me trapped firmly with my arms spread wide. My chest shook slightly as I tried futilely to get air into my lungs. The muscles of Callan's forearm shifted as he tightened his grip on my throat even though it was already impossible for me to draw breath.

At that moment, my life was entirely in his hands. And it was so fucking intoxicating.

My lungs burned, begging for air, but Callan's powerful fingers didn't let up.

He increased the strength of the vibrations. I threw my

head back, and I would've gasped if I could, as pleasure built exponentially inside me.

Angling his hips, Callan shoved his hard length deeper inside me.

Force magic pulsed against my clit.

My whole body was coming apart at the seams and my lungs screamed for air.

Callan slammed into me right at the same time as he increased the vibrations again.

White light exploded across my vision.

Just when the wave of pleasure crashed over me, Callan released my throat.

Air rushed back into my lungs as I sucked in a deep gasp while the intense orgasm racked my body, and in that moment, I swear my soul almost brushed the heavens.

My pussy clenched tight around Callan's cock as he continued pounding into me, and release exploded behind his eyes as well. His vibrating magic kept pulsing against my throbbing clit while Callan came inside me.

Dark moans ripped from our throats at the same time.

I gasped in another desperate breath as my heart slammed against my ribs while my body trembled underneath him. His eyes were filled with dark desire as he held my gaze.

Leaning down, he stole another rough kiss from my lips while the final tremors coursed through both our bodies.

And in that moment, the rest of the world might as well not have existed at all.

CHAPTER 32

Callan

Fireworks rose from the paper and popped in a few colorful swirls as one of the doormen opened our invitations.

It was such a ridiculous thing. Very few mages with that particular ability had contributed to the Great Current, which meant that these small tricks were all that people could accomplish. But it had made this mission disproportionately more difficult for us. I didn't even think they realized that adding something like that to a piece of paper made it impossible to forge since only the person who had placed the fireworks there knew what shapes and colors they were supposed to be. The heroes of Eldar just wanted something pretty to wow their guests, and because of that Audrey and I had had to jump through hoops to score these invitations.

"Masks up, please," the doorman said.

Audrey and I pushed our masks up so that he could see our faces. She was wearing a swirling golden mask that only covered the area around her eyes while I bore a silver one that hid the top half of my face.

A few seconds passed as the doorman looked between our faces. Then he smiled.

"Welcome to the ball," he said as he placed our invitations in the box behind him and motioned for us to step inside.

I glanced down at Audrey as we slid our masks back in place again. She had linked her arm with mine and there was a pleasant smile on her face as she looked up at me. It really was extraordinary what an accomplished liar she was.

"Well, come on then, husband," she said as she moved us past the men guarding the door, and took a step across the threshold.

Tearing my gaze from her, I swept it across the massive ballroom before us.

If I had thought that the Rose Hall looked magnificent on our last visit, it was nothing compared to now. All of the glittering chandeliers had been lit, and the thick red ropes that had blocked off the doors and the seating area were gone. Gigantic flower arrangements in pink, red, and green covered the empty spaces between the tables while the wide dance floor had been polished until it shone. The thousands of candles throughout the room reflected against the stained-glass windows as well as the clear crystal goblets that rested on silver platters along the tables. By one of the short sides, an entire orchestra was set up. Their music floated through the ballroom and mingled with the murmur of the countless people who already covered both the dance floor and the seats. Only the raised podium at the front of the room was empty of people.

A flash of dread shot through me.

This was it. This was our one and only chance to get Lance Carmichael before these insufferable heroes launched their attack on us. Everything had to go smoothly because we would not get another opportunity like this.

"Callan," Audrey said, and the edge to her voice sent ice raking down my spine.

"What?" I replied while we moved a little farther into the room.

"The door."

While keeping a neutral expression on my face, I slid my gaze towards the door to the left of the dais. The door that led into that small empty room and the exit to the gardens. The one we were going to use to get Lance out. Except, there was one problem with that now.

A thickset man in a dark suit was sitting on a chair right in front of the closed door. His arms were crossed over his wide chest, but even from this distance, I was sure I could see his eyes sweep back and forth across the ballroom.

Shit.

"Maybe he'll move," I said instead.

"Or maybe they noticed that you had messed with the lock on the door."

"Don't get so worked up. It's probably just a precaution until all the guests have arrived."

Though in all honesty, I wasn't so sure.

Keeping my grip on Audrey's arm, I steered us towards the seating area by the inner wall. I needed to find that waiter I had blackmailed. The colorful sea of people shifted around us as we moved. Audrey kept her mouth shut while we were in the middle of it, but I could feel her eyes burning holes in the side of my head.

As soon as we had reached an empty table, she opened that pretty little mouth of hers again. "I'm not getting worked up. If he doesn't move, we don't have a way out of here and our whole plan falls apart."

I released her arm and pulled out a chair for her. "He'll

move." When she just glared at me, I jerked my chin towards the dark wooden chair. "Sit down. You're making a scene."

Fire burned in her eyes, but she sat down and smoothened out her skirt. She was wearing a stunning gown in dark green and gold that matched both her mask and her eyes. I let my gaze drift down the tight bodice that clung to her curves while I moved to the other side of the table and lowered myself into the seat opposite her.

For a while, we just watched the mass of people around us. Or at least, I did. Her eyes were fixed on the burly guard in front of our escape route, as if she could get him to move by sheer force of will. Given everything I had come to learn about her these past couple of weeks, it wouldn't surprise me if she actually managed to accomplish such a feat. She had to be one of the most stubborn people I had ever met, and her mind was as wickedly sharp as her tongue. And she never backed down, which I found both infuriating and rather impressive at the same time.

A familiar face appeared between a cluster of women in colorful dresses and ornate feathered masks.

"There he is," I said in a low voice.

Audrey's sharp eyes shifted to where I was looking. "That's the waiter?"

"Yes. I'll go and make sure he's ready. Wait here."

She let out a dismissive huff at my commanding tone but said nothing as I stood up and made my way towards the skinny man in the white shirt. The sounds of clinking glasses and laughing people assaulted my ears as the crowd swallowed me. I kept my eyes on the waiter as he moved from table to table.

"I know, Lance is such a good friend," a female voice said from a table to my right.

Slowing my pace, I slid my gaze towards her instead. She

was sitting at one of the round tables along with two other people. The two girls were wearing glittering dresses and the guy sat proudly in a dark suit, but their masks were resting on the table in front of them as if they wanted people to recognize them. And all of them looked young.

"I'm so proud of him," she finished.

A small crowd had gathered behind them, and the brown-haired girl spoke loudly enough for everyone around the table to overhear.

"We all offered to come with him and help him fight," the other girl said. "But he didn't want to put us in danger, so he told us to stay in school."

"But we would have come with him otherwise," the guy finished with a firm nod. "After all, he is our best friend and we will always have each other's backs."

So, these were Lance Carmichael's precious band of friends. I marked each of their faces as I slunk past their table before continuing my hunt for the waiter.

A pair of wide gray eyes blinked up at me as I rounded a group of men who were congratulating themselves on something. Fear flooded the guy's face and he tried to edge a step away. I just closed the distance between us again while keeping a smile on my face.

"Remember me?" I asked.

Apparently, I had made quite an impression because he recognized me by my body and the bottom half of my face alone.

"Y-yes," he pressed out.

"Good. Do what you would normally do, but keep your eyes on me the whole time. The minute I give you the signal to approach me, you come running. Clear?"

He swallowed. "Clear."

"Excellent." I gave him a hard clap on the shoulder that

made him tip slightly sideways. "I'll give you the rest of your instructions then."

After watching him nod in confirmation, I released his shoulder and strode back the way I had come. Lance's friends were still bragging about his heroism to all the eavesdroppers nearby, as if just being friends with him somehow gave them the right to claim glory and righteousness as well. It was pathetic. The only reputation you had was the one you carved out for yourself. Skating by on someone else's accomplishments was a sure sign of weakness.

When the final part of the colorful crowd parted before me, I expected to find a pissed-off poison mage still waiting for me at the table like I had told her to. Instead, I found her standing a short distance away. With another man.

The stranger was tall, and from what I could tell beneath the golden mask that sat around his eyes, he was good-looking too. At least, he moved like someone who knew that he was handsome. His posture was confident and he leaned back a little when he laughed at something that Audrey had said.

I narrowed my eyes at him. Who the hell did this guy think he was?

As he straightened again, he stepped a little closer. Then he reached up and slid his fingers under a lock of Audrey's long black hair that had gotten stuck in her mask. After lifting it away from the golden swirls, he hooked it behind her ear and then drew his fingers along her cheek on the way down.

Rage roared up inside me like wildfire.

Stalking between the tables, I closed the distance to them in a few quick strides. Audrey saw me coming, but the stranger didn't. His damn hand was still trailing its way down her cheek when I came to a halt next to them and yanked up my own hand.

My fingers wrapped tightly around his wrist, keeping it in a death grip.

The dark-haired stranger snapped his gaze to me and opened his mouth, but he didn't have time to get a single word out.

"Back off," I growled at him. "She's mine."

Indignation flushed his face and he yanked against my grip on his wrist, but it did nothing to free his hand. So instead, he scoffed, "Yours? I have just as much right as you to flirt with a beautiful woman."

I tightened my grip on his wrist until a small whimper of pain slipped his lips. "Unless you want to find yourself at the bottom of a shallow grave tonight, I suggest you keep your hands off my wife."

"Your wife?" Alarm flashed in his eyes as he flicked them between my face and Audrey's. "I didn't know. She never said that she—"

"Leave," I cut off.

He tried to pull his hand out of my grip once more, but I kept it there for a few more seconds while I stared him down to make sure that he really understood.

Then I released him.

The sudden loss of resistance made him stumble a step back. After casting one last look at Audrey, he scrambled away while rubbing his wrist. I watched him go before turning back to Audrey.

"What was that for?" she snapped, her eyes flashing with anger.

I just grabbed her arm and started pulling her towards the dance floor. "Come on."

She tried to yank out of my grip until she realized that people were starting to stare. Blowing out a deep breath, she followed me willingly instead while I led us out into the middle of the shining floor.

From a short distance away, Elise and Carl Dawson waved at us and started forward as if they were planning on meeting up. We couldn't afford to get stuck with them since we needed privacy to kidnap Lance, so I just gave them a polite nod in greeting while continuing to lead Audrey towards the dance floor. They looked a bit put out by it, but Audrey managed a really convincing smile while she gestured apologetically between me and them before she finished it off with a shrug that seemed to say, 'what can you do?' A knowing smile spread across Elise's lips instead, and she gave us a nod before they disappeared into the crowd again.

Music from string instruments and a piano washed over us as I came to a halt in the middle of the dance floor and turned Audrey around while placing my hand on her back. After sliding my other hand down to hers, I moved us into the dance.

"We're supposed to be laying low," Audrey hissed at last, spitting out the angry words she had been holding in since the moment I got rid of that dark-haired stranger, but she still placed her free hand on my shoulder and followed my lead across the dance floor. Her green eyes glittered in the candlelight as she looked up at me, though it did little to hide the anger flashing behind them. "Threatening to kill someone is not laying low."

"Neither is flirting with some random guy," I threw back at her.

"It's called blending in!"

For some reason, that answer made me feel a lot better. I studied her face for a few more seconds before glancing away and clearing my throat. "Maybe I overreacted a bit."

Only the sounds of dresses rustling against the floor and violins playing heart-aching songs answered me. A scowl pulled at my brow when she didn't reply, and I dragged my gaze back to her.

Her mouth was slightly open and she stared up at me in shock. "Did you just admit that you were wrong?"

I snorted. "No."

"Yes, you did."

"I said that I might have overreacted a bit."

"Which is as good as admitting that you were wrong and I was right."

"It's not."

"By all hell, this is a night to remember. The night when Callan Blackwell at last admitted that he was wrong about something."

"Audrey..."

"If the history books don't mention this, I will personally write a strongly worded letter telling them that they have missed the greatest event in Eldar's history."

A huff of laughter escaped my chest.

"Ha!" She grinned up at me, her eyes truly glittering with only light this time. "See, even you agree with that. Then that means—"

Dropping my hand to the small of her back, I pulled her body tightly against mine and cut her off by pressing my lips to hers and stealing a long kiss from her. She jerked slightly in surprise, but then leaned into the kiss.

"Just dance with me, Audrey," I whispered against her mouth before drawing back again.

She looked up at me, but for what had to be the first time ever her talented tongue had no smart comeback. Shaking her head, she just let out a soft chuckle.

We danced for quite some time, and I knew that this would be the first and only time, so I savored the feeling of her body moving underneath my palm as I led her through all the dances. And through all of it, her eyes stayed locked on mine.

The people around us became a sea of color as we moved across the dance floor in tune with the music. Just when I was about to say something that I would have surely regretted, another sound interrupted.

Silver trumpets echoed through the vast ballroom, making everyone pause and turn towards the raised dais. A man in a sharp suit stood atop it. I released Audrey as we stopped dancing and faced him as well.

"Please welcome the stars of this night's magnificent ball," he called in a voice that boomed across the crowd. "The leader of the democratic parliament of Eldar, Chancellor Godric Quill."

A wave of applause swept through the high-ceilinged hall as a man with gray hair and intelligent blue eyes stepped up onto the stage.

"And the hero who will once and for all end the threat that the dark mages pose to our wonderful city," the man in the sharp suit continued as he swept his arm to the side. "Lance Carmichael!"

Deafening cheers raised the roof of the Rose Hall.

Audrey and I exchanged a glance.

It was time.

Now, we would finally get to see this faceless enemy for the first time. The student who thought he could use his power to change the world for the better. The young man who threatened to take away my freedom and everything I liked about my life, and force me back into an existence that I hated more than anything.

Lance Carmichael.

The Binder.

CHAPTER 33

Audrey

My heart thumped in my chest. This was it. At last, I would be able to put a face to the man who threatened to destroy everything I had built by forcing me to give up the powers that I had worked so hard to develop for so many years.

I snapped my gaze to the person striding up to stand next to Godric Quill.

We had ended up fairly close to the stage, so I could see the Binder clearly as he finally straightened and turned towards the eager crowd. At first, a flash of panic shot through me, and I had to remind myself that a Binder had to touch someone in order to lock away their magic.

When my mind had reasserted that he couldn't bind my magic from across the room, a wave of searing anger replaced the worry.

Lance Carmichael. He had golden blond hair that curled slightly at the ends, and bright blue eyes that shone with the ideals and truths about the world that he carried. It made me want to shove my poison magic down his throat. Why did he get to decide what kind of life everyone was supposed to lead? My path in life was no less valid than his.

"Thank you," Godric Quill said as he held up his hands to silence the audience. "Thank you all for coming here tonight to help us celebrate the start of a new era. It is not often that I meet someone as passionate and brave as the young man standing next to me. Instead of finishing out his studies these final months before he turns twenty years old, Lance Carmichael has agreed to spearhead our operation to at last deal with the dark mages who lurk outside our walls. Along with the entire might of our law force, he is going to ride out the day after tomorrow to end this threat to all of Eldar once and for all."

Another bout of cheering and applauding washed through the ballroom. Godric clapped Lance on the shoulder in a fatherly gesture and then motioned for him to step forward. When the leader of parliament held up his hand again, the crowd fell silent once more.

"Thank you for that, Chancellor Quill," Lance said as he gave the older man a nod while a bright smile shone on his face. "You are far too kind."

Clothes rustled and jewelry clinked as everyone seemed to crane their necks to get a good look at the hero of Eldar. I resisted the urge to cross my arms and scowl.

"My dear friends," Lance said as he turned back to face the sea of glittering guests. "Thank you for all your faith in me. I promise you that it will not be in vain. As soon as I realized that I was a Binder, I always harbored the hope that I would one day be able to change the world for the better."

A murmur of approval went through the audience.

"Magic is not meant to be hoarded jealously like treasure," he continued. "It is not meant to be something that only the privileged few can enjoy. It is meant to be shared. To be a gift to all people. For far too long have these dark mages amassed more and more power, selfishly refusing to share any of it with the ones who were born without it."

Calls of agreement rose from a few places in the crowd.

"But no more!" Lance declared as he pumped his fist into the air. "I give you my word that I, with the gracious help of Eldar's constable force, will find all of the remaining dark mages. I will bind their magic so that they can't hurt anyone, and then we will return them all to Eldar before I unbind their magic again so that they can complete the graduation ceremony that they should have done long ago, and add their power to the Great Current for all to share."

The people around us were getting worked up now and several of them clapped and whistled.

"These dark mages have terrorized our countryside for far too long." His voice was rising into a shout and determination blazed in his blue eyes. "They have kidnapped our people and forced them to become slaves out in their mansions in the hills. But no more!"

We had never kidnapped ordinary citizens and we didn't keep slaves. People sought us out willingly and offered to serve us because they wanted a taste of the freedom and power we had. But that, of course, didn't fit with Lance's narrative.

"They have tortured and killed all the heroic men and women who have previously gone into the hills to take them back to Eldar. But no more!"

Okay, that one was true.

"I will never understand why people who are born with power would refuse to share it with the less fortunate. Magic should be shared equally with everyone and these selfish dark mages who jealously hoard it all for themselves are nothing more than ruthless villains!"

People around us called out agreement.

"And I swear to you that I will bring them all back to face justice!" Lance finished as he thrust his fist into the air.

The entire ballroom exploded into cheers and applause and whistles. I studied the expression on Lance's face as he gazed out across the crowd. Blazing conviction shone in his eyes and he had that confident look that only young inexperienced people had. The one that came from thinking that they were immortal and that they could just go out and change the world as long as they had enough courage and passion. But that was not the way the world worked. Courage and passion didn't win any battles. Power and strategy did.

As I looked up into his smiling face and thought back on everything he had just said, I realized that I had never wanted to kill anyone as much as I wanted to kill him. Not even my hatred for Callan came close to the fury that rose inside me when I thought about Lance Carmichael's self-righteous attitude.

By all hell, I wanted to break him so badly. I wanted to shatter his spirit into a million pieces and grind it into the dirt below my feet and watch him weep as he realized that the world wasn't all sunshine and rainbows and people holding hands.

He called us selfish for not sharing our power, but we were not the greedy ones. The true greed came from all the entitled people who reached out like toddlers with their grabby hands and demanded that we give them something that we had worked hard to develop. Something that we had poured years of blood and sweat and tears into. Something that they hadn't earned.

I would get Lance Carmichael and I would break him, if it was the last thing I did.

"Audrey," Callan said.

Snapping my gaze to him, I almost bit his head off before I saw the same fury burning like black flames in his eyes as well.

So instead of taking out my rage on the one person in this room who, for once, wasn't actually the object of my anger, I blew out a controlled breath and adjusted the golden mask on my face.

My eyes drifted from the grinning hero who was leaving the stage to join the crowd and towards the door that led to the exit we had counted on. Dread drew its icy fingers down my spine.

"The guard is still blocking the door," I said.

"I know." Callan shifted his gaze between the ballroom's two short sides. "We're gonna have to improvise. That library you told me about, is it that one?"

The crowd around us was starting to shift as people returned to the seating area while others began dancing again when the music started back up. I discreetly turned to see where Callan was looking.

"Yes, but it's too far to jump out the window." I drew my hand over my jaw as a sudden idea popped into my mind. "Though, we might be able to make it work anyway. Listen up."

Rising onto my toes, I wrapped my arms around him as if I was giving him a hug, and then spoke softly in his ear. When I drew back, Callan looked down at me with raised eyebrows.

"You sure you'll be able to handle it?" he asked.

I arched an eyebrow back at him. "Are you?"

Huffing out a laugh, he dragged his hand through his black hair and then repositioned the mask across his face. "Alright, let's do it. I'll go find the waiter and have him send Lance to the library."

"Good. Let's get this over with."

"Be ca—" He cleared his throat. "Don't mess up."

Then he stalked away without another word.

I heaved an irritated sigh and slipped away in the other

direction. Moving stealthily through the crowd that had gathered below the stained-glass windows, I snuck towards the small library on the other side. The door was unguarded and there was no red velvet rope that marked it as off limits, so I assumed that I would be able to just walk inside. However, that of course also meant that there might be other people in there.

My suspicions were confirmed when I opened the door to find two people already seated in the leather armchairs. They appeared to be reading something, and they looked up in surprise when I entered. I slammed a hand over my mouth and sprinted over to the window. Throwing it open, I pretended to vomit right out through it.

The two men in the armchairs scrambled out of their seats.

"Oh, by the Current," one of them exclaimed from somewhere behind my back. "Are you alright?"

"Yes," I croaked, not turning around as I dry heaved again. "I'm just feeling a bit... sick. If I could just have a few minutes to—" I pretended to throw up again.

"Of course," he stammered. "We'll give you some privacy."

Their shoes thudded against the floor as they fled out the door and closed it behind them.

Straightening from the window, I turned back to the now empty room and let a villainous grin slide home on my lips. Men. They never quite knew what to do when a woman was unwell, so they almost always beat a hasty retreat.

I leaned back against the windowsill and crossed my arms while I waited for that waiter Callan had blackmailed to deliver Lance to me.

The minutes ticked away. Five minutes turning into ten which then turned into fifteen, according to the small clock on the side table. A few other people tried to enter the room, but I just pretended to vomit out the window again while begging them for some privacy.

When twenty minutes had passed, I was beginning to wonder if the waiter had just cut and run now that he knew exactly who he was supposed to lure here. But then the door was pushed open.

My eyes shot to the two people who became visible through the gap.

A skinny man with gray eyes and the white shirt of a waiter walked across the threshold while speaking over his shoulder. "Again, sir, I'm so sorry to pull you away from your friends like this, but this young lady was desperate to speak with you and she didn't want her husband to find out. As I mentioned, I think he might be abusing her so please be gentle."

"Of course," Lance Carmichael said from behind the waiter. "I will do everything I can to help her."

It was actually a pretty decent lie. Right now, Callan was posing as my husband, and given the number of times he had stabbed me and choked me and cut me and just generally tried to kill me over the years, he was definitely abusing me. Though, to be fair, I was just as abusive to him since I had done the exact same things more times than I could count.

I touched my hands together and then kept the magic hidden in my palms as the two of them finished walking into the room.

Blue eyes full of concern looked down at me as Lance approached while the waiter closed the door. The hero of Eldar opened his mouth to speak, but I never found out what he had been about to say because my magic shot through the air and down his throat before he even realized what was happening.

The emotions on his face shifted from concerned to stunned before his eyes fluttered closed and he toppled backwards. A dull thud rang through the room as he hit the floor back first.

The waiter slapped a hand in front of his mouth, presumably to stop a scream.

I moved closer to Lance and looked down into his unconscious face before glancing up to meet the terrified eyes of the waiter.

He swallowed before removing his hand from his mouth. "He said you'd let me live." His voice wobbled slightly and he stared at me with pleading eyes. "He said that if I did this, you would let me live."

"I know." I smiled, which made his shoulders relax and his hands drop to his sides. I gave him an unapologetic shrug. "But I made no such promise."

Slamming my palms together, I shot a lethal dose of poison magic straight at him. He only had time to suck in a gasp before it hit him right in the face and killed him instantly.

Another thud echoed through the small private library as the dead waiter hit the floor next to Lance. Surprise still twisted his features. I shrugged as I moved back towards the Binder.

We were about to abduct their greatest hero and the leader of their impending attack. We couldn't very well leave any civilian witnesses who would be able to identify us and tell the others exactly when and where we had escaped.

A hero would have just knocked him out and tied him up and hoped that he wouldn't be discovered until after we had gotten out of the city.

But unfortunately for the poor waiter, I wasn't a hero.

I was just a ruthless villain.

CHAPTER 34

Callan

Long black hair tumbled out and fluttered in the breeze as Audrey poked her head out through the window. Craning my neck, I looked up at her from where I stood on the grass in the gardens outside.

"You got him?" I asked in the lowest voice I could use while still making it carry all the way up to the window.

"Yes." Audrey yanked off her swirling golden mask and threw it into a bush outside. "Get ready."

She ducked back inside. Keeping my gaze on the now empty window, I moved into position right underneath it while also tossing my own silver mask into the same bush where hers had disappeared.

It had been beyond easy to get here. All I'd had to do was walk out of the front doors while saying that I needed some air. The doormen had said nothing, and no one was watching the garden, so I had been able to sneak around the building without anyone noticing. The fact that the windows in the Rose Hall were made of stained glass also helped with privacy, of course.

Getting here had been easy. Now, came the tricky part.

A head of golden blond hair appeared in the window. Then a pair of arms that fell off the windowsill and swung limply in the air. Audrey became visible above Lance Carmichael's back as she tried to haul his unconscious body up onto the windowsill and then out. Gritting her teeth, she looked to have her arms locked around his waist as she tried to lift him.

Impatience and a flash of worry shot through me.

"Hurry," I snapped at her.

If anyone walked into that library right now, Audrey was dead. There was no reasonable explanation for why she would be throwing Lance Carmichael's unmoving body out the window. And while I might be able to just sprint away through the garden if we were discovered, Audrey was stuck in a room with only one door, a window that was too high up to jump from, and the entire parliament of Eldar ready to charge in at a moment's notice.

"I am hurrying," she hissed back at me. "But he's fucking heavy."

With only a few months left to his twentieth birthday, Lance had the physique of a grown man. Tall and broad-shouldered and muscular. Audrey had said that she would be able to handle it, but based on the strained expression on her face, she was struggling.

Suddenly, Lance's chest slid over the windowsill.

Alarm flashed across Audrey's face. "Get him!"

The weight of Lance's upper body dangling over the edge was too great, making it impossible for Audrey to keep a hold of him. His legs slid through Audrey's arms quickly when she lost her grip.

I took a small step sideways while I tracked Lance's trajectory as he free-fell out the window. Bending my knees slightly, I held out my arms and then braced for the impact.

My body jolted as Lance's unconscious form landed in my arms. I let out a soft huff. Damn. He really was heavy. Now that I knew just how much he really weighed, I couldn't help but be a little impressed that Audrey had managed to lift him off the floor and push him out the window on her own.

After setting the Binder down on the grass, I looked up at the window to meet Audrey's gaze.

It was empty.

Panic burned through my chest.

"Audrey," I hissed.

No answer.

"Audrey!"

The window remained empty.

Fear and panic ran wild in my chest as I stared up at the building. Had someone walked in and seen her? Was she busy trying to explain her presence there or had they already captured her? The image of Chancellor Quill dragging Audrey away in handcuffs flashed through my mind.

I had already taken two quick steps back towards the front door before I stopped myself. Looking over my shoulder, I cast a glance at Lance's body. I couldn't just leave him lying out here in the garden for anyone to blunder into. But if they had caught Audrey, I had to do something. Fast.

My heart thumped in my chest and indecision raced through me. What if I hid him and then went back into the party? That way, I could—

"Heads up."

Whirling back around, I snapped my gaze towards the window just in time to see another blond head appear above the windowsill. Narrow shoulders and a skinny body slid over it a second later.

Confusion swirled through me as I watched the body fall through the air and land back first on the grass below. It was replaced by relief as I looked up to see Audrey's stunning face in the window once more.

"What are you doing over there?" she asked while climbing up on the windowsill. "Hurry up and get over here."

I quickly moved back to the spot below the window and held out my arms.

For a single second, uncertainty blew across Audrey's face as she looked down at me. It wasn't lost on me that this particular move required quite a bit of trust. If I didn't catch her, she would break her legs and be left crippled and unable to escape from the scene of a crime that was sure to go down in the history books as one of the most heinous ever committed against the city of Eldar. And all she could do was hope that I would catch her and not leave her to such a fate.

Then she jumped.

Her green and golden dress fluttered in the air as she plummeted towards the ground. I shifted my position slightly.

Relief flooded her face as she landed in my arms. I set her down gently on the grass, allowing her to smoothen down her skirt and hair before my hand shot out and took her jaw in a firm grip.

"What are—" she began but I cut her off.

"When I call your name, you answer," I informed her in a voice pulsing with authority. "Is that clear?"

She tried to slap my hand away. I stared her down for another second before releasing her. While glaring up at me, she stabbed a hand towards the skinny corpse next to us.

"Since I couldn't very well leave a dead body in the library for anyone to find, getting him out was more important than answering your incessant yelling." Before I could reply, she stalked over to the body. "Now, help me roll him under that bush."

After casting a quick look at the still unconscious Lance, I strode over to help her. Placing my palms against the dead waiter's side, I rolled him towards the nearest bush. A small flicker of approval danced inside me. I had forgotten to tell Audrey that she needed to kill him too. We couldn't leave any witnesses who knew that we were the ones who had taken Lance. But apparently, she had figured that out on her own.

"He said that you had promised to spare his life," she said conversationally while we shoved the corpse under the leaf-clad branches.

"Well, he should have known better than to trust a pair of ruthless villains."

She chuckled. Straightening, she wiped her hands before starting back towards Lance Carmichael. "Come on. Let's get him out of here before people start looking for him."

Warm winds smelling of flowers and damp earth swept through the gardens as I hoisted Lance's body up and draped his arm over my shoulder. Wrapping my other arm around his waist, I moved us forward while Audrey fell in beside us. From a distance, it would look like I was only supporting a friend who might have consumed too much alcohol. As long as we stayed away from the brightly burning street lamps and any crowded areas, we should be fine.

Tense silence fell as we snuck through the darkened gardens outside the parliament building. I wasn't usually nervous, but there was so much riding on this mission, which made my heart pulse hard against my ribs as I walked. If we were discovered, we would have to fight our way out. And that would be difficult while also carrying Lance's body.

Leaves rustled in the dark trees as another warm night wind whirled across the grass. We had almost made it to the edge of the gardens. If I squinted, I could see one of the small staircases made of white stone that led down the side of the hill. Taking the main steps was out of the question. But no one should be sneaking around the side steps leading to and from the garden. At least not at this time of night.

My muscles groaned at Lance's weight. Pausing briefly, I hoisted him a bit farther up and readjusted my grip.

Audrey's eyes slid to me. "You okay?"

"Yeah. I just need to—"

"Lance is missing!"

We whipped around and stared in the direction of the shouting voice.

"Lance Carmichael is missing!" the man bellowed again. "He was last seen leaving with a waiter to talk to some unknown woman, but now we can't find any of them anywhere."

"Maybe he just—" someone called back from farther down the main steps.

"No! We're not taking any chances tonight. Sound the alarm!"

One second of silence followed. Then the guard on the main steps started banging on the wide metal gong that I knew hung halfway between the parliament building and the city below. Deep metallic ringing split the night and echoed out across the whole of Eldar.

Audrey and I whipped our heads back around and faced each other.

Panic flashed across both our faces.

Shit.

CHAPTER 35

Audrey

The same flash of panic that had shot through me was mirrored in Callan's eyes. I flicked my gaze between Lance, the men banging the alarm somewhere on the other side of the bushes, and the shouts and clamor that rose from the entrance to the parliament building.

"We need to run," I announced.

"Agreed."

Clenching his jaw, Callan crouched down and then hoisted Lance up so that he lay draped over his shoulder instead. The force mage staggered a little when he straightened again, but then wrapped his arm over Lance's back to keep him steady. I knew how heavy Lance was, so I understood that running with him like that would not be easy.

"Are you sure you—"

"Just run, Audrey," he cut me off, and jerked his chin towards the stairs.

I took off. My dress flapped around my legs as I hurried down the steps. It wasn't exactly the choice of attire I would have picked for a sneaky escape, especially not since the gold shone every time we passed under an oil lamp, but there was no way for me to switch clothes until we reached the smuggler's tunnel. We had already stashed our packs there last night, so I'd be able to change into something easier to ride in once we got there. When more shouting rose from atop the hill, I had to force myself not to amend that to *if* we got there.

Callan's footsteps pounded against the stone steps behind me, twice as heavy now that he was carrying Lance on his shoulder. I cast a quick glance back at him. The unconscious Binder bounced up and down on Callan's shoulder, but the force mage still managed to keep up.

Light pooled on the ground from the street lamps as we reached the bottom of the hill and stumbled out into the wide road beyond. I whipped my head from side to side. If anyone spotted us like this with a body slung over Callan's shoulder, we would look incredibly suspicious. But if we reverted to the previous ruse of pretending to help a drunk friend, we wouldn't be able to move as quickly.

"Speed or stealth?" I asked.

"Speed," he pressed out after drawing a deep breath.

"Alright. I'll make sure the road is clear."

Only a strained grunt answered me as Callan shifted Lance into a better position.

Once he was done, he gave me a nod. I moved a few steps in front of him as we ran across the street and towards the cover of the houses beyond it.

Metallic clanking filled the night around us while constables yelled orders for all the curious citizens to stay inside their homes. I pressed myself up against the wall before glancing around the corner. Light from the oil lamps cast flickering shadows over the pale stone street, and a few trees rustled their leaves in the wind. I swept my gaze over the road again. Then I waved Callan forward.

Making sure to stay in the pools of darkness between the lamps, we snuck across another street and towards the city walls in the distance. My heart pattered against my ribs. I desperately wanted a distraction right now to draw the search away from us, but we were still too close to the parliament building to risk any unnecessary attention.

While fighting down the urge to just poison everything that moved, I kept my eyes flicking back and forth while we made our way through the darkness and towards the outskirts of the city.

Boots pounded against the street.

My heart leaped into my throat and I held up a hand to signal to Callan that he had to stop. After making sure that he had seen it, I slunk along the wall and peered around the next corner.

Five constables were running down the road, and they were heading in the direction of our cross street.

I whipped around and flicked my wrists at Callan while mouthing, "*Go back!*"

His chest was heaving with exertion and he looked like he would rather fight an entire battalion than undo one single step that he had already taken. Running up to him, I grabbed his free arm and pulled him towards the closest alley. Irritation flashed in his dark eyes, but he let me lead him towards the small opening between the houses.

The sound of running feet drew closer.

My pulse thrummed in my ears. Tightening my grip on Callan's arm, I practically hauled him the final bit into the alley right as the thumping boots rounded the corner.

We had to get out of sight before they passed by this alleyway as well.

I sprinted to the other end of it while Callan continued

staggering on behind me. The sound of voices reached me as I drew myself up by the wall and glanced into the next street.

Dread surged inside me.

Four more constables were heading this way.

Whirling back around, I made a shooing motion with my hands. Callan sucked in a deep breath and threw out a hand to brace himself against the building next to him. Lance's limp legs swung in front of the force mage's body as he tried to straighten again.

The thudding boots from the other side of the alley suddenly sounded far too close to us. I leaped towards Callan and Lance and shoved them flat against the wall before pressing myself into it as well. Blood pounded in my ears.

Please don't look in here. Please don't look in here.

The five constables ran past the alley mouth.

I held my breath.

Light glinted against their silver helmets as they passed, but none of them looked into this alley. Intense relief washed over me.

"Hey, who's there?"

That relief died in my chest as I snapped my gaze towards the opposite side of the alley and found the other four constables staring straight at us. Fire bloomed in the leader's palm before he sent it flying into the darkness.

The light glinted against the gold in my dress as it illuminated the whole alley.

"It's Lance!" the leader snapped. "Sound the—"

But I had already slapped my palms together and hurled a cloud of poison at them. Glittering green magic shot through the air and hit him straight in the face, cutting off his shout and making his eyes bulge in shock.

The other three who were standing behind him had

received an extra second before it reached them, and they managed to dive aside before it struck.

"They're here!" someone bellowed from around the corner.

I sprinted towards them to cut them off right as shouts rose from behind me as well. Cheating a glance over my shoulder, I found the five constables who had run past us on the other side. Magic blinked to life in their hands as they skidded into the alley.

Callan let out a vicious curse and dumped Lance's body on the ground before he whipped around to face them. Lightning crackled from that side of the street, but I couldn't spare any more attention on it because the three constables on my side leaped out from behind the walls.

Throwing myself sideways, I narrowly managed to evade the fireball that had been aimed at my chest. It sped through the air and hit the wall next to me at an angle, sending flames and embers flying into the night.

My shoulder hit the opposite wall. I pushed myself off it and slammed my hands together right as a lightning strike crackled through the air. While throwing a massive cloud of poison at them, I dove forward and rolled across the dusty stones to escape the lightning bolt. My magic wasn't suited for shielding, so I had to kill them before they could launch any more attacks.

Two of the constables hit the ground as my magic made contact, but the final one leaped sideways while shoving his hand forward.

A blast of wind hit me head on.

Air whooshed in my ears as I flew backwards. My flight came to an abrupt halt as I smacked into something hard and crashed down on the street. A muscular figure was visible above me.

"What the hell, Audrey," Callan snapped as he straightened and hurled a force arc at the three remaining constables on his side at the same time as he raised a vibrating wall to block the fireball that my attacker had thrown at us.

Still hidden behind Callan's legs, I pushed myself onto my knees and touched my palms together before shooting a thin line of poison magic down the throat of one of Callan's opponents. Shock flashed on the survivors' faces as they tried to figure out where it had come from. The moment of inattention allowed Callan to throw a half-translucent arc of force at them that cut the blond one's head off.

While Callan slammed up another force wall to block my attacker's lightning strike, I used the time he bought me to send another massive cloud at the guy. He blinked in surprise as his own attack struck the wall beside me, leaving a black scorch mark on the pale stone. But before he could recover, my poison magic hit him.

A thud rang out as he toppled backwards.

I sent a glittering green streak right up into the sky before sprinting towards the mouth of the alley.

"What the hell, Audrey!" Callan snapped again.

"Others will already have seen this battle so it doesn't matter," I called over my shoulder. "Wait here."

There was only one constable left on Callan's side now, so I knew that he would be able to kill him within the next few seconds. I had something to retrieve.

When I had glanced around the corner earlier, I had seen something made of metal glint in the light from the streetlamps. As I skidded around the corner, I desperately hoped that I had been right.

Victory sparkled inside me.

Hiking up my dress, I jumped the short wooden fence and landed in the small messy garden inside. Sunflowers ducked out of the way as I elbowed my way through them and grabbed the item that was leaning against the wall. With a firm grip on the handles, I raced out through the low wooden gate and darted back to where I had left Callan.

All nine constables were lying dead on the street. As I ran my eyes over them, I couldn't help but think how much neater my side of the battle was. My attackers were lying there intact, almost as if they were sleeping, while Callan's five opponents had been reduced to a bleeding heap with various limbs missing. Well, everyone except the one that I had so generously poisoned.

"We need to go," Callan growled at me as I came into view. "That flare you sent up is going to draw everyone here."

A deafening explosion cleaved the night.

Panicked screams and frantic banging on metal gongs followed it.

I grinned at the force mage. "I think they're going to be otherwise occupied."

The streak of green magic I had sent into the air had been the signal to start creating chaos on the other side of the city. Based on the noise from that blast, Henrick and his gang had really taken this assignment seriously. I wasn't sure if it was due to the dozen people I had killed in his presence or the blood-soaked heart that Callan had deposited in the tattooed gang leader's lap, but either way, I was pleased with the outcome.

"What are you doing with that?" Callan stabbed a hand towards me as I stopped right next to Lance's body.

"We need a faster way to transport him."

He looked between my face, the item before me, and the body that was slumped against the wall while disbelief blew across his face. "You can't be serious."

"Of course I am. Now, help me get him into it."

CHAPTER 36

Callan

I felt absolutely ridiculous. Running down the street like this made me feel like a kid in some kind of bizarre race. While we sprinted towards the next road, I glanced over at the poison mage next to me. There was a smug smile on her lips, as if this strange idea of hers had been pure genius, but lingering excitement from the fight also made her eyes sparkle like gems.

As we skidded around the corner and darted towards the next one, I had to admit that this was a faster way to transport Lance. I slid my gaze back to the brightly painted wheelbarrow that I was pushing in front of me. Lance's legs flapped up and down where they hung out over the edge and his head jerked from side to side as I steered. Yes, it was fast. But it still made me feel ridiculous.

Explosions echoed from the other side of the city. Whatever that gang of diversion experts were doing, it was working. We hadn't run into a single constable after that last battle, so they were all probably running towards the booming noises, thinking that was where we were trying to escape.

"Two more streets," Audrey called over her shoulder as she veered around another corner. "Then we—"

She slammed into a tall man with a silver helmet as he ran around the corner from the other side. The force of the collision sent them both sprawling. Screeching to a halt, I set the wheelbarrow down as seven other people rounded the corner as well.

A wave of exasperation rolled over me. Why did I have to jinx it?

The seven constables who were still on their feet stared in shock at us and the unconscious Binder that we had stuffed into a bright yellow wheelbarrow painted with smiling sunflowers. While they were still trying to recover, I threw a spinning force arc at them.

Five of them had the presence of mind to duck. The other two lost their heads.

Fire and lightning crackled through the air as they hurled attacks back at me. I timed my force wall so that I could knock the attacks away in one fell swoop. Flames exploded against the house to my right as the fireballs hit it instead. A moment later, white lightning cracked into the pale stone, leaving black spidering marks in its wake.

On the ground, the eighth constable had rolled on top of Audrey. She jerked her knees up and slammed them into him, but he was almost twice as big as her so it only made him wince slightly.

I threw another arc at the others while simultaneously trying to block their attacks. They were starting to coordinate them to the point where blocking with only one wall was becoming difficult.

One of them dropped to his knees next to the brown-haired man that Audrey was wrestling with. Working in tandem, they grabbed her wrists and kept her arms spread wide while they yanked her to her feet.

Flicking my wrist, I shoved two more fireballs off course with a force wall while jumping aside to evade the lightning bolt that I hadn't been able to block. Spinning back to face them, I threw an attack between their strikes and cleaved two of the constables right down the chest. The other three started up a merciless barrage while the two who had finally straightened began hauling Audrey away.

She kicked and thrashed against them, but without being able to bring her palms together and summon magic, she was no match for their physical strength.

Indecision flashed through me.

I stole a glance in the direction of the smuggler's tunnel while I continued parrying the hail of attacks from the other three constables. We were so close to the tunnel now. I could easily make it out with Lance at this point, even if I didn't have Audrey's magic to keep him knocked out.

This had been my original plan. To sneak into Eldar, get Lance, and then leave Audrey Sable to be captured by the heroes and stripped of her magic. So what had changed? Wasn't this the better solution? The easier solution?

Fire roared through my soul. No. I might hate Audrey more than anything, but she was still a dark mage. As my mind flashed back to Lance's speech in the Rose Hall, I realized that, regardless of our internal wars, I would always have other dark mages' backs against these insufferably self-righteous heroes.

Lightning cracked against the house on my left as I redirected two more bolts.

My eyes found Audrey's across the street.

Since I had no way of telling her what I was about to do, I just had to hope that she would come through for me.

Slamming my palms together, I hurled a vibrating arc of

force magic at the two men holding on to Audrey's arms. Since they were taller than her, it flashed through the air above her hair and severed their heads without touching her. However, that move had left me completely exposed to attacks from the other three constables.

The moment their grip on her arms slackened, Audrey rammed her palms together and summoned a poison cloud so large that it filled the whole street almost all the way up to me.

Fire and lightning died out as the three constables who had been about to take me out instead gasped in a lethal breath of her magic. She turned slowly. For a few moments, she just stood there inside the swirling green cloud, watching as the three men choked to death on her poison. I knew that she could have killed them instantly if she wanted to. But apparently, she didn't.

Long black hair rippled down her back as she raised her chin and stared down at the men who had now collapsed to the street. I could only see one side of her face from where I stood, but by all hell, I swore that she looked like death incarnate right at that moment.

The constables twitched on the ground at her feet for another few seconds. Then they stilled and the glittering mist disappeared as Audrey turned back to me.

Only the distant sound of explosions broke the silence for a while as we just stared at each other across the street full of corpses.

At last, she jerked her chin towards the two men who had grabbed her. "Nice shot."

I nodded at the ones who had died from her poison before their attacks could hit me. "Nice timing."

"Yeah." She dragged a hand through her hair and then slid her gaze to Lance. "Shall we?"

Tearing my eyes from her, I strode back to where I had left

the yellow wheelbarrow and the limp Binder inside it. After grabbing the handles, I pushed it in front of me as I followed Audrey the final distance to the smuggler's tunnel.

The entrance was located in an abandoned building, so I dumped the wheelbarrow a short distance away to avoid attracting attention to it, and then carried Lance the last stretch. While I dropped him on the floor, Audrey changed out of her dress and into a pair of riding clothes. When she was done, we hoisted our packs and then moved towards the trap door.

Audrey held it open for me while I slid Lance down the ladder. He hit the bottom with a thud. When he woke up, he was going to have a whole lot of bruises. But at least he was still alive. Though, when we finally got to our destination and I could get started on breaking him, he was going to wish that he wasn't.

Once I had climbed down after him, Audrey followed and then closed the trap door above us. Darkness fell.

We remained motionless in that cramped space, standing chest to chest, while we let our eyes adjust to the faint light of the crystals that had been set into the tunnel walls.

"I'll drag and you push," I said when I could see a bit better.

She nodded. "Alright."

Dropping to my hands and knees, I crawled into the low tunnel before turning over so that I sat on my ass. Then I grabbed Lance by the arms and dragged him in with me. Audrey's face came into view as she crouched down as well and placed her hands on the Binder's legs. While crawling after us, she helped push his weight forward.

Sweat ran down my spine as we worked to haul the heavy body through the narrow tunnel. Carrying him across the city had sapped my strength more than I wanted to admit. When we came up with this plan, I had assumed that Lance would be a gangly teenager and that I would have no trouble lifting him. I supposed that leaving the academy at fourteen had made me forget that all those young students actually became adults in time for the graduation ceremony.

My leg muscles groaned in exhaustion as I scooted backwards once more and dragged Lance with me. We still had an entire night of riding ahead of us before we got to The First and Last Stop inn. But after that, I would need a few hours to recover.

The tunnel opened up into the circular space that housed the other ladder. I blew out a deep breath as we heaved Lance into it. While Audrey crawled into the space as well, I got to my feet and climbed up towards the trapdoor before pounding my fist against it.

"John!" I called.

Barely half a minute later, something metallic slid across the surface above, and then the trapdoor was lifted open.

John barely had time to see who was inside before I climbed up.

Straightening, I turned to face him. "Get some rope."

"Uh, yeah. Sure." He drew his hand through his dark disheveled hair and then hurried to grab a long coil from one of the hooks along the stable wall. "What—"

"Are the horses ready?" I interrupted as I snatched the thick length of rope out of his hands.

"N-no."

My gaze snapped to him and I was pretty sure he saw his death reflected in them because he paled visibly and staggered a step back.

"I mean, they're here," he pressed out while raising his hands. "They're just not saddled."

"Then saddle them."

Before he could reply, I turned back to the tunnel and dropped the rope into it. While John scrambled away to saddle our horses, Audrey looped the long rope around Lance's chest and under his arms before throwing both ends back up to me.

As I grabbed them, it struck me that I hadn't even needed to tell her what I was going to do. She had just immediately understood how we were going to get Lance up the ladder and had stayed down there, waiting for me to throw some rope down, while I talked to John.

With a firm grip on the ends of the rope, I started pulling our unconscious prisoner upwards. Audrey climbed onto the ladder and helped push him up as well. I would never admit it to her face, but I was incredibly thankful for that because my muscles were already trembling with exertion after this night.

Lance's body created a rut in the scattered straw on the floor as I dragged his legs the final bit above the edge. As soon as he was out, Audrey climbed up as well and closed the trapdoor behind her.

A horse snorted from somewhere close by. I was just about to open my mouth and tell Audrey to help me get the ropes off the Binder's body when hurried footsteps closed in from the long corridor running through the stable.

"The horses are..." John trailed off as he skidded to a halt next to me and stared down at the floor. The small trace of color that had returned to his face drained right out of it again as his eyes widened. Staggering a step back, he whipped his head between me, Audrey, and the body on his floor. "Please, *please*, tell me that's not Lance Carmichael."

I locked hard eyes on the middle-aged smuggler. "You didn't see anything. Because if you did, your family will pay the price. We just abducted Lance Carmichael from the heart of Eldar... Imagine what we could do to a simple smuggler's family."

"N-no, I..." John stammered.

"That is, if Chancellor Quill doesn't execute you for high treason first. I don't think he would be very understanding of your involvement in kidnapping his precious Binder if you were to come clean about it. Do you?"

He swallowed. "No."

"Exactly. So what did you see?"

"Nothing."

"Indeed." I jerked my chin at him. "Now, tie him to the third horse."

This time, I let John do all the work of dragging Lance to the horses and hauling him up across the saddle. Since John was a muscular guy himself, he accomplished the feat relatively easily.

Once he had finished tying the blond hero to the saddle, I reached into my pack and pulled out a pair of handcuffs. They snapped shut around Lance's wrists with a metallic click that seemed to echo into the candlelit stable.

Next to me, Audrey rolled her shoulders and stretched out the muscles in her arms.

After checking to make sure that Lance's hands were firmly secured and kept apart by the metal rod in the middle, I walked over to my horse while throwing a glance over my shoulder. "Let's go."

"Don't give me orders," Audrey replied, but there was less poison in her words than usual.

I huffed out a low chuckle and instead just swung myself up on the horse. While Audrey did the same, John used a rope to tie the reins of Lance's horse to the back of my saddle. Then he hurried over to the door and opened the wide ones to let the horses out.

Clicking my tongue, I pushed my heels into my horse's

flanks and urged it forwards. The horse behind me followed as we moved. Audrey brought up the rear.

"Remember," I began as we rode past the smuggler.

"I didn't see anything," he finished for me.

"Exactly."

I spurred my horse on, taking off into the grasslands. Faint booms still came from somewhere inside the city, but the night out here was dark and quiet.

"Keep the gates closed," someone called from what sounded like the other side of the city walls. "We'll keep them trapped in here until we find them."

"What's that booming sound?" another guy called back, and this one sounded like he was standing atop the walkway over the gate.

"They were trying to blow their way out through the walls on the other side. The constables are fighting them now."

A smug laugh built inside my chest as we sped straight out into the darkness. They had no idea that there was another way out so they would waste days searching inside the city before they realized that we were no longer there. And by then, it would be too late.

Only moonlight illuminated the grasslands as we made our way farther out. We had to cut across the grass for a few more minutes before we could ride back onto the road when we were far enough away from the gate.

As we at last reached the Valdan Road, Audrey fell in beside me. I glanced over at her where she sat atop her dark brown horse.

I couldn't believe that we had actually pulled this off.

Letting my eyes drift over the poison mage beside me, I studied the expression on her face and the way her lips curved in a sly smile. Wind whirled through her hair and made it ripple behind her like liquid shadows, and the silvery moonlight glittered in her green eyes.

I had to admit, Audrey Sable was actually a damn good person to have at your side in a fight.

CHAPTER 37

Audrey

P ale red light fell across the grasslands as the morning
sun stretched its first tendrils over the horizon. I
looked between the unconscious man on the ground
and the inn a short distance away.

"I thought you said he was supposed to be waking up at
sunrise," Callan said as he crossed his arms and looked down
at me.

Meeting his gaze, I shrugged. "I estimated the strength of
the poison based on how quickly someone with a body type
like his usually burns through it, but there was more left inside
him than I had predicted. It's not an exact science."

"Then why didn't you say that?"

"I did. I said he *should* wake up by sunrise. But it doesn't
matter, I've pulled out the remainders of the poison now."

"Why can you never just admit—"

Lance let out a loud groan, interrupting Callan's next
taunt.

I arched an eyebrow at the force mage. "You were saying?"

He huffed out a dismissive breath, but didn't retort.

Another moan came from the Binder on the ground as he worked to shake off the lingering effects of my poison. Blades of grass clung to his golden blond hair from when we had just unceremoniously pulled him off the horse and dumped him on the ground while waiting for him to wake up. His clothes were dirty and rumpled, probably from when we dragged him through the tunnel, and fresh bruises peeked out from underneath his clothes. He was also still wearing that pair of stiff handcuffs. To sum it up, the great hero of Eldar had probably both looked and felt better than he did right about now.

Once I was sure that Lance was truly waking up, I met Callan's gaze again. "I'll get us a room. Make sure this one understands what will happen if he so much as breathes in a way we don't like."

"Oh don't you worry. I'm quite skilled at threatening people."

"Don't I know it," I replied with a huff of amusement.

While Callan smirked back at me, I grabbed the three horses' reins and started towards The First and Last Stop. It was morning, which meant that other people would be up and about too. We couldn't very well carry an unconscious man into the inn and expect no one to notice, so we had to make Lance walk inside while pretending that he was here with us of his own free will. But we didn't want people to get too good a look at him, so I would get the room first and then we'd just have him walk straight up the stairs to it.

After handing over the horses to the stable hand, I approached the front door. I hadn't told Callan that I'd be taking the horses with me, but I trusted him about as far as I could throw him and there was no way I was leaving him alone with Lance and the horses so that he could just ride off without me.

The scent of baking bread enveloped me as I stepped across the threshold. My stomach rumbled in response to it. It had been quite a while since I had eaten anything, and all the fighting and running yesterday had used up a lot of energy as well. I would need to get us all some food too.

Muted chatter filled the room as I started towards the pale wooden counter at the back. The whole tavern area was packed with people eating breakfast. I studied their faces as I walked.

When I reached the counter, I rapped my knuckles against the worn wood. "I need a room."

"Sure," the innkeeper answered as he turned around to face me while giving me a smile. "Any preferences?"

"The biggest you have."

"That one is quite expensive."

"Not an issue."

His blue eyes lit up. "Then I have the perfect room for you. It has a large double bed, a small separate room for baggage storage, and even a bathroom attached to it."

"We'll take it. And three full breakfasts too."

"Excellent."

While I retrieved some money from my pack and slid it across the counter, the innkeeper grabbed a large key from the rack behind him and held it out to me.

"It's on this floor," he said, and pointed in the direction I had come from. "Just across the hall over there, on the other side of the stairs."

Satisfaction swirled inside me as I nodded in acknowledgement and took the key before starting back towards the front door. The room was on this floor? That was perfect. We would be able to get Lance in quickly and quietly.

Warm summer air ruffled my hair as I stepped back out and gazed across the grass. Callan and Lance were standing in the same place as I had left them. Raising an arm, I motioned for them to approach.

Lance was walking next to Callan, and he looked to be carrying the force mage's pack. One of Callan's jackets was draped over Lance's hands, making it look like he had knitted his fingers together to carry the pack in his arms. I had to admit, it was a really clever way to hide the fact that he was actually handcuffed.

As I watched the way Callan's muscles shifted under his clothes while he strode towards me, I realized that this was it. This was the last day of our temporary truce. After this, everything would change.

"You got the room?" Callan asked as they closed the final distance.

"Yes." I slid my gaze to Lance. "Did he explain the rules to you?"

Lance's blue eyes were filled with both fear and anger as he flicked them towards Callan before meeting my gaze. "Yes."

For someone who was supposed to be the hero of Eldar, he was surprisingly easy to intimidate.

"Good." I jerked my chin as I opened the front door again. "Then follow me. Don't raise your head and don't speak to anyone."

Our feet thumped against the pale wooden floorboards as I led them across the hall at a brisk pace. After unlocking the door on the other side of the stairs, I held it open and motioned for them to hurry up.

A flash of panic shot through me when the sound of chairs scraping against the floor came from the doorway leading into the tavern area. But before that group of people could make it into the hallway, Lance and Callan had thankfully already crossed the threshold. I slipped inside after them and closed the door behind us before blowing out a long breath.

While leaning back against the door, I swept my gaze across the room. It was rather large for a simple roadside inn. A couple of drawers lined the wall beside me and there was a double bed next to the window on the other side. To my left, a wooden door stood open to reveal that small baggage room that the innkeeper had mentioned. And on the right, another door led into a bathroom. A small smile tugged at my lips. It had everything we needed.

Callan took his pack and jacket from Lance's arms, revealing the stiff handcuffs underneath. While he set them down next to the bed, I unslung my own pack and pulled out a metal contraption.

The chain rattled as I pulled it out before advancing on Lance.

Straightening from his own pack, Callan turned to look what I was doing. Amusement tugged at his lips, and he arched an eyebrow at me while nodding towards the item in my hands. "So that's where that one went."

"Yes." Placing a hand on Lance's chest, I shoved him towards the small baggage room. "In there."

He looked like he wanted to protest, but in the end, he just shuffled into the closet-like space. I reached up and snapped the metal collar around his neck before locking the chain to the horizontal metal rod that was supposed to be used as a clothing rack.

The contraption was one of the things that Callan had bought from that shady store in Eldar. Before we left our rented house, I had stolen it from his room and put it in my pack instead. I knew that we would need to lock Lance into the room when we stopped at this inn, and that it would be the perfect opportunity for that damn force mage to betray me and disappear with the Binder on his own. After all, we were both dark mages, and we took what we wanted from this world without being bothered by something as silly as a conscience. So I couldn't let him outsmart me.

Palming the key, I turned and strode back into the bedroom. Callan was still looking at me with raised eyebrows and half a smile lurking on his face.

"You have the key to the handcuffs," I said. "And now I have the key to this."

Callan smirked at me. "Still don't trust me, huh?"

"No. And I assume the feeling is mutual."

"It is."

"So, we have one key each."

"Fine." Callan huffed out a soft chuckle and then started towards the bathroom. "I'm taking a shower."

I tracked his movements until he disappeared beyond the doorway, then I strode back out to the tavern and retrieved that breakfast I had ordered too. While balancing three bowls of stew and chunks of bread on a wooden tray, I returned to our room and kicked the door shut behind me. After placing it down on one of the small side tables, I locked the front door but left the key in the lock so that Callan could still get out if he wanted to.

Water splashed against tiles from the other side of the bathroom door. I cast a glance at it before picking up a bowl and a chunk of bread on my way to the baggage room.

Lance Carmichael was sitting down on the floor, leaning his back against the wall and staring out at nothing. The chain was just long enough to allow him to lie down if he wanted to.

"Here," I said as I placed the food in front of him.

Suspicion swirled in his eyes and he made no move to eat it.

I rolled my eyes and then touched my palms together. Glittering green magic swirled around my arms while I shot him a pointed look. "If I wanted to poison you, I wouldn't need food to do it."

He seemed to see the logic in that because he picked up the spoon resting inside the bowl. With his handcuffs on, his movements were a bit awkward, but he began eating the stew.

Moving over to the tray, I picked up a bowl and a piece of bread for myself, and then sat down on the bed as I started wolfing down the food as well. From where I sat, I could still see Lance through the doorway.

"All that stuff you said in your speech," I began between mouthfuls of stew. "Do you really believe that shit?"

"Of course I do," he said, his voice brimming with indignation. "And it's not shit. Magic is supposed to be shared equally. Not hoarded by the select few."

"You really can't see any reason for why mages would want to keep their magic?"

"Only selfish ones."

Wood clanked as he stabbed his spoon into the bowl in a show of anger. I just cocked my head, studying him while I tore off a chunk of bread. For a while, we just ate in silence.

"So you really are fine with spending a decade developing your magic just to give it all to someone else?" I asked when his food was gone.

"Yes."

"Then why aren't you sharing all of your money too?"

Drawing his eyebrows down, he gave his head a short shake as if that should have been obvious. "Because everyone has a job and everyone makes money."

"Do they?"

"Yes." Righteousness blazed in his eyes. "But not everyone has magic. That's why we need to share it."

The sounds of splashing water that had been coming from the bathroom stopped. I finished the last of my food and pushed up from the bed. After grabbing his bowl and spoon as well, I set them back down on the tray. Then I drew in a deep breath and moved back to stand in the doorway above him.

"If you could have just kept your ridiculous ideals to yourself, you would have lived a wonderful and happy life in your beloved city. But you didn't." Touching my palms together, I called up a cloud of poison and then flashed him a smile sharp enough to draw blood. "I look forward to breaking you."

Before he could reply, I shoved the poison down his throat. He slumped down on the floor. The strength of it was enough to knock him out for at least eight hours.

After one last look at the hero of Eldar, I closed the door to the baggage room and left him alone in the dark.

Lance Carmichael.

He would come to regret his choices before the end.

I would make sure of it.

CHAPTER 38

Callan

While Audrey was taking a shower, I ate the food she had brought for me and then added another lock to the chain connected to the metal rod. I might have the keys to the handcuffs, but that wouldn't stop her from just slipping away with Lance regardless. And we were so close to the end of this mission. If she was going to betray me, she would do it soon.

But at least with this extra lock on, neither of us would be able to get Lance out of that room without the other person's key. Well, unless I used my force magic to cut through the metal rod. But that, she would surely hear. I had no idea where she had hidden her key while I showered, but it didn't matter. I was exhausted and I needed this day of sleep before we started our war again.

After I closed the door to Lance's small room again, I drifted back to the bathroom. I wasn't sure why I did it, but I pushed the door open. Crossing my arms, I leaned against the doorjamb and watched as Audrey finished taking a shower. I knew that she had heard me come in because she had cast a glance over her shoulder when I opened the door. But she just continued showering anyway.

Maybe she wanted to steal one last moment from our temporary truce too before it was over.

Her long black hair was tied up in a bun, leaving her entire body on full display. I ran my eyes over the curves of her hips and ass. My cock swelled in response.

Audrey Sable.

Working with her had turned out a bit different than I expected. I had come to understand why she had been able to survive this long as a dark mage. She was clever. And ruthless. And incredibly skilled with her poison magic. She also had an uncanny way of getting under my skin.

"Enjoying the view?" she said as she turned off the shower and spun around to smirk at me.

"Yes."

Surprise flickered across her face. Apparently, that was not the response she had been expecting. But she recovered quickly, and that smug smile curled her lips again as she raked her gaze across my bare chest before dropping down to my pants. Too late, I realized that she saw my cock straining against the fabric there.

A satisfied laugh rolled from her tongue as she twisted and grabbed a towel from the rack instead. After wrapping it around her body, she sauntered towards me.

I watched her. While leaning against the doorjamb like that, I blocked the way out of the bathroom, so when she reached me, she was forced to stop.

"You're blocking the door," she announced.

"Yeah. Wanna do something about that?"

Her hand shot out and she palmed my cock through my pants. "Want to do something about this?"

Blood rushed down to it, making it swell even more, but I

kept my arms crossed over my chest as I stared her down. "Do *you*?"

"It's been an intense day." She lifted one shoulder in a casual shrug. "I could do with some stress release."

A thrill rushed through me, but all I said was, "Same."

I stepped aside, finally letting her move into the bedroom. My heart started beating faster. Irritation shot through me in response to it. When had I become this addicted to watching the expression on Audrey's face as I made her come? To her naked body beneath mine? To the feeling of burying my cock deep inside her? It was ridiculous, and a sign of weakness.

Shoving the confused emotions aside, I tried to force my heart to return to its normal rhythm as I turned to face Audrey.

For a moment, we only watched each other from a few steps away.

"I'm still going to kill you once this is over," she announced.

"And I'm still going to take back my lands and then make you beg me for the sweet release of death."

"Good." A battle seemed to be taking place behind her eyes. Then she blew out a short laugh and straightened her spine as if she had made a decision. "Then I'm giving you a free pass." She spread her arms wide in a cocky gesture. "This time, and this time only, I will allow you to give me orders."

I blinked at her in surprise. It was followed by a rush of excitement that made my blood crackle like lightning. She *liked* it. Based on her actions last time we fucked, I had guessed that it was true, but this as good as confirmed it. Audrey Sable actually liked it when I dominated her in the bedroom.

"Then I intend to make the most of it." A sharp smile spread across my lips as I nodded towards the towel. "Take it off."

She moved her hands back and slowly undid the top of the

towel that she had rolled up. The thick white fabric brushed her skin as it fell towards the floor. For a while, I just left her standing like that, completely naked before me, while I ran my gaze over her perfect body.

Her chest was rising and falling at a quick pace and there was a dark hunger in her eyes.

I twitched two fingers at her. "Come here."

Another bout of indecision flashed in her eyes, as if she still couldn't really reconcile her sexual desires with her default setting, which was to stubbornly disregard anything that came out of my mouth.

Then she blew out a long breath. Oh what I would have given to know exactly what she was thinking in that moment. But she hid the rest of her feelings as she sauntered up to me and looked up with a cocky tilt to her chin. It just made me want to subjugate her even more.

"Get on your knees," I commanded.

Her mouth dropped open ever so slightly.

I raised my eyebrows in silent challenge.

Flames burned in her eyes, but she lowered herself to her knees before me. I had to suppress a sharp breath as blood pounded inside me, making my cock throb at the sight of her. By all hell, I wanted her like that every minute of every day.

"Take off my pants," I ordered.

She drew her hands up my thighs before grabbing my belt. While keeping eye contact with me, she slowly unbuckled it and slid it out of the belt loops. It produced a soft thud as she dropped it on the wooden floorboards.

Her fingers slid across the skin right above my pants. My heart stuttered before beating twice as hard when she started on the buttons. I drew in a deep breath as she curled her fingers around the dark fabric and drew both my pants and my underwear down my legs. What was it about her damn hands on my skin that made my heart want to shatter my ribs?

My hard length sprang free as she slid the clothes down. I stepped out of them and kicked them to the side when they bunched around my ankles.

Reaching out, I drew my hand along Audrey's jaw before placing my fingers under her chin and tilting her head back. "Good girl."

A small shudder coursed through her body.

"Now, show me how talented you are with that tongue."

She held my gaze until I removed my hand from her chin. Then she slid her hands up my legs again. Her fingers dug into my skin as she took a firm grip around my thighs and then leaned forward.

A low moan tore from my throat as her lips brushed against my cock. She took the tip into her mouth while she swirled her tongue around it, and I damn near came right then.

My hand shot out. Threading my fingers through her hair, I gripped it tightly as she teased my tip with her tongue yet again. She let out a smug chuckle that made me want to shove the entire length of my cock down her throat. Hell damn it, why did she manage to affect me like this?

She pushed her head forward, taking me deeper into her mouth. My chest heaved as she spent quite some time working her lips and tongue in a way that made white lights flicker in my brain. Tightening my grip on her hair, I blew out a steadying breath as she drew back before swallowing more of my cock again.

Pleasure built inside me like an explosion trapped in a glass jar.

Drawing back, she flicked my tip with her tongue and then immediately took me into her mouth. Her teeth grazed my skin.

My control snapped. Fisting her hair, I held her pretty little mouth where it was as I came down her throat. She swallowed it all.

I sucked in a shuddering breath as I finally released her hair, allowing her to draw back again. *Shit.* I was the one who was supposed to be dominating her. But here I was, falling apart at her touch.

While trying to piece my shattered mind back together, I jerked my chin towards the bed next to us. "Get on the bed."

She flashed me a victorious smile before wiping her lips and rising to her feet. Her hips swayed with cocky arrogance as she sauntered over to the bed and climbed up on the mattress. Oh, I would draw some really nice pleas from those pretty lips soon.

Grabbing the belt from the floor, I followed her to the bed while she sat down in the middle of it. The mattress creaked faintly as I moved onto it and then sat down so that I straddled her thighs. She raised her eyebrows at me.

A lethal smile played over my lips as I wound the leather belt around my fist a couple of times. Her eyes flicked between it and my face. I let the silence stretch, allowing her mind to run wild with the possibilities. Then she licked her lips and I just couldn't let her sit like that any longer.

After unwinding the belt again, I positioned it over her eyes and then yanked it tight behind her head. She let out a small noise of surprise. Putting my palm against her chest, I shoved her down against the mattress.

"Move your hands above your head and keep them there," I commanded.

"You're not tying me to anything this time."

That had been an order and not a question. But I had already expected that because it would have made it far too easy for me to just leave her tied up like that while I double-crossed her and disappeared with Lance. And Audrey wasn't stupid.

"I know." Leaning forward, I took her chin in a firm grip and slanted my lips over hers. "So move your hands above your head and keep them there, and stop trying to give me orders."

Her hot breath caressed my skin as she let out a dark laugh, but she raised her arms and placed her hands against the pillow above her head.

Once I was sure that she would keep them there, I released her chin and climbed off her, leaving her lying there naked and blindfolded on the bed. She turned her head slightly as if trying to hear what I was doing.

I just knelt next to her and watched her for a while because I knew that the wait and the uncertainty would just make her body more sensitive to my next touch.

When she started to squirm her hips, I reached out and flicked her nipple.

She sucked in a gasp.

I swung my leg over her body so that I was straddling her again and then braced my palms on the mattress on either side of her. My cock brushed against her entrance as I shifted my hips. She let out a dark moan.

Leaning down, I planted a kiss on her ribs.

Her body jerked slightly and she turned her head again as if trying to see through the leather belt blocking her vision. I kissed my way up her chest, making her squirm underneath me again. When I reached her tit, I drew my tongue along the curve of it.

A low groan tore from deep within her chest.

While still bracing my hand against the mattress, I traced the tip of my tongue over her sensitive skin and towards her nipple. Her chest heaved, and she clenched and unclenched her hands where they rested on the pillow.

I swirled my tongue around her stiff nipple before taking it into my mouth. A tremor coursed through her body as I ran my tongue around it again. I nipped at it with my teeth.

She sucked in a sharp breath and then let it out in a long shuddering exhale. Another moan dripped from her mouth as I continued my slow torture. Her breath was coming in fits and starts. While I rolled her nipple between my lips, I reached out with my other hand and positioned it right above her other tit. Just when a shudder of pleasure rolled through her, I gave her other nipple a hard flick.

A gasp tore from her lips. She wriggled her body underneath me, which only made my cock brush against her pussy again.

Her hands shot down. Since she was still blindfolded, she couldn't see what she was doing, and her hands slammed into my shoulders before she raked them down my back. A needy moan came from her throat as she tried to pull me harder against her.

I straightened abruptly and touched my palms together. While vibrating force magic appeared around the fingers of my left hand, I flashed forward and locked my right around her throat.

Since she couldn't see it coming, she drew in another startled gasp. I tightened my hold on her throat. Keeping my grip hard enough that she was forced to draw strained shallow breaths, I made it clear to her that she was only able to still breathe because I allowed it.

"What did I say about moving your hands?" I demanded.

"I—" Her words were cut off as I traced my fingers over her soaked pussy, letting her feel the vibrations.

"It's almost as if you want me to make you beg for mercy again."

"You—"

Shifting my hand, I pressed my fingers straight against her

clit. The pulsing magic around them made her buck her hips and drag her hands down my ribs. I adjusted my position so that the tip of my cock was resting against her entrance while I continued sending low vibrations into her clit.

A pleading moan spilled from her lips. Arching her back, she tried to wiggle farther down. I tightened my grip on her throat again.

While keeping the vibrations just low enough to tease her but not intense enough to make her come, I dragged my cock through her wetness before positioning it against her entrance again. She sucked in quick shallow breaths. I leaned down over her.

"I'll settle for some light groveling this time," I whispered against her mouth.

She tried to push harder against me again but I only shifted back. A small groan filled with desperation ripped from her throat. I traced my tip over her pussy again.

"Please," she gasped out in surrender. "Please, I'm begging you."

The breath from those intoxicating pleas danced over my lips. Her pulse fluttered under my fingers as I kept my hand locked around her throat, restricting her breathing to only strained breaths. Holding her life in my hands like that was mind-blowingly addictive.

"Callan," she begged in a voice trembling with need. "Please, I—"

I stole her next gasp from her lungs as I claimed her lips while shoving my cock inside her. She moaned into my mouth as she tangled her tongue with mine while I drew back and then thrust into her again.

Fuck, she felt so good. None of the other people I had used for stress relief had ever felt this good. This perfect. I wanted to feel her, taste her, claim her, take all of her and give her all of me. What was so special about this damn poisoner that she made me feel such a desperate need for her? Something that I had never felt for anyone else.

A groan of pleasure tore from her chest as I rammed my cock into her all the way to the hilt. I increased the strength of the vibrations.

As a shudder racked her body in response to it, I realized that I wanted to see her eyes when she came for me. Releasing her throat, I reached up and yanked off the blindfold. Audrey sucked in a deep breath while I threw the belt aside.

While still trying to blink her eyes back into focus, she locked her hands behind my neck and yanked my mouth back to hers. I kissed her savagely while I continued pounding into her. Then I increased the force of my magic again.

She gasped into my mouth and pleasure suddenly pulsed in her beautiful green eyes. Her inner walls clamped down around my cock. I kept sending vibrations against her clit while I thrust in and out of her tight trembling pussy.

Release exploded through me.

A dark groan tore from my chest as I came while she was still riding the wave of her orgasm. She slid her hands down to my arms, digging her fingers into my biceps.

Her cheeks were flushed and there was a slightly dazed and incredulous look on her face as her chest heaved while the final tremors of pleasure racked her body. And damn it all to hell, but I found myself wanting to see that expression again.

But instead, I pulled out and collapsed to the mattress beside her.

My chest was heaving too.

Tilting my head to the side, I studied Audrey's face and tried to commit it all to memory. Because this was it.

This was the last day before everything changed.

CHAPTER 39

Audrey

My riding boots thudded against the wooden floorboards as I walked back out of the tavern area and returned to our room. When I crossed the threshold, I found Callan standing in the open doorway to the baggage room, looking down at Lance.

"He's awake," Callan said.

Afternoon sunlight fell in through the open window and cast the whole room in a golden glow. After our final act of indulgence early this morning, we had slept for most of the day. And now, all that was left was to finish this mission.

"Good," I replied as I crossed the room and then stopped next to my pack where it waited right beside the closet. "The horses are ready too."

Callan grabbed Lance, who was still chained to the metal rod, by the arm and hauled him up. "On your feet."

I watched the way Callan's lethal body moved as he strode over to where his own pack rested against the wall by the door. Thoughts about what we had done this morning fluttered through my mind unbidden. I shoved the tangled emotions out. He was a good fuck. That was all there was to it.

The chain rattled faintly as Lance moved inside the baggage room behind me.

That sound helped me snap my mind back to the present. There was a mission to complete. I rubbed my hands and then shook out my tired muscles.

"If we ride hard," Callan began as he twisted towards me, "we should reach Essington's mansion by—"

The door banged open right behind him. He tried to whirl towards it, but two strong men had already grabbed one of his arms, while two more took his other in an iron grip. Before he could get a single word out, a fifth brawny man looped his arm around Callan's throat from behind, locking his head in a tight grip. Three more ran into the room after them. Fire and lightning flickered in their palms.

Callan thrashed against their hold, but between the five of them, they managed to keep him completely immobilized. Rage flashed across his face as he snapped his gaze back to me.

"It's nothing personal." I let a victorious smile spread across my lips as I cocked my head. "Well, actually, it is."

A snarl tore from Callan's chest. "You vicious little—"

"Thank you so much for helping us," I said as I swept my gaze over the eight other men in the room while my smile turned much sweeter. "I thought we were done for when this dark mage attacked the ball and abducted us. But you saved us."

"You told them I'm a dark mage?" Callan growled.

"Of course I did."

For a while, I just stared back at Callan from across the room. Rage flashed in his eyes and he yanked against the hands keeping him trapped, but they didn't let up. I flashed him a wide smile that shone with mocking victory.

"Now, boys," I said to the eight men, "please hold him while I get the handcuffs."

A laugh bubbled from Callan's chest.

There was a beat of silence.

Then the other eight men in the room started laughing too.

I sucked in a gasp and jerked back a step as the three people with magic already summoned aimed their crackling lightning and hissing fire at me instead.

My hands flashed forward.

A lightning bolt struck the floor right next to my foot, forcing me to jump sideways towards the wall instead of focusing on slapping my palms together.

"Oh I don't think so," Callan warned. The five men who had been holding him had released their grip and pointed magic attacks at me as well. "Keep your arms spread wide, or the next one goes into your chest."

Glaring at him, I let him see the hate that flashed on my face. But I slowly spread my arms while showing him my empty palms.

He brushed his hands down his rumpled clothes before meeting my gaze again. A mocking sense of superiority clung to his cheekbones as he smirked at me. "Well, don't you feel stupid now?"

"How?" I pressed out between gritted teeth.

"Do you remember our first day in Eldar? When I locked you in that room?"

"Yeah, I remember that. Vividly."

"While you were trapped in there, I went back to that place... What was it called?" He snapped his fingers. "The Black Emerald."

"So?"

"When we were there together, you made an entire room full of people get down on their knees and beg you to spare their lives." Callan spread his arms to indicate the people in the room. "So I recruited them. I told them they would be able to get revenge on you, which they were more than happy about, and then sent them out here to wait for us."

"You've been planning this since *that day*?"

"Of course I have." He cocked his head. "I've been trying to kill you for five years. Do you really think I'd let this chance slip by? Though, if it's any consolation, my original plan was to let you get captured by the heroes in Eldar. But then I decided that I wanted to take a more personal approach so that I could enjoy the victory longer."

"Fuck you."

"Yes, you did."

My gaze darted around the room, calculating the distance to all nine enemies before me. Callan tutted and shook his head.

"You're severely outnumbered. Not to mention that they already have magic ready to throw, which means that you won't be able to touch your palms together before their attacks hit you." Flashing me a lethal smile, he took a step forward. "Now, unless you want to get hit with a mass of lightning strikes that will leave you twitching on the floor for hours, keep your hands away from each other while I lock you in a pair of handcuffs."

A green cloud exploded into the room before me.

Panic flashed in the magic-wielding men's eyes as my poisonous mist shot down their throats, and their faces still bore masks of shock as their dead bodies hit the wooden floor in a series of dull thuds. I kept the poison in Callan's lungs at an intensity where it was impossible for him to raise his arms to summon magic, but just shy of lethal. He had also collapsed to his knees on the floor, and he was dry heaving while trying to keep his eyes locked on me.

"You thought you could double-cross me?" A wicked laugh dripped from my lips. "I recognized the people from The Black Emerald the moment I walked into the tavern this morning. I will applaud you for only recruiting the people who had been sitting at the edges of the room when I made them beg for mercy, but do you really think that I would have survived this long as a dark mage if I didn't make sure to mark the faces of *everyone* I humiliated?"

Only choked gasps answered me as Callan's chest shook with the effects of the poison.

"As soon as I saw them sitting here in the tavern when we arrived, I knew what you were planning to do. There were civilians in the tavern when we got here this morning, but now the only people in this entire inn are the ones you hired from The Black Emerald. And as soon as I unlocked Lance's chain and we walked out of this room, you were going to use them to take me down." I lifted one shoulder in a shrug. "Which was why I had to force your hand. By bringing them in here to capture you, I decided how and where this fight would take place. And since I knew that they would release you and turn on me, I had already rubbed my hands together and summoned my magic *before* they stormed into the room." Twisting my hand, I showed him a small green tendril that I had kept hidden behind the back of my hand the whole time. "Just a little sleight of hand."

Callan's arms hung uselessly by his sides as he doubled over while his body tried to vomit up the poison. Then he banged his knee on the floor in anger and snapped his gaze up to me again.

"And now, you're trapped inside my magic. Still alive only because I allow it." I huffed out a mocking laugh and shook my head at the kneeling force mage. "Did you really think that you could outsmart me?"

A cold hand appeared on my arm.

Every single drop of the glittering green poison cloud evaporated in a flash.

I staggered a step back and whipped my head down to stare at the five black rings that had appeared like tattoos around my forearm.

Shock clanged like giant bells inside my skull.

Callan pushed to his feet. A sharp smile spread across his lips as he locked eyes with me.

"Oh, sweetheart, I already have."

CHAPTER 40

Callan

I watched as pure shock pulsed in Audrey's eyes. With her mouth slightly open, she stared from me to the black circles around her arm and then finally to the golden-haired Binder standing behind her shoulder.

Lance Carmichael, who was still shackled by the neck to the metal rod inside the baggage room, looked back at her with blue eyes that were filled with both anger and hope. Her gaze dropped to his wrists. No handcuffs encircled them. While Audrey was still trying to process what had just happened, Lance flicked his eyes to me.

"And now you'll let my friends live?" he asked, though it sounded more like a plea. "You'll tell your men to let them go?"

Audrey snapped her gaze back to me.

I flashed her a wicked grin.

She thought that she had been able to outsmart me. But unfortunately for her, I had already come to realize just how clever she really was. I knew that she wasn't stupid enough to fall for that stunt. Of course she would recognize the people from The Black Emerald. Because, just like she said, there was no way that she would have survived this long as a dark mage if she couldn't remember the faces of the people she threatened. So they hadn't been the key to my main plan. They had been the diversion to set this up.

While Audrey had gone in to get us this room, I had told Lance that I also had his friends. Since I had seen them at the ball, I could describe them in great detail. And since Lance had been knocked out before he was thrown out the window of the parliament building, he had no way of knowing what had happened at the ball after he was rendered unconscious.

When Audrey went out to tell the now dead men to come storming in here, I took the opportunity to unlock Lance's handcuffs. Since he was still shackled to the metal rod in the baggage room, he would only be able to reach Audrey with his magic. And just as she had placed my pack by the door so that the men from The Black Emerald could grab me from behind, I had made sure that hers was right next to the baggage room, within easy reach of Lance.

Me banging my knee into the floor had been the signal since I knew that Audrey would use her poison magic against me. Hiding it behind her hand was a clever trick. I hadn't known exactly how she would do it, but I knew that she had set up her own ambush so that she would somehow manage to get her magic into my lungs. Once Lance had heard the signal, he had snuck out of the baggage room and bound Audrey's magic, just like I had told him to.

"You promised," Lance pushed. "You promised you would spare my friends if I did this."

"I—"

Audrey bolted.

Leaping across the bed, she threw herself out the open window. I slammed my palms together but she was already gone.

While spitting out a vicious curse, I whirled around and sprinted out into the hallway and towards the front door. Another group of people from The Black Emerald leaped aside as I hurtled past them.

"The blond guy still in the room," I barked at them. "Handcuff him and then bring him outside."

"Yes, boss!" they answered.

Boss. They had barely even started working for me properly. We'd see how well they performed their duties now, and then I would decide whether I would kill them or let them serve me.

The door banged against the wall as I shoved it open and raced outside.

Audrey was sprinting for the horses in the stable, because out in these grasslands, there was no way for her to escape from me on foot. Especially not without her magic.

While darting after her, I slammed my palms together and threw a thin blast of force at the back of her knees.

She crashed down into the grass as my attack hit its target. First, her knees slammed down, and then the momentum of her previous sprint sent her whole upper body smacking into the ground. A grunt ripped from her chest.

I closed the final distance between us right as she rolled over on her back.

Steel glinted in the afternoon light as she slashed a knife at my legs. It whooshed through the air right under my feet as I jumped to evade it. Since the strike missed, her arm ended up far to the side. As I landed on the grass again, I kicked the knife out of her hand before she could bring it around for another slash.

It sailed through the air and landed on the ground a short distance away while Audrey hissed in pain. I tried to move back into position, but she kicked her foot upwards between my legs, aiming for my crotch.

The move forced me to leap backwards to avoid a direct hit. Pain shot through me as her toes still made partial contact with my cock.

Using that second of grace, she pushed herself up to her knees and whirled around while trying to get to her feet. Touching my palms together, I sent another force wall straight at her back. She slammed chest first into the grass again.

Before she could recover, I rolled her over on her back and planted my whole weight on her hips as I straddled her. She yanked up her arm and rammed her elbow towards the side of my ribs. Letting the strike go through, I grabbed her other wrist while she was distracted. Another bout of pain pulsed through me as her elbow hit, but I kept my grip on her other hand and forced it down to the ground next to her head.

Panic rippled in her eyes and she bucked her hips to get me off, but it didn't even lift me. She tried to slam the side of her hand into my throat instead. I knocked her arm aside and used the second that bought me to yank out the knife I kept strapped to the small of my back.

Before she could bring her one free hand back for another strike, I pressed the cold edge of the blade against her throat. She stilled.

Her chest heaved, and fury flashed in her eyes as she stared up at me. "You made Lance bind my magic!"

"Yes." I grinned down at her. "And I have no plans on getting him to undo it."

"I should have poisoned you last night!"

"Yes, you should." Cocking my head, I looked down at her curiously. "When were you going to do it?"

Clenching her jaw, she just stared up at me in rage-filled silence.

I pushed the knife harder against her throat. "Answer."

"When we were halfway to Essington's house," she

snapped. "So that I wouldn't have to travel with both your and Lance's unconscious bodies that far."

"You really should have done it last night. Because now, you can't poison anyone."

Her gaze slid from my face and towards the black rings around her right forearm. Then to the knife at her throat. Then to my body pinning her to the ground. And then finally back to the tattoo-like circles.

I could see, second by second, as the reality of her situation became crystal clear. The realization that she had lost, truly and irrevocably lost, to me dawned in her eyes like the hopeless gray sky before a heavy storm.

Throwing her head back, she slammed her fist into the ground beside her. "Fuck!"

The word tore from her throat with pure desperation.

People appeared around us. I jerked my chin at one of the men from The Black Emerald. He approached. While I rolled Audrey over on her stomach, he locked her wrists in the stiff handcuffs he had been perceptive enough to bring.

Audrey just lay there, her cheek resting against the thick grass. Her long black hair fell down to conceal the other side of her face as well. I pushed to my feet.

"You will let my friends go, right?" Lance repeated from somewhere behind me.

I glanced over at him. He was handcuffed again, and another of my newly recruited men was holding him by the chain that was still attached to his neck. I didn't know how the guy had gotten the chain off the metal rod, but perhaps these people would be useful after all.

"That depends on your behavior," I answered before flicking my wrist at the man holding him. "Get him on a horse."

Crouching down, I hauled Audrey to her feet. Since her

hands were shackled behind her back, she had to jerk her head to get her hair out of her face. Then she turned to glare at me. I just stared her down until some other guys brought my horse forward.

After lifting her up into the saddle, I swung myself up behind her.

"This isn't over," she announced as I reached around her to grab the reins.

A huff of laughter escaped my chest. Pushing my heels into the horse's flanks, I urged it forward. "Yes, it is."

We rode the whole way to my mansion in silence after that. My new recruits spread out around me as if to keep watch, while a few of them kept Lance under control.

When we finally reached my mansion, darkness blanketed the world. Halfway to my front door, I was met by Henry and a few of my other guards. The new recruits handed over Lance's chain to Henry while I led Audrey forward. She kept her mouth shut but her chin raised as I marched her down to the dungeon I kept in my basement. Henry followed closely behind with Lance.

"Lock him in there," I told Henry, breaking the long silence, and jerked my chin towards one of the cells while I came to a halt with Audrey in the middle of the torchlit space.

"Yes, boss," Henry replied.

"But my friends," Lance repeated for what had to be the hundredth time. "You promised!"

"We'll see about your friends," I answered.

Metallic clanking filled the basement as Henry shoved Lance into the cell at the far end and began locking the chain around his neck into one of the metal hoops that were set into the stone. I turned to Audrey.

She was standing in front of me with her chin raised

defiantly. "So... You're going to take my lands now? My mansion?"

"Yes." A smirk tugged at my lips. "Though, technically, they've always been *my* lands."

After letting out a huff, she stared up at me in silence for a while. Metallic rattling came from Lance's cell as Henry continued to secure the Binder in it. I only looked down at Audrey, staying silent as well.

"And now you're going to use Lance as a weapon against both the other dark mages and the heroes," she said at last.

It was more of a statement than a question, but I answered anyway. "Yes."

"Clever. That was what I was planning to do too."

"I assumed as much."

Another short silence filled the air between us.

"So..." Audrey began. "What happens to me?"

For a while, I didn't reply. I only continued looking down at her. Her eyes never left mine, but she didn't push for an answer. And I was incredibly impressed by the fact that no matter how long I let the silence stretch, there was still no fear in her eyes.

"I haven't decided yet," I replied at last. "But for now, I'll let you live."

The cell door banged shut. Henry locked it before starting towards me. I kept my eyes on Audrey.

Our job was finished. The mission was complete. We had managed to abduct Lance Carmichael and get him out of Eldar before he could launch his campaign to wipe us all out. The threat against all of us dark mages had been neutralized.

What's more, I had what I wanted. A weapon that would keep both the other dark mages and the heroes in check.

And I finally had Audrey Sable right where I wanted her.

Handcuffed and powerless in my dungeon. Entirely at my mercy.

So why didn't I feel more victorious?

"Congrats, boss," Henry said as he came to stand beside me. "This mission was a complete success."

A success?

I looked down at Audrey where she was standing before me with that stubborn tilt to her chin and that fire in her eyes that told me that this wasn't over. That she was going to try to kill me the first chance she got. It made those confusing feelings swirl inside me again.

And suddenly, a truly dreadful realization seared through my chest like a burning blade.

No, this mission with Audrey had not been a success.

It had turned into my worst failure ever.

Because I had fallen for her.

Bonus scene

Do you want to know what Audrey was thinking during that shocking last chapter? Scan the QR code to download the exclusive bonus scene and read the final part from Audrey's perspective.

ACKNOWLEDGMENTS

I told my dad and uncle not to read this book. Before *Ruthless Villains*, I had mostly written fantasy books where the romance wasn't as... descriptive. My dad and uncle always read every new book I release, so you can imagine my anxiety while I was writing all the bondage and knife play and choking and other kinky sex scenes. When I was getting close to the end of this book, I realized that there was only one thing to do. I had to tell them straight out that they are not allowed read this book. And I did. So, I would like to start this acknowledgment section by thanking my dad and uncle for **not** reading this book.

And of course a huge thank you to them and the rest of my family and loved ones for their support too. Mom, Dad, Mark, thank you for always being there for me. I truly don't know what I would do without you. Lasse, Ann, Karolina, Axel, Martina, I'm so glad I have all of you too. Spending time with you always makes me happy.

I would also like to thank my amazing best friend Oskar Fransson. Thank you, both for always filling my life with light – and also for your help with some research questions.

To my amazing copy editor and proofreader Julia Gibbs, thank you for all the hard work you always put into making my books shine. Your language expertise and attention to detail is fantastic and makes me feel confident that I'm publishing the very best version of my books.

A huge thank you to Claire Holt, the incredible designer from Luminescence Covers, who made this absolutely gorgeous cover. Your talent for creating beautiful covers is out of this world and I'm so lucky that I get to work with you. Find Claire at www.luminescenecovers.com.

I would also like to thank Franziska Stern for the stunning hardback design. It is even more beautiful than I could have hoped for! Franziska can be found at www.coverdungeon.com or on Instagram @coverdungeonrabbit.

I am also very fortunate to have friends both close by and from all around the world. My friends, thank you for everything you've shared with me. Thank you for the laughs, the tears, the deep discussions, and the unforgettable memories. My life is a lot richer with you in it.

Before I go back to writing the next book, I would like to say thank you to you, the reader. Thank you for reading about my two stabby and violent, but also maybe a bit loveable, villains.

If you have any questions or comments about the book, I would love to hear from you. You can find all the different ways of contacting me on my website, www.marionblackwood.com. There you can also sign up for my newsletter to receive updates about coming books. Lastly, if you liked this book and want to help me out so that I can continue writing, please consider leaving a review. It really does help tremendously. I hope you enjoyed the book!

CPSIA information can be obtained
at www.ICGtesting.com
Printed in the USA
LVHW100308300523
748352LV00017B/59/J